"The Selection meets X-Men meets Incredibles. I cannot recommend this book enough."

JENNIFER, GOODREADS

"I loved this book! ... I am looking forward to the next book in this series"

PAM HARRIS - AUTHOR OF FALLEN GODS

"A solid fantasy tale about an unusual girl who is more than she appears ... it's cute and well-written"

GOODREADS REVIEWER.

"I have fallen in love with the super hero genre ...I'll be looking for sequels. "

KINDLE CUSTOMER

"…the story has great characters but it also has some great villains which include some brilliant twist and turns."

"This is an amazing read and dayum! You gotta pick it up if you like superheroes and angst and action and falling for someone you aren't supposed to. So good. Really."

"Mina Chara has a winner! Hero High is out of my normal genre, and it took me a couple chapters to get into the book, but the writing and flow of the story sucked me in."

"If you want to read something new and unique, check out Hero High. You will love it! ."

"Starts off strong and doesn't let up until the very end … non-stop action … imagery was very masterfully used to make sure the reader felt like they were a part of the novel."

C. GONZALES

"This book is fantastic … to be honest I thought the book would be predictable and it wasn't. The story kept me guessing until the very end."

JENNIFER, GOODREADS

HERO HIGH

FIGURE IN THE FLAMES

MINA CHARA

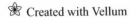

For my Family

This book is a compilation containing the first three Friday Fitzsimmons stories and contains the whole of the 'Figure In The Flames' story arc.

Denial

Anger *and*

Bargaining

CONTENTS

PROLOGUE: MAKE THEM GOLD

I N THE YEAR **1930** the world experienced strange lights in the sky; a comet, gone rogue, fell into Earth's orbit and pounded our blue planet with bright, shooting stars. In the same year ordinary men and women began to exhibit super powers and by 1939 the connection was clear. In the moments before death the Comet gave powers to those with an overwhelming desire to live. Object D/1930 X1 was given a name: the Heroic Comet.

In the war years that followed, those affected by the comet saved thousands, but life in peacetime wasn't easy. One hero, Stronghold, found the solution; he designed and built Icon City, an island homeland for heroes.

By the year 1950 the world knew comet given powers could be used for evil as well as good, some of the heroes turned to crime and this sent the world into panic, so in 1959, as the first group of heroes prepared to retire, the International Heroes Group was formed with a simple mission: recruit and train new heroes.

The group did well. New villains and heroes arose and in 1979 Captain Fantastic joined their ranks where he battled the most desperate villain of all: Dr. Dangerous. They clashed for many years until the Doctor's plans grew more and more gruesome and the public demanded action. In 1986, Captain Fantastic took the lead; he killed Dr. Dangerous on live television and surrendered to the police.

One year later, his plea of self-defense was upheld and Captain Fantastic, now even more popular, was released. He spent the next five years urging the world to keep a close eye on superheroes through a dedicated television channel, and as part of his efforts he opened a school where the next generation of super powered heroes could be trained.

He called it **Hero High.**

I grew up with stories of that school and the heroes who passed through its doors.

Now I get to write one about *my* hero.

————

"Ms. Fitz?" I hold out my hand to her, and she takes it with a firm, reassuring grip, almost as though offering congratulations.

"You want to write a book about my life?" I sit down next to her in her family restaurant and café, the atmosphere warm and friendly with just a touch of refinement. It's early in the morning, a misty pink sky above us.

"I'd like to write how you became what you are today Ms. Fitz."

"Call me Friday," she tells me over a mug of steaming soup.

"Of course. Friday, I was thinking, maybe a story about your early days? How you got here."

"Do people care about that?"

"Of course! You're a household name."

"I am?"

"Of course ma'am. Everyone knows the stories, it's just they're a little…"

"Sparse?"

"Sparse, exactly. I'd like to write something more substantial."

"I wouldn't know where to start."

"At the beginning. Tell me your story from the very beginning."

"The Cliffnotes version, or ..."

"As much detail as necessary."

She adjusts her position, gets comfortable in her seat and stops for a moment to think before setting her mug down to snap her fingers. "Got it. It all started when-"

————

HELLO

THERE WAS SOMETHING ABOUT touching the glass that made me feel like I could reach the horizon. Just for a moment, I stopped shaking and the anxiety lifted. Icon City lit up everything around it; the lights reminded me of stars. I could see them moving through the streets while helicopters buzzed around the skyscrapers, their lights blinking in the distance.

Could I really do it? Really live here? Part of me was bursting with excitement; I longed to wander the streets,. The other part of me was scared to walk those streets because I wouldn't be invisible. All the other kids on the plane, my classmates, they were practically jumping out of their seats. It was years since I'd been this close to anyone my age, other than Jake and my sister. My dad hadn't called, or even seen me to the plane, which wasn't surprising. My sister was there. Those days everything was about my sister. The most I'd said to my father in years was, 'are you okay?' He almost never replied.

Jake stayed next to me on the plane, his legs bobbing up and down. It was easier, having him with me. He'd always been the someone to make me happy at the end of the day.

"Day, that's it! That's the city!" I took a deep breath that seemed to plummet downwards. "Day? You okay?" he asked, looking away from the window.

"Just nervous." Jake took my hand in his and although my nerves didn't settle down, I felt braver. I leaned over to get a better look: It seemed like every inch of Icon City held a skyscraper, each one brighter and more intricate than the last. This was a city that came alive at night, when lights flashed with brilliant color. As we got closer I caught glimpses of the statues in the cobbled market streets, the carvings on the buildings, and the hi-tech trams moving fast past candlelit cafés.

Jake pulled out a tourist pamphlet with his spare hand and set it on the table in front of us. His eye's lit up as he started to read. "The city was built in 1947," he said, looking over, "Stronghold, the guy who built it, said he wanted it to look like a city from before the war."

"Well if you want to be specific," I said.

"Which you always do," he replied.

"Which I always do," I agreed, "Stronghold started making plans in 1945, but he didn't get permission to start building until 1947."

Jake shrugged, and flipped the page. "Okay, what about this?" he stopped flipping, let go of my hand, held the book up for me, and started quoting. 'I wanted it to be a haven of beauty and art, I wanted Icon City to be colorful and artfully deco, like the buildings I'd loved once when I was young, before the war.' What do you think he means by that?" he asked.

"Well, he grew up in Lupiac in France, then moved to Paris in 1922, when he was seventeen, so he's probably talking about Deco since it originated in Paris in the 20's and 30's, and then waned during the Second World War."

"Thanks superhero encyclopedia!" he laughed.

"Shut up." I muttered, giving him a nudge on the shoulder.

Jake filed away his book, and leaned over to my laminated guide of Hero High. "Does it list your classes in there?" he asked.

"Sure, maths, english, gym."

Jake raised a brow as he continued. "So it really is a school? I always wondered, I guess they film for the show at weekends, and in-between you take regular classes," he said, turning pages.

"We're beginning our descent into Icon City." buzzed the plane's intercom.

Jake put the guide book down and strapped in with a smile on his face. The frustration in my bones came back, I needed to *do* something, but this time there was *just* enough excitement to distract me. The Super Structure went by in an instant as the plane began its final descent onto the runway. The landing was smooth and perfectly executed. Our stationary windows overlooked the airport's mall.

A woman, clip-board in hand moved down the aisle. "Okay kids, get your bags and line up in single file. We're heading straight to the Super Structure." A girl right at the back raised her hand. "You have a question?" Her puffy hair bounced as she stood up and her bag tipped over, showering gift shop trinkets on the floor.

"Aren't we supposed to be getting an allowance?" the girl asked.

"Yes," replied the woman flipping through her clip-board sheets, searching for the girl's name. "Ms. Asimov, is it? We got you all on the 'plane a little late this year, so you'll get your allowance in the next couple of days, and we'll schedule a trip so you can shop for what you need. Don't worry, you'll survive. Anyone else have a question?"

A boy shouted from the back, not bothering to raise his hand. "What's gonna be in our dorms?"

"I'm glad you asked," the woman replied. "Basic toiletries, utensils, simple furnishings, a pre-planned wardrobe, that sort of thing. There's a lot more information actually *in* your dorm rooms. Bottom line, you can survive without buying anything for a couple days. So," she smacked her pen on the clipboard back and forth, "no worries."

My mind started racing, I wanted to be sure I'd gone through everything I needed. A gift for my new team mates!? What about food? What if I didn't like the food in my dorm? What if I didn't like any of it? My chest felt like it was vibrating. All the other students stood up with their suitcases, standing in single file. One boy across from me had a single plastic bag, nothing more. How could he be prepared for one of the world's largest, most active cities? Others had clearly overpacked, some had three suitcases, one or two had even more. I tried to reach *my* suitcase, but as usual my arms fell short.

"Want me to get that for you?" Jake teased, as I reached up on my tip toes.

"No! I can do it!" I insisted. My fingertips brushed the bag, but couldn't reach the handle. Jake ignored me, and used his extra inches to reach up and put it in front of me. It wasn't huge, but it was quite big, it held all my jackets and cardigans, the necessities of life. I needed something between me and the rest of the world, like that second layer of clothing was armor. I knew we were supposed to wear what they picked out for us, but I never was crazy about being told what to wear, that's one thing that hasn't changed at all with the years.

I clambered off the plane with Jake, directly behind the boy with three suitcases, watching him try to pull them all along. The boy with the supermarket bag pushed past him, and all the other students, sick of waiting, did the same. I'd almost decided to follow when I remembered where I was. I didn't plan to start by ignoring someone in need. What sort of hero would that make me? I picked up my luggage and walked over to help him.

"I've got it!" he snapped at me.

"I'm trying to help!" I growled

"Like you could."

Jake pulled me back and shook his head. "Calm down." A scream of frustration came from behind me as

Jake steered me away. My heart sped up. I could hear the other students, shouting with excitement. I took a deep breath and stepped into the terminal, determined to keep a straight face in case this was the first time the cameras caught me. I planned to keep a low profile, play an extra on the show, but still I had to *have* a profile, a picture, maybe a coaster with my face on it.

All the willpower that kept my face straight faded in an instant. The ceiling must have been four or five stories above me. Palm trees decorated the mind bogglingly large room. Thousands of people were coming and going, shops lined every wall, six or seven escalators were going up and down. Glass elevators sped upwards to far-away floors, and in the center of it all stood a huge neon sign bearing the single word 'Welcome!'

The boy from earlier pushed past while I was frozen. The barricades in place for us split off. Stewards checked things over, and began to give directions.

"All handlers this way!"

Jake looked at me and pulled me into a hug that was over in seconds. "Good luck Day." I pulled him into another hug, but still, I had barely any time to wrap my arms around him. "I'll see you tomorrow, you'll be fine, okay?" he said it like a command, an order not to fall apart, like he wasn't nervous at all.

I nodded like I wasn't scared. He was a handler, I was a hero and the stewards were waiting to take him away. I thought Jake would make a great handler, he'd always wanted to be a hero, but had never developed any powers of his own. Being a handler was his way of being involved. Giving advice to heroes as they fight, being a hero's structure and support. Jake was a great friend, and he'd have been an even better handler.

The woman with the clip-board and booming voice pointed a firm finger at me, and motioned me over, then she held up her hand demanding silence. I took a moment to study her features. The mole by the side of her mouth, gave her authority and presence, like a star from a vintage movie, but her unwashed hair and battered jacket told a different story. It looked like she'd been working for longer than was ethical, but in that case so did everyone else. Like the woman with the clipboard they all had an earpiece in place and their clothes were much the same.

"We have your names, ages, and powers," the woman told us, "we need you to walk in single file in front of the camera and then, you'll be evaluated, you'll be introduced on stage for the first episode, and once we come to the Super Structure, you'll have a few moments to mingle with working heroes before your tour, and finally, room assignments. Then, I promise, we'll let you go. Okay?" She turned away, and then stopped, looking back. "I should have mentioned. I'm Veronica Lagar, I'm the senior producer for the 2005 season. Let's get started."

Hero High had a tradition of going through each student in the first episode of a new season, even if it meant using a ten minute time slot. I did *not* want to be on TV, but I knew there'd be no getting round it. We all stood in a line and tried to walk naturally towards the exit, trailing our suitcases behind us. I was pretty sure as the camera panned over me that my face was as stern and uninviting as possible. My bitch face would go down in one of two possible ways. One, they would ignore me, or two, they'd wonder why I looked so angry, and forever I'd be the creepy girl in the corner.

Veronica Lagar herded us out. She led us past the expensive shops while various privileged by-standers turned their heads. Every time we passed a café, I had to hold myself back. I wanted to charge in there and demand their largest doughnut. I was *so* hungry I'd have eaten anything, but the one shop that stood out was the chocolatiers. Other students in other years had the time to stop there, but not us. I'd never seen anything so delicious looking back home, but, I had to let it go.

The doors of the terminal opened and the cold wind

rushed in. A line of photographers braved the cold September night, trying to catch the new students at Hero High. People behind them waved a sign, and screamed for autographs. It seemed so pointless. They had no idea who we were but it made no difference, the city was so alive.

Vertical walls of glass reflected the brake lights of the cars like a street after the rain. Never had I heard such a mix of noises; cars running past, taxis honking at each other, students shouting and chatting, the wind, the photographers screaming. The buildings were so tall, so far above me, brightly lit in blue, pink, and purple lights, or sculpted into hard metal lines like a work of modern art. I'd never felt so lost.

We hurried onto double decker busses that waited by the curb. The inside was laid out much like the 'plane with bright pinks and blues, large leather chairs, and candy bars reminiscent of a dream I had not too long ago. I took a seat next to a girl with a sneer.

As the busses pulled out, Veronica stood up and took out a microphone. "Once we get there, the very first thing you'll be doing is team assignments, and mandatory, that's *mandatory* powers tests." Everyone on the bus groaned in response. "I know you've already done it, but now you have to go through it for the cameras. That's just how it is."

We'd already done a power test when we submitted our applications. I could barely prove I *had* a power, it only ever came in handy when solving a problem or taking a test. In the end I'd passed because I could solve a pile of algebra problems in what to the judges seemed like the time it took me to *read* the questions. As Veronica sat back down, I tried to clear my mind, and focus on the buildings rushing past my window. I wanted to vomit, but being sick on television didn't seem like an option. If I was lucky I'd be one of those that didn't make it into the show. I'd have to make myself as boring as possible, something I didn't think would be difficult. The sights of the city pulled me away from my nerves for a while, but the journey didn't take long. In no more than fifteen minutes we'd reached our destination, Super Structure; the home of Hero High.

The square outside the Structure was littered with people clapping and waving and holding welcome signs. The busses stopped behind the Power League stadium, and we all got off one by one. Across the square, the Super Structure was strangely shaped, but it was also one of the largest buildings in the city. It looked like a narrow archway, built from two separate skyscrapers that joined only at the top. The shorter building on the left was for the students, with classrooms, dorms and gift shops for fans. The taller of the two, the building on the right, was the realm of real superheroes. There they monitored villains, produced new tech, and supervised superhero missions. A small sphere sat between the two towers, like the pin in a clock while the pathways that held it in place mimicked the hands.

Veronica sent us through the barricaded trail, to the front of a stadium where the center was plastic flooring rather than astro turf or wood. There was no audience in the bleachers, just the jumbo screen, and the goals left over from the night before. The stadium floor was filled with weights, benches, and various types of running machine. One by one they gave us athletic gear and pushed us into the locker rooms. I waited until everyone had finished and the locker room was clear before I changed out of my clothes.

As soon as we all stepped out Veronica clapped her hands, and took her place on a small stage where all of us could see her. The camera crew stood next to her, reading their equipment and someone fiddled with a pack attached to the back of her skirt. She straightened her back and looked up. The light on the camera went red, and Veronica was suddenly *very* chipper.

"This is your first appearance on Hero High! We will determine exactly what your powers are, how useful they'll be, and rank them. At the end of the examination you'll be given a letter. Open it and you'll find your team assignment, power name and recommended career path! This will determine what mentor you're given. Are we clear!?" We hummed in agreement, and Veronica nodded. The doors to the room banged against the wall as they opened to a flood of extra cameras and commentators as men and women with clipboards directed us to the first trial.

I was pushed onto a running machine with everyone else, a black band strapped to my arm. The treadmill started without warning and I did my best to keep up as the speed increased. Other students had already moved on, and were working on the long jump, dead lift, and high fall. One of the men holding a clipboard turned my treadmill up as high as it would go, and my breath was reduced to short harsh puffs. "Stop," I yelled. "Stop it!" He paid no attention, so I jumped off and ripped the band from my arm. "We're done," I told him. He shook his head and scribbled something down before directing me to the deadlift. I managed to lift forty pounds before my arms felt like rubber, the long jump was a disaster, and I couldn't throw anything fast or far enough. The high fall wasn't so hard, so long as I took my time, I dropped from the grappling hook and landed squarely on the ground, but a tall stocky man with a whistle disapproved.

"If you take that long to get down, the bad guys gonna be gone already! Come on kid, step it up. You're a superhero, not a girl-scout, I won't be givin' out extra points for being careful."

A man leaned over and grabbed the clip board from the assistant who'd been shadowing me, and flipped over every page. A siren sounded, and a spotlight blasted light on the circular platform in the middle. A jumbo screen across the room flashed with the words 'power test'. A presentation purely for the show. The new guy shadowing me pulled me over to the side as each student got on the platform, waited for the camera and demonstrated their power with whatever props they needed. I recognized the guy, but I just couldn't put a finger on who it was.

The boy with three suitcases lifted his hands and mushrooms scattered across the floor, rising from their spots, like they were animated. The jumbo screen behind him showed an animated slot machine and all of us waited to see his school ranking. Each slot hit into place, he was ranked eighty eight. The crowd cheered, but not too loudly. The lower the score, the higher the rank, the number used to pit us against each other, something to make us compete.

The man shadowing me pushed me up on stage and joined.

"Can't run, can't lift, can't fly, damn! You might have an even lamer power than I do. So, what is it? Can you make it rain confetti? Or maybe you can play dead."

I thought for a moment wondering why he seemed familiar. "Oh my god," I said, "you're Flat Boy!"

He smiled for a moment, and then suppressed a glare. "Call me Coach Flat."

"What? Why? You used to be The Captain's side-kick! You were great, your power's amazing." His eyes narrowed, as though he was making sure I wasn't joking, and then smiled once he was sure I was sincere.

"So, what's your power?" Coach Flat asked.

"I can pause things."

The man narrowed his eyes, and sighed. "Elaborate."

"I can speed up how quickly I think, to the point that everything looks like it's stopped, and play things back, run possible scenarios in my head." I tried to sound confident, but as powers go, it wasn't likely to make good television.

"So. You're a super speedster?" asked the coach.

"No, I can't move fast," I explained, "it's just my mind. My body's frozen."

"Wow, that's the worst power I've ever heard!" said Coach Flat, "I love it! Can you show us?"

"Not really, in the application office they made me solve algebra problems for a day, to prove I even *had* a power."

"How fast could you do it?" the coach asked.

"From their perspective? As fast as I could read the question." I told him, "from mine? It seemed like hours?"

Coach Flat shook my shoulder. I expected encouraging words but instead all he said was "Sucks to be you. Give us her ranking." The slot machine on the screen spun, and landed on two hundred. As I stepped off the stage passing a tall, cheerful girl, Veronica tutted.

"Here's your contract," she said, sliding a large pile of papers and a pen my way. "Got to sign a contract if you wanna be on TV," she said with a sigh.

"But, I haven't read it," I told her.

Veronica snorted. "Sign it."

"I can't sign something I haven't read," I said again.

She frowned, narrowed her eyes, and reached under the table to pull out a large file with my name on the front. "Let's see," said Veronica, flipping through the pages, "here we are. Here for monetary reasons, yes?" I swallowed, and nodded wondering what difference it made. "Sign," ordered Veronica, "if you don't, no money." She smiled as though this was the only part of her job she enjoyed. In other circumstances I'd have spent a week carefully reading and re-reading the contract, but they'd sprung it on me at the very last minute and my family needed that money, so I signed. Before she could pull it back, I flicked though the pages, and blinked, catching a glimpse of the words, breach of contract … twenty thousand … fine.

"I don't understand," I told her. "I can't even demonstrate my power. Why didn't I score three hundred?"

She sighed, and put her clipboard down. "Because you're not ugly. I mean, hell kid! You could be a commentator or a teacher, some kids, well they're just too gross. Don't get me wrong, you're not exactly pretty, and you could do to lose some weight, but I don't hate looking at you."

"Thanks. You piece of shi-"

Coach Flat took my arm, "Come with me, shorty and don't say somethin' you'll regret, " he said, steering me away as fast as he could.

"I'm not short!" I insisted, despite the evidence.

"Sure." He groaned.Coach Flat pulled me over to the other side of the room where a small number of students were waiting around a mat. He dropped my clipboard onto a pop up picnic table and sat on the edge while another much larger, more imposing figure emerged from the crowd of students. Dressed in suburban father attire and glasses, this was the one and only Captain Fantastic.

My body locked.

Every one of the kids looked up at him in awe; the greatest superhero ever known, right in front of us. Everyone else around me sunk into nonexistence the moment I saw him.

"So, is this all of them Frank?" The Captain asked.

Flat Boy nodded briefly. "Yes Principal, it is."

"Good, good."

"That uh..." Coach Flat glanced down at the clipboard and pointed over at me. "That Fitzsimmons girl over there has the most passive power I've ever seen."

Captain Fantastic smiled and nodded in my direction. He looked at me. He looked at me! "Well," he said, "it's not the powers that make the hero."

My brain melted at the sight of his smile, and a blush powered across my cheeks. The girl standing beside me looked me up and down and sneered. I gave her a quick glare in response. So what if I was a fan?

"Partner up, and we'll see what you can do." said Coach Flat.

The sneering girl stepped in front of me without a

moments notice. Coach Flat started to speak, rattling off advice on how to handle a supervillain, and how to fight while The Captain stood at the edge, his arms crossed. My partner looked me up and down again, reached for my jacket, and opened it to see the lining. I pushed her away and readjusted it on my shoulders.

"That's a designer jacket," she said, "how much did it cost?" somehow she made a simple question sound like a threat. I straightened my back and bent my knees preparing for fight.

"A lot?" I replied. She scoffed and ground her teeth. "Look, it's just a jacket, okay?" I held up my palms, as though showing I didn't have anything in them.

"Why are you here?" she said, circling round me.

"What's that supposed to mean?" I asked.

"It means, if you're rich, why are you here?" She settled in front of a thick blue sparing mat.

"Being well off doesn't mean you don't have to work." I told her.

"Please, like this is work." She scoffed.

How could she say that? Being a superhero was a way of life. Not a walk in the park. "This is a job, we get paid," I said.

"Exactly, and we don't have to *do* anything." She checked the ends of her nails, though I was still ready to fight.

"Our job is to help other people!" I insisted, stiff with anger.

"I guess," she said, making the concept sound trivial.

"I guess? You and I have to give up our lives to help other people, that's what this job means," I told her.

"Relax, don't get so pissy about it." she hissed.

"I haven't relaxed since I was eight!"

"Take a chill pill," the girl said, "you need to calm down, I asked an innocent question, what is it, that time of the month?"

My fists clenched at my side, I didn't want to look at her.

"What? Gonna cry, then go home to mommy?"

Without so much as a moment's thought, I shoved her down onto the mat. "No one talks about my mother!" I said in warning from above her. The cameras swerved round just in time to catch her screaming.

"My arm! I think it's broken!" she cried, her head swishing about like she was trying to make sure the cameras caught the red gleam of her hair. The Captain pulled her up and several nurses rushed over to take her away, but The Captain stopped them at the door, giving her a brief check over as she leaned on him. "It's broken! She broke my arm!"

"Your arm's fine," said The Captain as he sent her

away. There wasn't a scratch on her, but she still clutched her arm like I'd broken it. As soon as she was gone, I knew she'd wanted me to punch her, not shove her. She was playing the cameras.

"Now I remember you!" shouted Coach Flat as he moved towards me, flipping through my file. "You're the girl that punched a guy in the face, so your dad sent you away," he put an arm around me and smiled, "you're a tough cookie, I like you."

"I didn't mean to do it," I said, and it was true. "It just happened."

"Sure you meant to," the coach insisted, "the guy probably deserved it."

"Frank!" yelled The Captain, glaring down at his friend, "It doesn't matter what someone was doing, *nobody deserves* it."

"The girl lost her temper," said the coach, "it happens." He looked at me, his lips pressed into a stern, straight line.

"I didn't hurt her," I said.

"She think's she's broken her arm," said The Captain.

"That's bullshit. All I did was shove her."

"I know what it's like to lose your temper young lady, I've been there myself," said The Captain, "but I will not tolerate this sort of behavior Ms. Fitzsimmons, do you understand?"

"Yes sir." I said without a moments hesitation, as though I was being scolded by my father. My voice came out gently and overly sweet, all because it was *him*, he stopped to look me up and down for a second, and sighed.

"Good. And Fitz?"

"Yes sir?"

"I'll be watching you." he said it with an ounce of concern, as though it was a warning, but not a threat.

"Yes, sir. I'm sorry."

He nodded to me, because he believed in my sincerity, and I *was* sincere. I would *never* have lied to The Captain. A bell rang and our clipboards were collected and tallied. We lined up, the cameras moving through our ranks, stopping to ask us a single question and see who looked best on camera. I opened my letter and found an overly large red D sitting next to my name. My team was blue, my rank in the class was bottom, and the recommended job was support. I could have made a good support hero working in the control center, thinking of plans for each hero in need, but the truth was I wanted to be out there with them, not cooped up in an office. I needed to work, I needed to *do*.

Jake had wanted to be a superhero since we were

kids, but he'd settled for helping heroes instead. The school for handler training was in the other part of the Super Structure, so superheroes and handlers never really mingled. I would be the first super powered handler. I sighed and pulled my letter out all the way, so I could read the name of my mentor, dorm house number, and power. Hyper Synaptic Activity it was called and in brackets it said, 'blinking'.

A few kids whistled and hollered as they received big red A's, and superhero job recommendations. The red-haired girl I'd shoved had a card that said 'spacial replacement' with a great big A on the front and a recommended superhero placement. Aya, the bouncy haired girl from the plane held a B card, which read 'Object Transportation' and the boy next to her held an A card which said 'Rapid Heat Transference'.

A tall, burly girl with bright green eyes had a power called 'Mirrored Dust Production and Manipulation', a boy wearing a name tag and with a book under his arm had a power called 'Integral Internal Substance Mutation' and lastly, a girl with sharp eyes and a regular frown held a card that said, 'Zone Production and Traversing'. There were other kids with D's, C's and B's; I could read the names of their powers but they didn't make much actual sense. I'd never realized it before, but maybe I *did* want to be a hero. Maybe I *wanted* to be like The Captain after all.

Veronica sent us to put our normal clothes back on, and threw us into the arms of frantic stylists. None of them changed our clothes, they just adjusted outfits on racks, placing numbers on tops and bottoms as they looked us up and down. One woman walked up to me taking note of my clothes and measurements. She stopped when she got to my earrings.

"Pink mother of pearl? That's a bit dated, don't you think? You should really change those."

"They were my mothers," I told her.

"Even so," she insisted, "pink's really not your color-"

"They're special to me, I don't care if they're dated." She shook her head, scribbled down a list of colors and stuck it to a rack of clothes with my name on. I'd hoped that we were finally done but no. There was more.

Veronica signaled us to follow and together we crossed to the building opposite. Inside was a stage, the curtains were still drawn and we stood together in the darkness ready to give the fans their first look at the new class. The unseen crowd roared, a man ran on, straightened his tie and checked the index cards in his hand while nodding to the assistants as they scrambled about. It was only when he turned to face us I recognized Carey Fry, his hand raised in greeting. Carey Fry had been on the Hero Channel for a while, he was their go to guy for the opening ceremony, quiz shows, interviews, you name it. I felt like I'd known him since I was a kid and though he did look a little older in person he was still handsome. He certainly knew how to wear a suit seeing as it was all red. And I mean, *all* red.

"Listen up." The chatter and mumbles faded out. "This segment will take five minutes at most, so don't worry, we'll let you go soon. Everyone, this is Carey Fry," said Veronica who'd wandered on next to Carey, "you've probably seen him before, so let him do the talking. Oh, and this segment we're recording is at the end of the episode, so shout goodbye to the cameras." With one more nod she left, and the stage went silent.

The curtains rose and the cameras pinged red as Carey shot into action. The crowd didn't roar, they *screamed*. The audience was huge, the theater was almost the size of a stadium. We all waved, and Carey quieted the audience down. As the cheers subsided into the occasional whoop, he gave a short speech about this year's students. Each one of our faces flashed up on the screen and someone in the back announced our names, our rank and power. People cheered for a few of the kids they'd seen before, Carey wished us luck, and told us to wave as the camera pulled out. The class erupted, obediently cheering goodbye as they waved at the camera, and who ever would be on the other side in the future.

Once we were done Veronica pushed us on, past the opening ceremony being held in the streets, past Jean-Claude Nakata singing, past the Hero High tower, and into the Real Heroes tower on the Super Structure where a party was being held on the first floor. Real Heroes was our sister show, and it was the start of the school year, the start of the new season. Investors, toy companies, studio executives, all had to be included, it was time for them to meet the next generation of superheroes.

Nerves tingled in the pit of my stomach. I hated all the attention and didn't want to answer questions. All I wanted to do was disappear before my nerves made me barf all over the floor I could barely see for all the busy feet. It was too much, there were too many people.

I drifted away from the group before anyone could notice, searching for something to drink or eat to get my mind off everything. The food was carried by serving staff on oval silver trays. I wanted so much to grab some, but somehow I didn't dare.

A waitress struggled through the crowds until an old man stopped her, holding her in place. I took a few steps closer and watched as she struggled with the contents of her tray; my stomach flipped again. I thought I was going to be sick for sure. A glass was about to topple, I "blinked" as they put it, only to calm my nerves, and reached out to catch the glass just in time. The waitress gasped.

"Nice catch."

"I guess." She gave me a smile and offered a thank you as I distracted the old man so she could scurry away. As soon as the distraction was over, I felt sick again. I pushed through the crowds like a speed boat tears the ocean, pushing people out of the way as my heart throbbed and nerves shook my body. Stay under the radar, that was the plan. I ducked down, almost crawling like a thief, to stay out of sight. It didn't help. Most people looked confused. Just why was a girl crawling about on the floor?

I ignored them. Just as my legs began to cramp, I saw a door marked 'EXIT' and sprinted straight for it.

Closing the door behind me I took a deep breath and welcomed the night air, the relative quiet, the wind as it moved through my hair. I was standing in a small garden walled off from the street by simple green hedges. Warm yellow lighting underlined the building and made it stand out against the vulgar pinks and greens of the other skyscrapers; my legs felt like they'd crumple any moment, I had just been in the Super Structure! *The Super Structure*. My lips turned up despite the churning in my stomach, when the whole superhero thing didn't work out, at least I could say I'd been there for a party, only to run outside and spend the night on a bench. I glanced to one side and froze. There, in the corner, was Captain Fantastic and a *very* tall boy. I pushed myself up against a bush, trying to hide.

"So. Excited?" beamed The Captain.

"I suppose," said the boy.

"You suppose? You're going to be a superhero!"

"I know. I'm very happy to have you as my mentor," said the boy but his voice was void and empty. The Captain's smile faded. He opened his mouth again, and I leaned forwards, trying to catch their conversation, only the bush rustled, and The Captain turned round.

"Ms. Fitz?" I raised my hand like a kid in class. "That was real nice what you did for the waitress."

"Thank you," I stuttered as he smiled and held out his hand, I took it without hesitation, forgetting that my hands were clammy with nerves.

"You're cold, that's not great," he said, sounding worried. It was reassuring, like a parent should sound.

"Nope. I'm a big fan, Sir, sorry, I mean, I just," I took a deep breath, "I saw your rescue during that hotel fire, I saw the time you saved the mayor from assassination, my favorite was when you saved Missy Mittens from jumping off that ledge."

"She certainly was a tricky kitty," said The Captain with a smile, "always finding a way to climb skyscrapers."

"I watched her show all the time growing up!" I told him.

"Missy Mittens was always causing trouble," he told me, "the entire city was on the edge of their seats every time she escaped the studio."

"Who needs a cat called Missy Mittens to help them cook anyway?" I added.

"Exactly," he replied with a smile.

"What's your name again, little lady?" he asked taking the seat next to me.

He'd called me little lady! "Friday Fitzsimmons," I replied.

"What did they name your power?" His tie was a gentle periwinkle blue, slightly too loose, and his jacket a little too large. He'd dressed himself. No stylist for this event.

"Hyper Synaptic Activity," I said. "It allows me to think fast. It's super lame."

"Just as long as it's super." It seemed like he was waiting for a laugh and I was happy to oblige.

"Good one, Captain." Over his shoulder I could see the tall boy roll his eyes. The Captain waved his hand at me as though to say I was too much.

"You use your power with the waitress?" he asked.

"I don't think it really helped."

"I'm sure it did. Just in ways you don't understand yet," he said. I was talking to Captain Fantastic, my nerves had been replaced with disbelief and awe. "It's good to meet you," he said, and sounded like he meant it.

"Even if I broke a girls arm?"

"You didn't break her arm. She's just," he waved his hand around, trying to find a word, and then abandoned the sentence. "I wasn't exactly gentle in my youth. I don't expect you to be perfect on your first day."

When he smiled, his white teeth were like a ray of sunshine. My face twisted in the most awkward way as I tried not to smile back and show mine, they were *far* from perfect. His were *super* perfect, which is appropriate, since he was *literally* super. I loved Captain Fantastic! Don't tell anyone I said that.

"Can you promise me something?" he asked, his tone suddenly serious.

"Anything." I didn't think, I just said it.

"Promise me you'll *try* to not let your anger get the

better of you. Okay?" I opened my mouth and closed it again. Was it that easy? "I had the same problem when I was your age, I still do. But we have to try. Will you try?"

"Yes sir. I want…" He set his glass down on the paved stone, and leaned on his knees, waiting for me to go on. "I want to be good. I wanna be a superhero." Those words made my eyes hot, I did the best I could to hold back the tears. I was *not* going to cry in front of him. I'd wanted this for so long.

"Then try to be."

I nodded, and he sat back up.

"How exactly did you get your powers Friday?"

I didn't want to tell him the truth so I kept it vague.

———

"How did you get your powers?" I ask.
"A car accident…" Her head drops, and then rises again, a smile on her face. "Nothing special, we'll get to it I'm sure. After all, it's why we're here."
I nod, and she goes on.

———

"I, uh, I don't know. I felt fuzzy and fizzy, and then my

brain did a thing, and I thought for a real long time, and then I did it. And now I'm talking to Captain Fantastic! Not that I'm excited about that. I'm not really into superheroes." it all came out in one long, fast, mess of words.

"Really? You're not into superheroes? Because you're gonna be one yourself."

My cheeks flared red. "Pfft, gijhh, ha. Oh you! … I'm not a fan…"

He laughed, louder this time, like I was a cat doing something hilariously stupid. He flashed his beautiful white teeth again, and the laugh lines on his face deepened. He was one of the most experienced superheroes and you could see it in every weathered line of his face. He'd been working for the city for so long; watching his wedding on TV was one of my earliest memories. Years of stress and pain, but there was hope in his eyes. "This is my mentee, Ashley. Ashley Friday, Friday Ashley. He's a first year just like you."

I leaned forwards to cast an eyeball over The Captain's mentee who nodded. We both rushed to say. "Hello." His voice was deep, strangely so, it almost didn't match his features. I'd expected a doppleganger, the next Captain Fantastic, but Ashley looked nothing like him. He was far taller than The Captain, and The Captain had to be six feet at least. He was long limbed, even gangly, and his shoulders sat almost impossibly straight. The Captain had icy blue eyes that glittered, *Ashley* had a long face with a nose that looked like it had been set too straight after a break, if that makes any sense. As Ashley stared down from behind his horn rimmed glasses, he struck me as underwhelming. Captain Fantastic's personal mentee? He didn't have the same warmth, the same charm. He didn't garner the same reaction. In fact he wasn't even close. "You uh, you've never had a mentee before. All the previous years?"

"Well, Ashley here is special," The Captain said.

"I guess he must be." Ashley said nothing, he only looked me up and down.

"You should get back in, it's cold out here." The Captain got up and held the door open for me. I waddled back in with one of the world's most famous superheroes behind me. The eyes of the party spun round and it caught me off guard, sending my heart racing for the second time. The throb of its beat pounded in my ears, the room started to twist and turn as my chest heaved. The next thing I knew I'd collided with a much larger body, and was tumbling down to the hard marble floor. Ashley's hands reached out to catch me like I'd caught the glass from the tray. He pushed up his glasses with his spare hand, and without so much as a smile, set me back on my feet again. Ashley was huge. Unreasonably so. And lanky.

"Thank you," I said.

"Do you have the time?" he asked. He checked his watch with a heavy sigh. "My watch is broken and I have a meeting, so, do you have the time?"

"Your watch is broken? Let me look at it." He refused to look me in the eye, like the suggestion was pointless. "Please."

He un-buckled the blue leather strap and dangled it in front of me as though it was something of mine he'd taken. "How do you intend to help?" he asked as I set it to my ear.

"My father's an inventor, there was a time he built all-weather watches for military use, so I learnt a bit about some different types of watches."

"Your dad builds things for a living?"

"He used to, now-a-days I do it. How old is your watch?"

"A little under a hundred years, maybe eighty. Why?"

"I think it's your hairspring." I shook the watch vigorously, something a lot of people do without under-standing why. "I can't fix it completely now, but..." I paused and shook it harder, checked, and the hands started to move again.

"How'd you do that?" he asked taking it from me.

"Like I said, it's your hairspring. I'm afraid it'll keep getting jammed, shaking is only a quick fix."

"So what do I do?"

"You could let me look at it another time. I have some tools, all I have to do is set the hairspring back in place."

———

"So," I ask, "you fixed things for a living?"

"Fixed and built things," she replies, "whatever the customer needed."

"You were a kid while you were doing this?"

"I pretended my father was sick, or away, while I ran his company. I signed his name and spoke for him."

"Why?"

"He gave up," she says, looking at me, stone cold, "I didn't."

———

The Captain called for his mentee.

"Thanks," said Ashley, as he secured his old blue watch on his wrist and stepped away towards the center of the crowd. The Captain wrapped an arm around his shoulders. Ashley was already busy, laughing and smiling, just as someone should over champagne and caviar, but my time was done.

Veronica stormed in, and several of the stewards ushered us outside. "Okay kids, time for a quick tour, and then you can settle in. Follow me!"

I checked over my shoulder, wondering why some of the other kids weren't coming with us, but it seemed that students like Ashley, mentees of the big name heroes, Black Magic, Mistress Widow and The Lightning Kid, they all got to stay at the party. Some kids at Hero High had been groomed for the school for years; something told me those kids didn't need a tour. None of us were given any time to get our bearings. Viewers at home just wanted to see the new students, and figure out which one they were rooting for. In a large cluster we all left the Real Heroes tower, crossing the courtyard to Hero High. Despite being part of the same building the only way to cross from one to the other without leaving was through the sphere on the top.

In the city square the stage cleared. Jean-Claude Nakata was scheduled to sing for the rest of the evening once the live cameras left us. The huge gold archway doors of Hero High were famous, fake, and etched with images of Stronghold, the city's founder. One by one, we moved through the revolving doorway in their center. The art in Icon City was so angular and elegant; I'm not sure what I expected when I walked in, maybe clear white surfaces? Lots of clear, uncluttered glass? No. Hero High was nothing like that, it looked most of all like a hotel mall. The air was humid and sticky, it rained in icon City almost as often as it did in Hawaii. It'd get colder soon, just enough for it to snow by Christmas, but the rain was all year round.

Pillars stretched up from the second level, palm trees lined the sides, amber marble walls stood in stark contrast to the glass of the shop fronts. Lights shaped like fans emitted a warm yellow glow, while the real lights were concealed in the ceiling. The place had been cleared, but you could tell it was made to hold thousands of people. The ceiling was maybe six or seven stories high and the walls were lined with Hero Channel themed shops. It smelled of fresh counters and cinnamon buns, as opposed to the hard scent of diesel and faint flavored afterglow of cigarettes outside. Most people don't like the smell of gasoline and cigarettes; they've always reminded me of exciting trips to big cities.

Various banners and posters the size of small houses were hung over the railing of the second and third floors. Captain Fantastic's was the largest, of course, and below that was a shop filled with superhero endorsed perfumes and colognes. Other posters hung for Hero High, Real Heroes, Super Variety Hour, Power League, and Hero Colosseum.

Pop music filled the mall, some recorded by heroes. Large glass cases held together by gold lines acted as elevators, and lined the walls like pillars while escalators moved up the levels like the laces on a shoe. Further down the long hallway were a few twists and turns, but eventually Veronica pointed to a café. It sat at the end of a hallway, as large as your average chain restaurant.

"This kids, is where you'll work if you want to earn extra cash while training." She waved her hand for all of us to go in. The majority of the place was childishly pink, there was so much pink it looked like a Barbie pop up café. The walls facing the entrance were all made of glass, and the back was lined with merchandise, key rings, mugs, backpacks, and back to school kits. Each rail was graded by year. The year one rack was blank, cleared out, for our stuff the moment it came in. "You'll serve coffee, tea, deserts. We have an in-house chef, so no cooking, just waiting on fans. There's no photography in here, and you're only permitted to sign photographs when officially paid for by the customer."

A couple of the kids looked at each other with

raised eye brows but Veronica moved on, further down the mall, where more and more shops were dedicated to Hero High. Each year had a shop, so year one's was currently empty. There were costume shops, full restaurants, and an emporium filled with figurines, plushies, and detailed action figures. There were normal stores too, a few chain restaurants, and a couple of clothing stores I'd heard of. Veronica stopped at a set of gold covered elevators that reached so far up they seemed to move into the ceiling, and beyond.

"These are *your* elevators," she told us. "All gold elevators are yours to use and are not open to the public. Once upstairs you'll receive your Hero High issue phones, you'll use them to slide against the lock, and it'll let you up." She pulled out her own phone, and demonstrated. "You can skip the shopping center alto-gether by taking one of the elevators on the outside. Everyone in, one by one. We're going to the lobby."

We filed in, in groups of ten. The elevator interior was pretty damn big, even with benches. One of the girls in front of me started inspecting the buttons. I reached around her, and pressed L.

"Hey! I wasn't done looking."

In normal circumstances I would have said some-thing back, but I was too tired. The doors pinged open with a clean crisp, electronic greeting, and everyone stepped out into the lobby.

The colors were the same, but the atmosphere was immediately different. The lobby was lit like a hotel bar, the walls were etched with gold bars arranged in hard, abstract, angular lines. A reception desk, with keys on hooks almost grew from the gold tracing on the walls, but right in the center stood a huge cylindrical fish tank that cast over the room a whisper of blue, projecting ripples onto surfaces like a theater showing the ocean on loop. It made the place look like an aquarium themed bar I was *not* old enough to drink in.

"This is where our tour ends for now. You've probably seen the rest on the show, and if not, well, then ask someone else. Get your room keys from my assistant, and get some sleep." Veronica turned on her heel, and left in another elevator with three of her personal assistants. The fourth waved us all over and referred to his clip board before shouting a team color. The members raised their hands, he gave them their room key and each team wandered back into the elevators. I split off from the crowd for a moment to investigate the vending machines hidden in the back. A few of the employees gave me funny looks, but I ignored them and bought myself some candy. I was just about to consume all that chocolatey goodness when Veronica's assistant called for the blue team, and only I raised my hand.

"Looks like you're on your own Ms...Fitz? Blue team, number six."

I looked at the keys and then back at Veronica's assistant as the rest of the students stared. "So wait, am I *all* of team blue? Why?"

"I don't know exactly," he said, looking down at his clipboard. "I think it was requested by someone."

I shrugged, way too tired to argue, and collected the gold key that said six. A few of the kids sniggered as I passed by, and someone whispered something I couldn't make out. I drowned out the unwanted comments with the crunch of each bite, pressed the buttons in the elevator for one of the dorm floors; forty six. The floors for housing went from forty six, to fifty. As the doors closed, I sighed with relief. At least I was alone.

I stepped out again, expecting a hotel hallway, but instead I was greeted by a street of small houses set around a faux stone courtyard. Each house was pristine, the stone walls barely weathered. It looked more like the set of a music video than a real street and the floor did nothing to hide the fact that it was part of a building. The courtyard and wood paneling effect seemed more like a resort gimmick than anything else. Small street lamps lit the way, and the door to each house showed its number and the color of the team to which it belonged. I walked further and further, down similar streets of houses, until I found the one that was mine; there was a huge blue patch on the door, my name, and the number six.

I actually found myself liking the faux cul-de-sac as I stepped up to the porch of my miniature house. I could hear banging and rattling, the sound of celebration coming from the other dorm houses. I took a deep breath as I turned the knob, and braced myself for what was inside. I knew the first night was going to be hard. Missing my home, missing my room. I needed to stay calm, make sure I didn't over react. Why was the idea of sleeping somewhere else so scary, nearly heart attack inducing? Maybe lying down to sleep meant I wasn't going to catch a train back home in time for sunrise.

I sighed, and checked my phone for any messages from my dad or my sister, but they hadn't so much as texted. The mess of emotions in the pit of my stomach lurched as the door swung open. At least I was living alone and no one else would see me cry. I found myself wishing Jake was there, the one thing I'd brought from home when my dad kicked me out. Inside there was a table for keys, hooks for jackets, nothing exciting. The dorm house was rustic and retro. For a moment I mused to myself about how it wasn't really my style, only to realize I'd no idea what my style *was*. Decorating at home had always fallen to me, Dad never cared, and my sister was too young. All I ever did was what the magazines told me; our whole house had been shades of off white, accented with mountains of glass. I fell onto the leather sofa. The evening sky was dark, but the lights of the city were so bright you could barely tell.

The kitchen behind me wasn't as big as back home, but still a good size. I rifled through the drawers, but found nothing much other than basics like salt and sugar, no doubt we were expected to buy our own food and decor as the show progressed. There was a miniature coffee maker, too bad I don't like coffee. A bread box, four plates and matching flatware. On the center island was a huge basket wrapped in plastic. My eyes lit up like I'd just seen a chocolate store with the sign FREE in the window. A gift basket, a glorious, *free*, gift basket. Oh man I loved free things. My hands grappled for the scissors on the counter and cut through the plastic like a mad man so I could see all the free stuff!

Inside was a huge bar of chocolate, a set of key rings, some money to get me started, various cookies, and sodas of all sorts. I sifted through it all, setting aside ear buds and a flip phone. The last thing in it was a huge Banoffee Pie. I *loved* Banoffee pie, it was my favorite food in the whole world. I set it in the refrigerator and picked up the phone. The label on it read, 'Hero High Communicator'. I opened the phone and found contacts already loaded, and an itinerary set on the calendar. On top of it was a letter, with the title, 'your mentor'. I opened it immediately. Which poor superhero had been stuck with me for the next four years?

Your sister told me you're mad about Banoffee Pie, so I wanted to get you one from a bakery downtown, I hope you like it. I look forward to working with you! -Your mentor, Sense.

Sense! Sense had been around for nearly twenty years, she was *the* longest working superhero in history. Sense was amazing! I scooped up some of the pie, and pulled out the letterman jacket at the bottom of the gift basket. The sleeves were a baby blue, with a space for the team name once I'd decided on it. Although, it wasn't really a team was it, if it was just me? I loved the jacket all the same.

I kicked my suitcase down the slim hallway towards four doors one of which was labelled with my name.

The colors of the room were eye searing; a mess of hot pinks and blues. The room was the epitome of two thousand and five, the walls were covered in ugly decals you might put in a tween's bedroom. How old did they think I was? I was seventeen, not twelve! I pulled in my suitcase and duffle bag setting them on the bed. The room was snug, but I liked that. The desk was built into two bookcases standing at opposite ends, and the bed sat on the opposite side of the room, covered in furry lilac pillows.

The whole room design was sickeningly trendy, right down to the hot pink shag rug. It screamed 'designed by a forty year old who thinks they get the youth of today'. The part I liked least was the huge round mirror that engulfed far too much of the room. I started unpacking my clothes, and had moved over to open the closet when I found another message taped to the door. The piece of paper held one word: 'clothes'. I threw my jacket back onto the bed, and opened the closet. It was full of outfits, all with numbers attached. These were the clothes the stylist had selected. Another piece of paper on the inside read:

Must be worn when called to all TV events.

Wear them as they have been numbered, each number corresponding to a matching top and bottom. The clothes you have worn will be replaced at the end of each month.

I turned the page to see a detailed list of the clothes with their prices next to them. Three hundred dollar skirts, thousand dollar jeans, and jackets even *I* would never be able to afford. The very last page of the letter was advice on what to wear if I wanted to buy clothes for myself, and a comprehensive color evaluation, telling me what colors I should and shouldn't wear. In bright red letters it said.

NO PALE PINK

I rolled my eyes and put *my* clothes away in the drawers instead. No one was taking my earrings off me.

A small window led out onto an even smaller balcony since I was right at the edge of the building, but actually, I liked it. I liked how disgustingly trendy the room was too. I'd never set foot in a place like this before, but it made me feel like this was an adventure. I pulled back the white curtain and gazed out into the busy night, watching cars hurry from place to place, seeing the theatre signs as they flashed, watching as the penthouse restaurants sparkled. I'd done it, I was there, in the big city. I could see it all, but for tonight I was safe and sound, bursting with excitement to start the new day, if only I could make the night pass in a flash!

I couldn't sleep, I *couldn't*. I was...

Too,

too,

awake.

———

WAKE UP

THERE **I** WAS, STILL misty eyed, and in my pajamas, but hey I was up and eating breakfast with everyone else in the cafeteria. Actually, I wasn't the *only* one in my pajamas; the school wide bell had woken us all up at six thirty, and cameras had come barging into our houses to catch us at our worst. Now the camera crews stayed at the sides, checking their equipment while the producers talked among themselves. Jake sat beside me at our shared table, flashing his handlers badge to everyone that would look. Hero High's cafeteria was trying to look like a fifties diner, with neon pink lights above our heads, and aqua blue leather booths lining the walls. The checkered floor continued up the stairs and onto the balcony of seats above. The clatter of knives and forks, and the whirring of the air conditioning filled the place with a regular hum of white noise.

"Friday!"

I shook my head and zoned back in. "What is it!?" Jake smiled and grabbed my morning cookie. "Not in the morning Jake, give it back."

"It wouldn't kill you to lose some weight. You're gonna be on TV. Cameras add pounds," he said patting my stomach. I gave him my most intimidating glare as the other students started to pack up their things. There were times I *really* hated Jake Jepsen and this was one of them, but hey, no-one's perfect, and it wasn't the time to lecture him. He picked up my tray and threw it in the trash. My fists clenched. If Jake Jepsen had been anyone else, he'd have received a swift punch to the groin. I put up with his crap, and he put up with mine.

"That tray was still full," I said.

"You weren't gonna eat it," he pointed out.

"Still," I protested, "it was full, and perfectly good. Such a waste."

"It's Hero High, they can afford it."

"Still-"

"Jeez! Let it go 'Day, look at the rankings."

He showed me his phone where my photo was displayed along with many others, sitting at 205. I'd gone down five points in popularity and all I'd done was sleep. "I've gone down? I haven't done anything yet!"

"Exactly," said Jake. "Look around, the other kids are already working the cameras."

He was right. New recruits were gushing to the cameras, telling sad stories designed to make strangers care. I gave the phone back and sighed.

"Ask me about my new digs," he prompted.

"Digs? You mean your room?" I'd been so occupied with myself the question hadn't crossed my mind and Jake knew it.

"Yeah! Just ask me," he said.

"Umm, what are your new *digs* like?"

"Why do you have to say it like that?" he said, laughing, "you sound like a dork. Okay fine, I'll tell you," he said as we moved to the elevator and sped upwards, "they're not as fancy as this, but still, they're pretty great, and I got this gig working at the snack stall, so I'm pretty nervous about that. Oh, and I met this cute girl." He stopped, and looked over at me, wiggling his eyebrows.

"Okay?" I said, "so?"

"So, ask me about her."

"What's she like?" I shouted out in exaggerated interest.

Jake smiled as he tilted his head at me, deciding

whether or not to call me out on the apparent sarcasm. I smiled back, and he cleared his throat. The story was more important than a lecture. "Okay so get this," he said moving closer, a spring in his step, "she's so much fun, she likes comic books, and she's all like, deep and stuff."

"Alright," I said, wondering where this was going.

"And get this," he said, "she does yoga."

"What does that mean?"

"It means she's super flexible," he said, rolling his eyes at me.

"I still don't-" I said, shaking my head.

"It's hot," he huffed.

"Oh, cool." After a beat, I reached up to ruffle his hair, and a laugh tugged at his lips. His hand pushed mine away as the elevator doors opened, and I started down the road of dorm houses. "Do you not get that I am a *straight* female? If you want me to, I *can* appreciate her aesthetically when and *if* I meet her," I told him.

"I get it, I get it."

I ran into my dorm house, pulled on my clothes, and my letterman jacket. Jake pulled open the door as I stepped out, ready to face the day.

"So, are you gonna ask her out?" I asked him.

"Nah," he replied, "we've got to focus on you. We need to get your ranking up."

"And how exactly are we gonna do that?"

"I have a plan," he said with a laugh and wrapped an arm around mine as we walked back to the elevator. "Okay, so I didn't ask you anything about you, and I took away your breakfast. So, what's your dorm like?"

"Nice," I said, wondering if I should have given him a tour. "all the walls are exposed brick, I'll show you later."

"I checked ahead to make sure I knew where the classes were."

"Really?" I yawned. Even for Jake it was an impressive start.

"Of course, I'm your handler, it's my job." He poked at my nose like we were still kids, and handed me my time table.

Breakfast

    History class w/ Mrs. Adkins.

    [The Pacific Theater During World War II.]

(NO super heroes. We're not learning about super heroes!)

    Social studies w/ Dr. Diamond.

[How to interact with others and charm the cameras.]

(Please refrain from bringing home made super suits to class, and deciding on your own names. It's just embarrassing.)

Social studies w/ Dr. Diamond. (Double Period)

[Trust exercises, to improve hero team work.]

(It's not funny when you let your team mate fall. Stop doing that. I'm looking at you, Joey.)

Lunch

Gym w/ Coach Flat.

[Sparring, and self defense, aided by Lightning Kid.]

(Get set to get wrecked, tiny adults!)

English w/ Mr. Andersson.

[Continuing with class reading of *The Caves of Steel* by Isaac Asimov.]

(Jenna, please stop insisting everyone in the book is secretly gay, Elijah has a wife.)

Maths with Ms. Lyngstad.

[How to calculate an agent's percentage, fees for speaking engagements and merchandise licensing agreements.]

(Stop writing boobs on your calculators. It's NOT funny.)

End of School Day

. . .

I folded it up, and Jake unwound his arm from mine as I joined the crowd of first years, "I'll see you at lunch."

I had expected to start class with, well, a *class*, but, instead I found myself in a large room filled with clothes, makeup, and cameras. Veronica appeared with her assistants, and handed something off to one of them. "Okay kids! Gather round! Your first period starts in an hour's time, so before that we're doing all the photography for your debuts!"

One assistant, clipboard in hand, climbed up on a box and shouted out team names. One by one the teams went through hair, makeup, photography, and editing. As each one finished, they were excused, and directed somewhere else, but when my turn came, time had almost run out; they slapped concealer on my face, and didn't bother to change my clothes. They took exactly three photos and the message was clear; I wasn't worth their time.

Still wiping the makeup off my face I pulled the glass doors open to find all the other students with Captain Fantastic. It took me a moment to remember we'd already met, and there was no reason to be as star struck as I was. His eyes darted through the crowd, and settled on me briefly as he smiled. I resisted the urge to clutch my chest like a tween swooning at the sight of their favorite pop star. Almost all the girls were still wearing their professionally applied makeup, not willing to waste the opportunity to look good all day. Captain Fantastic clapped his hands, and everyone turned.

"Hello! Hi. How is everyone? Okay?" There was a general hum of agreement. "Good, good. So, things you need to know. Hero High is a normal school, maths, science, art. You do superhero stuff, *after* school, on the weekends, and in gym. Variety show episodes are filmed on Saturdays and Sundays. Let me make this very clear," he said clearing his throat, "your studies are important! Training to be a superhero is not everything! Okay!?" Everyone nodded, and he clapped his hands again. If that was how he felt, then why were we woken up at six, to have strangers take pictures of us? Why have cameras invade our bedrooms? "Great! Then I'll finish with... Um, hi, I'm Captain Fantastic, and I'll be your principal for the next four years. Good luck, and off to class with all of you!"

He nodded again, and pointed to the doors as he left. Schedules were handed out along with backpacks which contained everything we could possibly need. Each bag was color coded, and so were all of the utensils. Math class was nothing special, a few heroes taught some of the regular classes. Only Coach Flat taught gym.

I was exhausted, I'd been thrown into a completely new world. So I practically ran into the cafeteria, eager for some fuel. Handlers were already there and eating, there were two cameras, moving through to each table, and interviewing students about their first day.

I covered my face with my bag, as Jake waved me over and handed me a tray. "You're not gonna tell me to skip lunch too are you?" I asked.

"No. I don't think you'd get through the day." He mumbled.

"Nice." I repled.

"What?" He laughed. I nudged him in the side, but he only chuckled.

"Okay, so let me give you the low down, I've been studying up," he said as we turned round with our plates full, and he passed me his phone. "Checkout the website for the rankings."

I tapped my way to the Hero High website and found the up-to-date popularity rankings on the front page organized by year. All the new kids sat with their newly assigned teams, getting to know the older members.

"Okay. Team gold: all first years, all groomed beforehand, and not surprisingly, already front runners," said Jake pointing to the table in the center of the room. Gold team had three members, and they seemed to enjoy each other's company in a very laid back way. I checked the phone. It already placed two of them at one and two in the freshman year rankings.

"That's Aya, the guy next to her is David, and the other one is Ashley."

I bit back the urge to tell him I'd already met Ashley because we hadn't *really* spoken, so I looked at the other members. Aya was a tall slender girl, beautiful by any standards. Her hair bundled on the top of her head in twists like a crown. Her skin was dark and rich, like wet earth, face shaped like a heart, and eyes sharp like the headlights of a sports car. David was the everyday image of rising star. Broad shouldered and handsome he had the strong 'superhero' jaw. His chin was thick, his eyebrows darker than his hair, and his skin took on the tone of oak wood.

Veronica stood behind them, pulling David's arm over Aya as the cameras faced them and Veronica started the silent countdown. Aya and David looked awkward in each others arms as the camera started to roll.

They smiled and introduced each other as boyfriend and girlfriend before going over their time at camp, and who their parents were. David talked about his dad, who'd retired many years ago, and was now working in the Canadian government. Aya spoke about her mother and father, and their continued humanitarian work. Veronica eventually nodded, realizing she wasn't going to get a sob story out of them, and asked them for a quick kiss on camera. Aya declined, saying she'd just eaten a slice of garlic pizza, which made everyone laugh as the camera moved on to Ashley. Veronica took a seat behind the camera and slung question after question at Ashley, as though she didn't know what to do with him. She asked him if he had famous parents, he said no. She asked him what made him special enough to be the captain's mentee, he said he didn't know. She asked him if he had his eye on any of the girls in his class, he said he was focusing on his studies.

Veronica was losing her patience. I turned to Jake as we stepped away from the food line, and he muffled his laugh.

"What, what is it, what are you laughing about?" I asked looking for a table.

"Ashley. I mean, who names a kid Ashley? Ashley's a girl's name," he giggled. I rolled my eyes, and pointed to a booth at the back.

"Is it?" I said, setting my tray down, and looking out the window overlooking the city.

"Duh. It doesn't matter, point is, they're gonna be the next big thing, I'm telling you!" said Jake.

"Okay."

"I mean it. When Aya starts selling her merch, I swear I'm buying! She's already number one in the year!"

"Really?"

"Aya and David were in the public eye before Hero High, they're legacy heroes," Jake told me. "Rumor says they went to Camp Hero, and that's how they met!"

"Keep your voice down," I hissed.

"Okay, okay. Over there." Jake pointed to a table full of kids lifting objects two and three times their size, and claimed they were called 'the buffs'. The handlers sat at corner tables, studying non stop and another, large round table held all the heroes destined for Hero Control. Methodical and organized, their powers were not particularly useful in a fight.

Right at the back were boys and girls who appeared to be brooding, next to them were a few bubbly team mates, and off to the very center were all the kids that were guaranteed to be popular by the end of the year. Most of them would switch teams to create a gigantic heap of popularity which everyone predicted would be the gold team, and then, there was me.

Where did I fit in? Why exactly was I in a team by myself?

Jake stumbled and rammed into one girl's back. I caught his tray in the nick of time, but the girl's clattered to the ground. The cameras interviewing students spun round, and the producers went silent like a documentary presenter trying not to disturb wildlife. Jake had walked straight into her, and she stood, glaring at both of us. I felt sure I could hear a growl as she looked down at her ruined lunch, and back up at Jake. Like someone navigating a tight rope, I stepped in between them, and Jake tensed behind me. It was the girl who'd cried about her totally *not* broken arm.

"'Day, what're you doing? Move!" said Jake.

I ignored him and held out my tray to the girl, offering her some of my food.

She looked directly at me, her right eye twitching. "My lunch," she said, moving her gaze back to Jake, and I realized the whole *room* had gone silent, "how dare you!"

"Relax lady," said Jake stepping out from behind me. He put his hand on the girls shoulder and I heard whispers from the other students. Her name was Mary Mayberry. "Take a chill pill. Okay?"

Before I knew it, she'd grabbed Jake by the collar, and the students were up in their seats, wondering if they should run to fetch a teacher. Not a single member of the camera crew tried to call for help or step in to stop what was happening.

"What did you just say to me?" said Mary raising her fist.

Not hesitating as I blinked. My heartbeat slowed, and then stopped, forming that tiny pocket of time that allowed me to think for as long as I needed.

What could I do? I could put the tray in-between her fist and Jake's face. Would that really stop her though? No, and Jake would still get hurt, plus I'd throw away all my food. I told myself to be real, that I was probably going to lose my lunch if I got into a fight with this girl. I could ram myself into her, that would be fast enough to throw her off balance, but once again I'd lose my food. But... It was all I could think of.

The world snapped back into acton, and I rammed into Mary as fast as I could, my tray and all my precious lunch falling to the floor. My body hit a table, and all the kids sitting there screamed at me for falling on them. I pushed myself up, only to have one boy at the table shove me backwards. I heard another plastic tray clatter to the floor. It was Ashley Ang, dressed in an up-tight sweater and tie combo, the glint of his glasses obscuring his eyes. His gaze shifted to the lunch I'd knocked on the floor.

"I had to *pay* for that," he said, looking genuinely distressed.

"Apologize, freshman," called Mary Mayberry.

"Yeah, that was *so* not cool," agreed another girl.

I considered it for a second, but with everyone's eyes on me, expecting me to grovel, something in me refused. I was trying to help. If the producers wouldn't do it, I *would*.

"I'm waiting, freshman!" shouted Mary, again.

"I have a name," I replied.

"Like I care." She snorted.

That was it. I picked up a glass of cola, and poured it straight onto her head. She screamed like I'd stabbed her and threw a pie in my direction, but instead of hitting me, she hit the boy behind me. He threw something, and then his target threw something, and in seconds the room erupted into a full on food fight. The cameras rushed back and forth from one person to the next trying to keep up. For a moment I thought I could escape, until I saw Jake lobbing a slice of cake at Mary. She thrust her arm into the air, then she charged towards Jake, slashing small holes of swirling light. The cafeteria roared as the older students raced for the corners, escaping Mary's power. Everyone watched Jake run round the room like a dog on a race track, dodging Mary's attacks as each hole tried to pull him in, only to be plugged with tables and chairs.

I blinked again.

Mary had to have a weakness, she had to have a quirk. What exactly was her power? Black holes? No. Superpowers are specific, scientific. I'd seen her card on my first day, it said, 'space exchange'. So she wasn't a black hole, she could exchange one space for another with a slash of her hand. The air that sucked and blowed out of the hole's in space were simply air displacement, which was great, but didn't help me. Could she control where to send someone? I looked at each lingering hole out of the corner of my unmoving eyes. One led to grey skies, another to blue, they weren't in the same place. What did that say about her? That she could control it? If so, then why those places? Was it random? I didn't know, and I didn't like not knowing.

I could run an experiment, and find out, but I didn't have the time. I'd just have to try manipulation and see if I could throw her in one. It was a long shot, but it was all I had.

I blinked back in, and ran for someone's apple, chucking it at Mary's head. Once I had her full attention I backed up against the cafeteria wall, my eyes scanning the crowd. How could I get her to think of somewhere specific? All I could think of was the Power League theme song. "P-p-p-p-power league! P-p-p-p-power league! Using super powers to play a sport!"

There weren't any actual lyrics for the power league theme, I'd made them up. Mary's brow raised as she slashed through the air and I could see on the other side, the power league stadium. She'd be able to get out if she could focus, but it would keep her occupied enough for me to hide. I ran forwards to push her in, but she grabbed me by the collar.

"That's enough!" Captain Fantastic's voice boomed through the cafeteria, and the cameras ran to catch it. "You two, *detention*. Everyone else, get back to classes, now!" The Captain ordered. The room cleared in a mumble of complaints and curse words, mostly from the producers. The Captain strode towards us, and forcefully removed Mary's hands from me. "Ms. Mayberry, Ms. Fitzsimmons, what happened?"

Mary clenched her jaw and narrowed her eyes.

"I tried to stop her from punching Jake," I told him, "and well, things escalated. She was going to punch Jake!"

The Captain sighed. "I can see that Ms. Fitzsimmons. I was hoping you'd be one of the good ones."

Jake looked back from the doorway, and gave me a thumbs up before leaving.

Had he bumped into Mary deliberately? Was he giving me a chance to prove I could fight with the power I had? Jake had always had faith in me, but now it seemed like I was in trouble. He'd come laughing and smiling into my life when we were only two years old and as soon as I realized there was a difference between boys and girls I'd had a crush on him. Jake had even been my first kiss, a kiss that had led to nothing, as first kisses should. He'd stared at me awkwardly, and acted like it never happened. I'd taken it as a polite no thanks', but to be fair, we were both ten at the time. I sighed at The Captain's words. "I just didn't want her to start a fight," I said.

"So you started one of your own? Really?" The Captain said in a tone of pure disbelief.

"No-one got hurt." I insisted.

"You need to learn how to resolve things peacefully, Ms. Fitzsimmons," said The Captain.

"I'm sorry, Captain." He looked so disappointed in me my heart broke. Mary sneered in my direction.

"Clearly Ms. Mayberry doesn't think it's possible to resolve things peacefully."

"Oh no, I *do*," said Mary, "I just think that's funny coming from a murderer."

The Captain's face tightened, and he took a long deep breath before tearing his gaze from Mary.

"*Detention*, after school, my office, both of you," he stated firmly.

"You want to put us in the same room together?" I cried, looking back and forth between them.

He paused, and nodded to himself. "You have a point. You two will serve detention in different rooms." He said to himself.

Mary re-adjusted her jacket, smoothing out the collar, but didn't seem to want to change her wet clothes. She stomped down the hallway. My stomach rumbled. I was *not* going to skip lunch. I put the last penny of my weekly allowance in the vending machine, and got myself a sandwich. I was about to tear up the packaging when I saw Ashley talking to The Captain who clapped him on the back as he left. Ashley just stood there as though he had no-where else to be, like he'd turned off, waiting for orders. My stomach rumbled again. Jake had ruined Mary's lunch, but *I* had ruined his.

Ashley was a long way down the hallway as my grip on the sandwich tightened. I sighed, and threw the sandwich at his head, hoping he'd catch it. It hit him in the center of his back, with a faint plastic slap. He swerved, his lips pushing against each other, his features almost shaking.

"I swear to God, Fitz, if you want to start something-" his index finger extended towards me like I was a dog. It really pissed me off; but then he caught sight of the sandwich on the floor. He shook his head as he knelt down and muttered something under his breath, all I could make out was, 'at my head'.

"Sorry about your lunch!" I said. His eyebrows twitched upward and his eyes widened, as though I'd spoken a different language.

And then I left.

————

The rest of the school day went as expected, I was terrible in English, but couldn't wait to get to Math, it had a way of making me feel at home. Either you're wrong, or right, no in-between. Not to mention my power helped a hell of a lot, I could think through all the problems with no time limit.

As the bell for the end of the school day rang, everyone collected their color coded bags, and headed out the door.

I'd almost forgotten about detention until I saw The Captain at the end of the hallway blocking access to the elevators. In my old school if I'd got detention, no one would have come looking. In fact, I don't think I ever went to detention when I was told to, and none of the teachers ever brought it up.

The Captain though, he seemed more hands on. I kind of hated *and* admired that. I'd never had an adult *force* me to do anything before, but there he was, *forcing* me to go to detention, and you know what? I was happy about it.

He held out his arm down the hall, and followed beside me. A few students gave us some strange looks, I was the kid who got detention on the very first day. We stopped at a set of glass doors etched in large black triangles. The Captain pushed them in, and went to sit behind his desk.

The walls of his office were black and gold just like the lobby, and the chairs behind his desk were an off white color, their backs and arms like a U. It all seemed just a little too flashy; he'd always been a man of the people, a man's man and this, apart from the pictures of his wife on his desk, wasn't very, *him*.

I took my place in the U shaped chair opposite his desk, and saw Mary already sitting in the other. The Captain signed something then looked up to the both of us, pushing his paper work aside. "So. We need to figure something out between you two." He groaned. Mary refused to look away from the wall, or even acknowledge that I'd joined her. She wasn't wet anymore, someone had dried off her clothes, or the school day had done it for her. "We don't need to talk about who did what, we just need to discuss the emotion behind the fight. The others say you used your powers Mary, why was that?" The Captain asked, leaning forwards.

"That handler was pissing me off," she spat.

"Good, but why was he pissi- I mean, annoying you?" he replied, the tone far too calm.

Mary didn't reply for a moment, she looked at me briefly.

"Maybe I shouldn't be here," I suggested, "maybe you could call us in one at a time or something?" Mary's sneer reappeared and Captain Fantastic chewed on his bottom lip.

"Now now Ms. Fitzsimmons, there's no need for that," he said. "Mary?"

"It's none of your business," she growled.

The Captain's face dropped, and he sighed. "Well, in that case I really am going to have to give you two detention. You realize you're giving this young lady detention too Ms. Mayberry?" Mary didn't reply so The Captain got up, opened a classroom door and shook the hand of another teacher. "Mary, this is Coach Flat, he'll be overseeing your detention period." Coach Flat tipped an invisible hat to her, and then to me. The Captain extended his hand, showed Mary to her seat and then closed the door behind her. He led me to a different door. It opened into a slightly smaller classroom with exactly two desks, one for me, and one for a teacher. Instead of a teacher, Ashley Ang sat at the front.

"Ms. Fitzsimmons, since I'm Mr. Ang's mentor he'll be overseeing your detention. Don't start any more fights." With that, The Captain left, closing the door behind him.

Even as I sat down Ashley didn't look up from what I assumed was his homework. I spied a small camera in the corner of the ceiling that probably linked directly to the website, they knew someone would be having detention in there, so no doubt they had a live feed. I kept my gaze firmly on those frosted glass doors, but I could feel Ashley's eyes flickering up and glaring at me, sneering, frowning, whatever. There was nothing, *nothing* in the room to entertain me.

I counted the tiles on the ceiling, I tried to unscrew my desk with my finger nails, but by the time I looked to the clock, only fifteen minutes had passed. I let out a sigh. The only interesting thing in the room was Ashley.

He hunched over his work like the gawky giant he was, almost too big for the chair he sat in. This was Mrs. Adkins class room, and she was about as tall as me. Nothing in this room was the right scale for someone his height, he looked like an adult at a toddler's tea party. Why did he have to be so dull? He had no hair on his sweater, or the paint on his jeans, there wasn't a speck of anything on Ashley Ang. His tie was deftly aligned, his shirt pressed, and his sweater, bright, but not *too* bright, heaven forbid someone would notice him! No, Ashley Ang was profoundly DULL, and it was annoying as hell. I bet he was the kind of guy I could lob a spitball at and he'd ignore me.

Don't do it Friday. Don't do it.

You're just going to get into more trouble.

I had to do it.

I took a spare sheet of paper, crumpled it up into a nice neat ball, and in my boredom, I threw it at his head. The paper bounced right off his shoulder, without even so much as a flinch. I knew it. Ignore at all costs was his policy. Boring.

I tapped my toes against the floor, and sat up. So, his clothes were pressed and pristine, what did that say about him? What could I figure out about this guy? A choice in hairstyle or lack thereof says a lot about a person. I had messy, puffy hair, and a fringe straight out of the eighties. I work a lot, so I keep it short, you can tell just by looking at me that I'm a hands-on kind of person. Jake is the kind of guy that likes to flip his dirty blonde bowl haircut. He does it because he likes to be trendy, but he also says the style is really easy to maintain. Captain Fantastic had an old fashioned comb back, in a glorious strawberry blond. Not that I was a fan or anything like that. Ashley, his hair was the kind of black that looked blue under the light. It went to the nape of his neck, combed back, with a gentle kink in it. It was actually kind of nice. Soft looking, whatever. He wasn't interesting.

I pulled out my phone to check school rankings, but everything was the same; Ashley sat comfortably at number five for the freshman class. I cycled through all the cameras currently live in the school and found the feed to the room we sat in but watching it was weird, so I looked to see if they'd put my face on any of the games in the app store.

The moment my phone rang and chirped like a tribble as I pressed a button, Ashley's head shot up with a look like a wolf. I nearly jumped off my chair at the sight, Ashley's eyes didn't leave me as he stood up. It was like one of those towers in a theme park where they drag you up to the top and then drop you, the straighter his legs got the closer I felt to the top of the needle. Ashley might as well have been the same height as one of those rides; watching him stand over me filled me with just as much dread. His hand slammed down on my desk, but I didn't flinch.

My head tilted to the side in question, and my hand still gripped my phone like whatever was on it was far too important to miss. Ashley leaned over me and reached for my phone. His body was like a mountain blocking out the sun, or in this case, the single light fixture.

His hand wrapped around mine and I forgot what he was doing for a moment as a curious kick ran through me. My breath hitched, and my hand went loose. My phone slipped from my hand to his.

"Hey! Give that back," I blurted.

"This is detention, not after school day care," he turned on his heel as though he'd no other reason to look at me.

"What's your problem?" I demanded. His shoulders tensed and his body stiffened. He gripped my phone tighter and pulled the cable from the live feed before muttering under his breath.

Was he allowed to do that?

"What's *my* problem?" his jaw clenched as he turned to meet my gaze and I stood up to try and level the playing field, before remembering the disparity between our heights. "My problem is I don't like stuck up little brats playing at superhero." He said it in a gentle way without a hint of satisfaction in his voice, as though it was something he'd said a million times before, and was starting to grow tired of.

"Stuck up little brats? I'm not," I insisted, but actually, I kind of was. "Ferrari, check. Water bed, check. Ocean side villa made mostly out of glass, check. Raised by nanny, check. Impractical white furniture, check. Huh, well what do ya know?" I mumbled, "I guess I am a spoiled little brat." I shrugged and turned on my happy go lucky switch that dulled the regular frustration. "Whatever," I said with a shrug and what would have been a skip in my walk, had I been walking. I reached for the phone and he pulled it back. "Just give it back you, you giant! It's not like I'm in here for a *good* reason, I've detention because I tried to stop a fight, how is that worth punishment?"

"So you're just going to decide *not* to punish yourself?" he asked.

"Yes."

"That's not how the rules work." He gritted.

"Rules, shmules." He gaped at me as though I'd just said a string of curse words. I sighed, and gave up reaching for the phone. My arm was getting tired.

"Do you have *any* regard for the rules set out?"

"Not really."

He scoffed at me, and put my phone into his pocket. "How do you expect to be a superhero?"

"By doing good?"

"And breaking the law?"

"Breaking the law doesn't make you a bad person. Lots of good people have broken the law, sometimes without knowing. The law doesn't determine who's good and who's bad, it determines who's a rule breaker and who isn't."

Ashley shook his head, and moved round his desk, pulling a large file out from the door while I sat back down in my chair. "Finally your file makes sense."

"My file?" The large blue binder had, "Hero High" stamped on the front. Ashley plowed through it, and stopped at a page I could tell he'd reviewed before. "How could you ever be a superhero?" He said. It was the smudge of hate that made me sit up in my chair, and turned my face cold. "You set a water tower on fire!" he said pointing to a page as he read it out. "Because, and I quote Ms. Fitz, 'My friends bet me I couldn't set water on fire.'

"Hey don't knock it," I told him, "I got a few hundred bucks out of that, it paid for my new jacket." It was actually an out of commission water tower no one used anymore, and the money I'd got from it had actually only paid for my family's water bill, but there was no way I'd tell him that. Ironic. Maybe? Is that how irony works?

"Oh, I'm not done yet!" he said, clearing his throat before he continued, "you crashed a sports car, and when asked for a reason, you said you were bored."

I'd done that to try and get my fathers attention. Not a good reason in retrospect, plus, it didn't work. "That was an accident," I told him.

"You once skipped school to go to Paris for dinner."

I had to skip school for a company meeting my father refused to go to, only a few months after the "accident" with the car. It was the first time I'd filled in for my father as CEO. That was when I realized I couldn't go to school anymore. "I needed some alone time," I told Ashley.

"You bought a house with your father's money-"

"My money!" I said, and covered my mouth as fast as I could. I wasn't fast enough.

I'd signed those papers, I'd done the work, I'd read all the proposals, done all the presentations, talked to all the investors. I ran that tiny company, *not* my father. That was *my* money. I'd earned it. But that's not what I said.

"I mean, when you're a family, it's no one's personal money, right? It's everyone's. That's why you earn. So if you look at it properly, it was totally just as much *my* money as it was *his*." Why did I say that? Ashley looked at me like a tragedy that'd blown his house away, as though I was something he simply couldn't comprehend.

He shook his head, turned one last page, and pushed his index finger down so hard on it, it started to go white. "You started a fight club."

He had me there. There were *some* things I could try to justify, but others I couldn't, *that* was one of them. What could I say? I wanted to hit something. I was frustrated, I was always frustrated. And rather than hitting innocent bystanders I chose to hit people who'd agreed to it? I didn't need to tell him about all of those occasions, or my reasoning behind them.

As I sat there being verbally eviscerated, I knew I was done playing the game with him, interacting with him, looking at him. It was tiring. I had enough to worry about. I got up to leave, throwing my backpack over my shoulder.

"Detention's not up yet," he said.

"Bite me." Just as my hand reached for the door it swung open to reveal a smiling Captain Fantastic on the other side.

"So kids how was tha-"

I shoved passed him, regretting it only seconds after as tears pricked at the edge of my eyes. I'd shoved

Captain Fantastic, the most perfect man in the world. What was wrong with me?

"Hey you can't do that!" Ashley shouted.

"Did something happen?" The Captain asked, looking to Ashley. He frowned at The Captain, as if everything I'd done was his fault. "It's alright Ashley, go get something to eat. Let me talk to her."

"Don't waste your time Captain," Ashley said as he headed towards the elevators. The Captain squared his shoulders and smiled

"I see you and Ashely are getting along well," said The Captain as he caught up with my short stride.

"I hate him," I blurted.

"You hate a lot of people don't you?" he hummed, and clapped me on the back, and the elevator pinged. The Captain extended his arm like a hostess, but in this case he introduced an almost middle aged woman with a carefree expression and some brilliant red kicks.

No wait!

It was Sense!

"This is Lisa Kisaragi. She's your mentor, Sense. I thought this would be a good time for you two to do some bonding."

I'd met a few superheroes, but I never imagined I'd meet Sense!

———

"Wait, uh, Ms. Fitz, I mean, Friday?"

"Yes?"

"You knew Sense?"

"Duh! Sense was the longest working superhero in history." Her eyes light up as she speaks, as though these are all her heroes.

"Sense was older than Captain Fantastic?" I ask and she thinks for a moment before shaking her head.

"The Captain took five years off after the Dr. Dangerous trial. Surely you know that?"

I didn't, but I wasn't about to admit that to Friday. The trial took place before I was born, along with a good chunk of Sense's career.

"So what can you tell us about Sense?" I ask her.

"Her name was Lisa Kisaragi. She was tall and athletic, with a bright smile and black, bouncy hair held back in a ponytail." Friday searches for what to say next, as though pitching her favorite show or book to me, trying to make sure I leave wanting more. *"She'd been working since the age of fourteen, and she had two kids. She wasn't the most popular hero in the world, most people didn't know much about her, but people knew her. She was a constant people could always look for, like the Captain."*

"So, you were a fan?"
"Boy was I?"

———

"I'll take it from here," she said, wrapping her arms round The Captain in a quick, familiar bear hug. "Come on then!" and keeping an arm on my back she led me into the elevator. I was standing next to Sense! Sure, I'd met a lot of superheroes, but still. She was *really* someone you could look up to.

Back on the lobby floor Jake ran up to me, wrapping me in a half hug, before Lisa took notice of him. "Who's this, your handler?"

"Jake Jepsen at your service," Jake said as he tipped an imaginary hat and held his hand out for her to shake.

"Well Jake I was just about to take Friday here to some family dinner, how about you come with us?" Sense suggested.

"I'd love to, but I can't, I've got work to do." He wiggled his eye brows at me, and I knew he had a date.

"Well then perhaps another time," said Sense.

"Another time." Jake pulled me into another hug, and Lisa dropped me off at my dorm to change. She leaned against the door as I hurried in.

The sun was starting to set, and it would be dark by

the time we got back. I pulled on a jacket and a nice scarf, something worthy of a big city, and ran back.

Lisa led me down, showed me how to get out of the building without going through the mall, and pulled me into a parking lot. Her car was a sensible mini van, the back seats littered with snacks and toys.

"Sorry, it's so messy," she said, "I haven't had time to clean."

"No worries," I said, climbing into the beige interior. I closed the door and Lisa pulled out, into the streets of Icon City.

"Friday, right?" I nodded to her, suppressing a smile.

"So Friday, what do you want to know about me?"

I already knew everything. How was I supposed to say that without sounding weird? I settled for, "I know a fair amount of stuff."

"Oh, like what?" She smiled.

"Well, I know you've been a hero for over twenty years," I told her. Most heroes didn't last for ten. I mean, they were always in the public eye, but being a superhero is like being an athlete; at some point, you just can't keep up. Most heroes retire in their early thirties.

Lisa smiled. "So, you're probably wondering how old I am, right?"

I knew. She was thirty seven. It was written on her trading card and I'd brought all my trading cards with me.

"I'm thirty seven," she continued, "not old, by any means, but the Hero Channel disagrees. I joined right out of middle school, I've been a working superhero since I was fourteen, but I spent my first two years essentially being a water boy." She said it like the job had been a hassle, but still, she smiled at the memory. "I have two kids, I work almost full-time and my hobbies include, well, being a superhero, being a mother, and now, being a mentor."

"So, not much free time then?" I said, stating the obvious.

"Between the city and my kids? No. Not much. But I don't mind, that's how I like it." Lisa smiled in a way that told me she was far too confident to care if anyone had a problem with her. She pulled the car into an inner city Family Fries, and pulled out her phone, scrolling through a long list of regular orders.

"What do you want?" She asked. I told her to get whatever she was having.

I took the drinks and spare bags as we were handed the food. It took every ounce of self control not to reach into that bag and eat, just *one* french fry, but I ignored the rumble in my stomach and concentrated on Sense.

She wasn't an obscure superhero, but she'd never really been front and center. The media always favored the younger generation. As a kid I'd never understood why. I'd seen her save a school bus on TV, and fight off a super villain single handed.

"I've seen some of your, stuff," I said, but it was a lie, I'd seen *all* her stuff. "Why do the cameras-? - I mean, they never-"

She nodded, knowing exactly what I meant, and launched right in. "There are a few reasons. My handler blames the lack of general public interest on my suit: he tells me a fire truck red color scheme isn't friendly, and I don't show enough skin."

Lisa's super suit still had elements from her early days as a hero, so it looked a little dated next to the others, with its visor and shoulder pads.

"The Captain's suit is red," I told her.

"Exactly! So what? It's just not okay on me? And then *I* say, when you're a full time mother and a super-hero it's difficult to maintain a swimsuit ready body, so that ship's already sailed."

"Are all the handlers like that?"

"Most of them. I remember when I started out they thought it was important my suit had boob plates, even though I told them repeatedly it just redirects force to your vital organs. Amateurs."

"Boob plates?" I asked. I could guess what it meant, but had never heard the term.

"Yeah, you know, armor that molds around your boobs, because when you're fighting, it's so important your opponent knows you're a woman."

Lisa slowed as she rounded a corner, and eventually pulled into the middle of a neat city street among other family houses. As we pulled into her driveway, Lisa stopped the car under the warm amber lights and waved me out. I picked up the multitude of fast food bags and climbed up to her front door. And I do mean *climbed*. Her house sat on one of the steeper hills in the city. The moment the door opened the smell of jasmine and antiseptic wafted through the air. The experience was surreal in a way, it felt like those times I'd been over to other kids houses when I was younger, and it just seemed so odd to be *in* someone else's home.

"Mom!" Two kids came rushing up, she dropped her handbag like a brick, caught both of them just in time, and gave each one a kiss on the forehead.

"Come in kid, in you come." She muttered without realizing I'd been standing on the other side of the door, too cautious to step in. I tiptoed inside, Lisa slammed her keys down on her kitchen surface, and started handing out the food.

Her home was like a safe haven of warm calming

colors, a cave somewhere far away that lived in the light of the setting sun. The ceilings were two stories high, and a small balcony looked over the living room, where the odd toy or pen had been thrown on the floor. My eyes flew across the room and settled on her family photos. In a crowd of pictures of her kids was a single frame of her and a man. And that was it, one picture, everything else was the kids.

"James. That was his name," she said putting her hand on my shoulder.

"I uh, I'm sorry, I didn't mean to pry."

She shook her head and smiled. "It's okay, I'll tell you about him sometime. But not tonight. Today's not a day for crying." Her kids, Julia and Andrew, had always supported her career, their pride in their mom was obvious. They were far more mature than other kids their age and had often cooked family dinner despite only being eleven. Lisa told me she had married at nineteen and had the kids at twenty five; Julia and Andrew were the best behaved kids I'd ever seen.

Lisa sat down with them and her hamburger, sighing as they switched over to the Hero Channel. I settled down next to them feeling exhausted, then all of a sudden, one commentator started talking about Sense.

Lisa's head snapped round, smiling like her children

as she shoved a french fry into her mouth. "See kids, I told ya mama would get there! Turn it up!"

The blonde woman on TV straightened her papers, and began to speak. "Also in today's news, the B class hero Sense, will become part of one of the few duo teams on the Hero Channel, others include Silver & Gold, The Sharks, and the occasional team up of Black Magic and Captain Fantastic."

Lisa's smiled drifted into a frown as her hand fumbled around in her pockets for her Hero Program issue phone, panic in her eyes.

"Didn't you know?" I asked, "wasn't this planned?"

She looked round to me, stepped up from the sofa and started dialing like she was trying to kill the phone. "No, I did not know this was happening." The TV showed a young man standing behind a podium as he spoke about his new partner Sense. "He's a debut hero! I'm not working with a child!" said Lisa. Her head spun round to me. "No offense, kid."

"None taken," she nodded at me, and pressed the phone to her ear.

"Why is this happening?" Lisa asked as I stood and pressed my ear to the phone.

"Lisa, you're twenty years in," said the voice on the other end, "if you want to keep going, we need a reason to keep you. This operation costs some serious dough."

"Why give me an eighteen year old?" asked Lisa, pacing the room while I tried hard to follow, "if you want people to fund me, put me in a god damn bikini, I don't care anymore, this is how I earn. This is how my kids get to go to school, and it's an expensive school!"

"You're forty," said the voice as Lisa stomped to the fridge, she didn't even care I was trying to follow.

"I'm thirty seven!" she said as I tried to listen in but she held the phone away, and looked at me. I expected her to scold me, instead she said, "can you believe this guy?"

I shook my head, she pressed the phone to her ear again, and I followed.

"And besides," the voice continued, "he's not an eighteen year old, he's twenty six. He didn't register for a couple of years, went into training late."

"So you're going to put me next to a twenty year old?" Lisa asked, "fine. I get it, it's been decided."

"There's nothing I can do, Lisa," said the voice, "my hands are tied, you'll just have to make the best of it." With a click, he hung up and Lisa closed her phone.

Andrew and Julia shook their heads at the phone call, like this sort of thing happened all the time. I fell back onto the sofa and Lisa slumped down next to us with a sigh, engulfing her kids in another hug.

"Well kids, Mommy has a new partner. Let's hope he's reasonable."

"I'm sure it'll be fine," I said, trying to sound confident, "I mean you're the more experienced one, I'm sure he'll listen."

"I hope so. Sorry about this Friday, I'm supposed to be your mentor, and I'm not doing much mentoring."

"Are you kidding me? You're great. You're a full time superhero and mom. I'd say that's pretty amazing."

"Thanks for saying so, but-"

"I mean it. It's nice to know you can have a family, and do this job. You're a cool lady." I declared.

"Well, thanks kid," she said, giving my shoulder a pat.

Lisa's phone rang like an alarm bell, and her kids heads whipped round. "What is it, mom?"

She sighed at the dance of lights on the cover of her phone. "Trouble downtown kids."

Julia shot up from the sofa and threw her mother her jacket, while Andrew ran to the door. I was utterly confused for a second but Lisa nodded, and pushed her self up. "Brush your teeth and then go to bed, kids," she told them, "if I find out you haven't, there'll be hell to pay."

"Don't worry, Mom, jeez."

"Friday, you're with me," said Lisa. "Time for you to see what the job entails. Let's boogie."

Andrew threw my jacket expecting me to catch it, but it fell on my head like a wet dish cloth. He giggled as Lisa pulled me out the door and the change of scenery hit me; her home had been so warm and cozy, and now I was out in the cold starless night, with the light show of skyscrapers above me.

"We're gonna have to run," said Lisa as she started to tear ass down the road and I did my best to follow, but the hollow in my stomach was slowing me down, how was I supposed to run when I hadn't eaten anything all day?

Lisa kept up the pace for a couple of blocks until she skidded to a halt as a large city bus two stories high came into view.

A door in the side opened, and Carey Fry reached out a hand for Lisa and then me. The bus was huge, the size of a living room. Lisa went straight to a changing room. Two people, probably handlers, or supporting heroes sat at tables working on their computers. Carey held out his hand to me, and I took it, trying to make it look like I knew what I was doing.

"I remember you, you're Friday Fitzsimmons?" He smiled.

"That's me," I replied.

"And Ms. Kisaragi is your mentor. She's a good find. Once saved an entire school bus of kids single handedly. Diamond in the rough that woman," he said nodding.

"It sure looks like it, Sir." I agreed.

"Carey. Call me Carey. Are you going out with Lisa, or just staying to observe?"

"Going out," I said, though I wasn't sure what was involved.

"In that case I believe we have some armor for you, put it on and get out there quickly. She doesn't wait around for anyone." He laughed.

I nodded, and disappeared behind the curtains. A piece of modern plate armor sat in the back, it had no size or gender, so I strapped it on. As I was about to run out the door, Carey grabbed me by the shoulder, and handed me a domino mask.

"You're gonna need this if you wanna be a super-hero." Putting it on was like becoming a whole new person, as though just a mask could make me feel more confident. Carey put on an ear piece. "Move it," he said, indicating the door.

"Yes, Sir, I mean Carey. Big fan by the way."

"Thanks," he said and smiled as he held the door open. "Now get going."

I joined Lisa who was already out the door, and

rolled my eyes as I experienced the same sensation as before; going from the dimly lit warm interior, to the cold night air of the city.

"First test, get there in time," said Lisa as she waited for her red bike to appear from under the bus.

"Hold on, you're not taking me with you?" I asked.

"When I started out, I had a bike, not a motor bike, a pedal bike," she told me as she climbed into the saddle. "Figure it out kid."

———

"A pedal bike?" I ask and Friday smiles.
"Lisa started out fetching water and help for other heroes. She used a pedal bike."
"You're serious?"
"I believe it was pink and they stuck flower stickers all over it," she tells me as she sets her cup down. "In those days they had her in a pink tennis skirt and sneakers. It was her job to just run about from place to place, like a messenger."
"But she got a real bike eventually?"
"When she was sixteen, during the highway collapse of '84. She saved a school bus full of kids along with Captain Fantastic."
"What happened?" I ask, resting my chin in my hands.

"The Dr. set a bomb on an elevated highway, it hadn't been opened-"

"But there was a school bus on it?"

"They say the driver took a short cut, or maybe he just didn't see the sign," she says, taking a sip. "Whatever the reason, there's a school bus on the highway. Lisa hears about it and pedals out on her pink bike to find them, and the captain just runs."

"And they saved all the kids? How?"

"Well, rather than go after the bus, Lisa went after the bomb, which made sense, only she didn't know how to defuse one."

"So?"

"So, she threw it to the captain, and he threw it in the air."

"And everyone was okay?"

She tuts, and sighs. "The blast was enough to crumble a small part of the highway, but Lisa and the Captain had bought enough time to get the bus away before it collapsed."

"That's amazing," I say.

Friday smiles. "It certainly was. They made her a real hero after that. No more running errands. That's when she got her bike."

———

The bike roared into life and Lisa disappeared down the road. I nodded to the passers by as I stood there, in the middle of the street, wearing armor that made me look like I was ready for a nerdy convention. I decided to power through it, and just run there. I sped down the streets as fast as I could and considered stealing a plate of food from a café as I passed, but I had to get to wherever it was I was going. Eventually I reached an elevated highway, and saw Lisa, who'd left her bike, standing in the middle of the city traffic. People were being held back by police, trying to get a glimpse of what was going on behind the barriers.

I pushed through the people and the policemen let me go as far as they could. Lisa was in the middle of the road facing the wreckage of a car. A man and a girl were inside and in-between them, on the road, was what looked a person on fire. *Literally* on fire. For a moment I thought the man had been involved in the crash, but he wasn't rolling around or trying to put the fire out. I couldn't make out his face, but he *was* a man, standing there, covered in flames, and he seemed...

Fine.

The air was filled with the scent of burnt cloth, and dripping gasoline. The lights around me spun out fo control, and the crowds blared in the background. It was pure panic, people screaming from behind the barricades, the city still running and bright despite the horrible crash.

The sight was so strange I stumbled backwards and looked away. For only a second I skimmed the roof of a town house and spotted something black. It was a man, dressed to blend in with the city night. The only thing that set him apart was his bright yellow hair.

I looked back to Lisa making sure she was still there before I moved forwards.

"Get away from the car!" Lisa shouted. The Figure in the Flames took a step back, and the little girl in the car screamed. The Figure sparked, like he was flaring his nostrils, turned his back to Lisa, and stepped forward towards the wreckage. Oil leaked from the car's engine.

"Stop!" I screamed. My mind shut off; I couldn't think of anything except running forwards. A car crash had changed my life, I had to help that little girl and her dad. The man on fire flinched at the sight and his fire flared, knocking me back like a leaf in the wind. The world spun, and my insides felt like clam chowder. A moment later, Lisa was beside me.

"You okay kid?"

I nodded automatically without really thinking, I was about to point out the man on the roof, only to find he'd disappeared, and when I looked back to the wreck-age, The Figure was gone too.

"Help me get them out," said Lisa. I nodded and tried to stand up. The man in the car pulled at the seat belt like a baby trapped in a high chair, and his daughter just cried. Lisa and I gripped the car's frame, as though our touch would somehow prevent it from going sky high. "Calm down," Lisa told the man, "everything's fine. We'll get you out, okay?"

The man let go of his seatbelt, and nodded. I leaned over to Lisa and whispered, "Isn't the car in danger of-"

She bared her teeth at me, willing me to shut up, then pulled out a knife and started cutting at the belt. I climbed into the back of the car, where the girl's seat was upside down. "Sweetie, you've got to undo your seatbelt," I told her. She shook her head at me, and gripped her stuffed bunny tighter.

"I'll catch you," I said, "trust me."

"I'm scared," she mumbled, opening her eyes.

Her father yelled, telling her to move as Lisa dragged him away into the crowds, but still, she shook her head.

"Hey kid," I said and she looked at me, the long ears of her bunny swaying in the cold night air. "It's okay to be scared. You can't be brave if you're not scared. So please, be brave, and trust me."

She nodded, wiping away the tears, and I held my hands out, bracing my arms for her weight.

"Fitz! Hurry up!"

"I'm on it!" I called back, "come on sweetie, you can do it!" Her belt came apart with one loud click and she fell straight into my arms. I held her as tightly as I could as I pushed my way out of the car, but it all took time. Lisa had dropped the girl's father at the edge of the crowd and he, immediately, tried to crawl back to his daughter.

"Move kid!" Lisa screamed, running towards the two of us.

I ran as fast as I could until I heard the little girl cry. "Mrs Mine!"

I froze, and looked back. "Who's Mrs Mine," I asked.

"My bunny," the little girl replied. As a small child I had a stuffed bear and stupid as it was, I knew how she felt. That bunny was a member of the family. I dropped the little girl and pushed her forward.

"Run!" I yelled. "I'll get your bunny."

Lisa scooped up the girl and reached out to drag me back but she was too slow.

"Fitz!" Lisa screamed as I ran back towards the car, blocking out every sound, not letting my self think. I dropped to the floor and grabbed the toy like it was a baton in a relay race. I could hear each drop of fuel hit the road like the pounding of my pulse. Something blurry in the sky started speeding towards us and Lisa made a run for me again. Just as my fingers whispered across hers a voice boomed from above.

"Get down!" A man in a super skeleton suit flew down from the sky and wrapped himself round the two of us, deploying a shield from his back. It wasn't a moment too soon. The car erupted in an awesome display of fire and the crowd oohed and awed at the spectacle as though they were watching New Year's fireworks. I opened my eyes to the masked, super suited figure above me.

"Partner Kisaragi, it's good to finally meet you." Lisa turned away from his face, only inches from hers, and mumbled something under her breath that might have been "show off".

Barney Baxter was definitely a show off. The moment the coast was clear he put away the shield on his back and stood up to receive the roar of the crowd, waving as though they'd thrown roses and asked for an encore. Fireworks spun from his hands, his very own severely limited power, which was why he'd been given a super skeleton. It didn't cover his whole body, it was more like a backpack with various panels and bracelets on other parts of his body. Not many heroes used them, they didn't last long, but Barney didn't have much of a choice.

The first thing I heard after the explosion, was the high pitched wail of sirens.

I lay still on the pavement, trying to get my bearings and held up the bunny like a trophy after a mile long dash. The little girl collapsed on top of me, pulling me into a hug.

"You saved Mrs. Mine!" She squeezed Mrs. Mine like she was the most important thing in the world. I sat up, and the little girl smiled. "My name's June." She held out her hand for me to shake and said politely, "Thank you for saving me. What's your name?"

"Everyone calls me Fitz," I told her, "but just between you and me, my name's Friday."

"That's silly," said June, "Friday's a day of the week."

"That's rich coming from a month." I laughed.

She giggled as I gave her cheek a poke.

"Fitz, get up." Lisa stood in front of us, shaking her head at me.

"Huh?"

Lisa sighed, and took June's hand. "Say goodbye June."

"Goodbye Friday."

I held up my hand in a quick salute as Lisa guided

the little girl back to her father. I sat there for a moment, my stomach growling, until someone pulled me back onto my feet and though I wobbled, steady hands held me in place. I looked up to try and find something to focus on and found Ashley's stern face and large nose.

I groaned inwardly. Despite the fact that he stood next to a burning car wreck he looked composed and clean in a crisp white shirt and tie that looked far too old for someone his age.

"What are you doing here, Fitz?" Ashley asked.

"Superhero stuff, obviously," I replied, dry heaving half way through.

"You look like an idiot. Why did you go back for a stuffed toy?" He didn't sound confused, only angry I'd done it. I'll admit, it wasn't the smartest thing I'd ever done.

"I don't know! The little girl, June. She wanted it. Who knew you were a connoisseur of hero technique." I drawled.

"Are you done?" he asked.

"No! Where's Lisa?" I cried. I looked round and found her pointing a firm finger at her new partner. She was fine. I felt so sick, the adrenalin, the nerves, the shaking. My heart was going a million miles an hour, and suddenly, I couldn't breathe. Lisa pushed herself away from Barney who flashed the cameras a dazzling white smile. I pried myself from Ashley's grip, taking deep breaths in and out.

I didn't know where I was going, but I needed to get away from the lights and sirens. It felt like a million eyes were on me, making my bones shake with frustration. I couldn't focus on anything. A panic attack. That's what it was.

Tears sprang from my eyes, not because I was scared but because my mind and body were bursting with emotion, crying was the only way to get it all out. There was nothing wrong with crying, I told myself, but I felt pathetic as I did it. How could I explain to anyone I wasn't used to the outside? I wasn't used to talking to people, I wasn't used to life outside of a big house or without someone monitoring my every move. I took a deep desperate breath and stumbled down the street trying to stand straight backed. I was a full block away from where I'd been and I couldn't hold it in anymore. I leaned on my knees, and vomited my guts out in a long clear stream.

I'd vomited on the streets. Was that illegal?

"Fitz?" I spun round to find Ashley, holding an umbrella over his head as the water from a gutter tumbled down over him, and the orange yellow street lights played on the hard planes of his face. He stood a good few feet away as though he preferred to observe me rather than hold my hair back like he'd do for anyone else.

Rather than reply I pointed to the pile of sick and said. "Is that illegal?" My voice came out shaky and drunken.

"No, it's not illegal to vomit in the street," he said.

"Shouldn't I clean it up though?" I asked.

"It's fine."

"Great." I cringed at the taste in my mouth, and sighed as the rain soaked my hair and brought it out in messy curls. I was a complete wreck. As I stood up, he came up behind me, and handed me a napkin without a glance. Instead, he looked at my pile of sick.

"At least you didn't lose any food." he grumbled.

"I haven't had any food *to* lose."

"What are you talking about?" his voice was sharper, like only now he was paying attention. He adjusted the umbrella to cover the both of us, not that it really made a difference, I was already wet.

"I gave you my lunch, *remember*?"

"You didn't eat lunch at all?" he asked.

"Obviously not."

He frowned. "What about breakfast?" he asked.

I shook my head. "Dinner? Sorry, I was busy." I said pointing back to the car wreck.

He sighed, took my hand and began pulling me down the street.

"What are you doing?" I murmured. He stopped across from a convenience store, and checked both ways.

"What are you doing?" I asked again.

"Stay here." he said, without looking at me.

It was as though he wasn't even listening. Who was he to tell me what to do? He crossed the street, disappeared into the store. For a moment I considered walking away. It was weird standing in the middle of the street by myself. I didn't want to vomit again, but then Ashley emerged with a bag in his hand, and once again, checked both ways. He joined me under an awning, and put away his umbrella.

"Here." He put the bag in front of me, and inside I found a chocolate bar and bottle of water.

"You bought me snacks? That's real nice and all but-"

"No." He said reaching into the bag. "The chocolates are to get some sugar in your system and the water's because you should never eat without drinking. It helps digestion." He nodded towards them as he held them out, his voice entirely void of comfort. "Eat."

"What are you, a doctor?" I looked up to see a smile and the gentle light playing on his face once again.

There was a split second when my chest felt light and for a moment, I thought I'd been wrong about him looking plain, very wrong. He had one of the most interesting faces I'd ever seen. He was *strange* looking, but in a dignified way, that made you stop and look. He wasn't *handsome*, just *interesting*.

"Eat." He said again with a nod at the food and so I took the chocolate bar and water. "Water first Fitz, it'll wash down the sick," he stated.

"I know," I said defensively.

"Good."

"Why didn't you get cola?" I wondered.

"Because it's fizzy, you don't need that right now."

"It's sugary. If you'd bought cola, you'd only have needed to buy one thing, it would have cost less."

He fell silent as I unwrapped the chocolate. "Shut up and drink," he told me.

I was happy to comply and gulped down half of the bottle before digging into the chocolate like I'd been waiting my whole life for it. I'd finished most of the bar before he spoke again.

"Feeling better yet?" he asked with a tilt of his head.

"Much. Thanks."

"Don't mention it, Fitz." The way he spoke he

sounded as though he was bored, or waiting to leave. "Do you want to tell me *why* you vomited?"

"What do you mean? It was adrenaline," I added with a shrug.

"Right. Sure."

"Why the hell does it rain so much here? All the time on Hero High, it's always raining," I said.

"You're changing the subject," he boomed, "we're a small island. It rains a lot."

"We?" I questioned.

He nodded at me. "Well. I guess you could say I'm a native. Second generation immigrant."

An awkward silence hung over us as the sirens in the distance died out, and the lights left the street darker than before, with only the neon of the city reflected in the windows.

"What did you do with that house?" Ashley asked, his voice stern.

"Huh?" I said trying to cough out the taste left on my tongue.

"The one you bought with your fathers money?" It took me a minute to realize he was talking about my file.

"I bought it for someone who used to work for my father, they ended up in debt trying to get their kids through college. Had to sell their house, so I, bought them a new one. No mortgage, nothing."

"And you think that makes it okay?"

I glared at *him,* as *he* scoffed at *me.* "I'm not buying into your little Robin Hood fantasy. Did you ever stop to consider maybe that family thought it was condescending to have you buy a house for them?"

"Condescending?"

"Yeah, condescending. Some people don't *need* your money."

I stood up as tall as I could, my head still only just reaching his shoulders, and pressed him against the wall with my finger. "And here I was thinking that pride wasn't a good enough reason to go homeless!"

He shook his head at me in disbelief. "Why is that even your job in the first place?"

"Because my father won't do it. He hasn't done anything, not in years. I know I'm not perfect, but shit! I'm not nearly as bad as you think I am!" My head hung, the shadows of the alley blocking any line of sight he had to my watery eyes. "That's a lie," I whispered.

I saw him nod out of the corner of my eye, I was about to tell him off for it, but then he said, "And I'm not nearly as *good* as you think I am." He was The

Captain to be, he was going to *be* The Captain someday. "Finish the chocolate before I take you back."

I looked up at him, bewildered. "You're going to walk me back?"

"We live in the same building," he said with a shrug.

"But… But we just shouted at each other," I said.

"So? Finish the chocolate. It's time to go."

———

NEED SOMEBODY

THE HERO HIGH GYM was a room like nothing I'd seen before. It filled an entire floor. Above, a huge TV screen reflected a faux blue sky above us, and right in the center was a football field. A camera crew was already in place to film as the whole first year shuffled in together. The older students were on the field practicing cheerleaders at the side. We walked round Coach Flat who stood in front of a large white board marked 'Practical Hero Training'. Ashley stood next to him.

"Today, we're sparring to warm you up," he waved his hands in the air for emphasis, "line up to get your gym equipment." He chuckled. Taking out a list of names he designated each one red or blue and pointed from one student to another to let them know they were working together. The pairs had been planned before-hand, matching power to power to make a good first sparring session, but when he came to me he didn't seem sure what to do. "Go stand next to Mr. Ang for now." he said, I wanted to ask why I wasn't going to risk getting in trouble again. I took my place next to Ashley and his team mates did the same.

Aya leaned over and held out her hand, "Hi I'm Aya."

"Friday," I replied.

"That's David," she smiled as their last team mate waved from the end of the line and I waved back. "You can practice next to us," she told me, "let me know if you have any questions, okay?"

"Sure." I told him, "have you done this before?"

"I'm a legacy kid, my parents have been trainers at Hero High for a while. David's a legacy too, that's how we met," she said with a tilt of her head, David nodded in agreement. "Good luck."

"Thanks."

Coach Flat wandered into the crowd of students, telling each pair how to work with each other while I bounced on my feet like a kid waiting for their lunch. Once he'd gone to every group of kids and they were happily sparring, he finally came back to me.

"Fitz, you're in a tricky situation." He yawned.

"How so?" I grumbled.

"Your power is possibly the most passive we've ever seen. I mean," he put his hand out in front of him, and I heard a small pop as it flattened, it was as thin as paper. "Even I can use my power to cut stuff," he said and demonstrated by passing his hand through the corner of the whiteboard. It was such a thin cut he had to poke it before the corner fell, but all the same, he looked pleased. "Even Mr. Ang can *kind of* blow stuff up, but I don't know what to do with you." He drawled.

"Teach me how to fight like a normal person," I suggested.

"Can you even throw a punch?" he asked steering me away out of earshot of the rest, "I mean, you've got a real disadvantage. The other kids, they have super armor, vortices, weird string shit that comes out of their skin, I don't know what that's about. Plus, I'm pretty sure I saw this one guy who's power was killer babies. You've got thinking real fast. You're gonna get hurt, kid, there's no way round it."

"I know," I said with a heavy sigh. Maybe I should have resigned myself to life as a support hero, but even support heroes did their four years of schooling as though they were going to be working heroes. I didn't plan to give up within two weeks, even *if* my power was crap. Coach Flat threw me my armor with a proud smile, and did the same for Ashley. "You'll spar with Mr. Perfect here, at least I know he won't kill you." With that he pushed us through the door to the changing rooms, and yelled "Try not to have sex in there kids!" before leaving us all alone.

My mouth hung open.

Ashley just pushed up his glasses. "What the hell is his problem?" I blurted at Ashley, who didn't seem bothered in the slightest, though really I couldn't tell for the glare on his glasses.

"Coach Flat's just a weirdo to trying to make people think he's interesting when he's not. He's just trying to make up for his lack of dick," Ashley huffed, and went to hide behind the lockers, slipping off his jacket as he went. Had Ashley Ang really just said that?

I moved into the corner, and inspected all my clothes. The shoes, trousers, top, hard vest, were all the same blue color. I checked round the corner to make sure he was far away, the lockers rattled.

"What are you doing Fitz?" he called.

"Nothing!" I yelled.

"Interesting," he said, "because it sounded like you were coming out of your corner. And I'm *changing*."

"I wasn't looking!" I insisted.

"Did I say you were?"

"I was *checking*," I told him.

"For what? *Me* looking?" he said sounding almost offended.

"No!" It was a bad idea anyway, fully clothed was as good as it got.

"Why not?" he replied.

"Why not what?" By this time I was properly confused.

Ashley sighed. "Why *weren't* you looking for *me* looking?" he said in tone that was just a little too playful, at least for him.

"I, uh, um. S-should I have been?" There was silence for a moment.

"Of course not," he replied, returning to his normal deep monotone. What? Had I imagined that? I must have. The scuffle of clothes returned and I decided to just do it, get it over with, so I whipped off my clothes, pulling on the uniform as fast as I could. It was all on in record time, and Ashley still hadn't appeared. I was counting my lucky stars. What did he mean by 'of course not'? I shrugged and reached for my hard vest. The back was all straps. I unclipped everything, lay it on my chest, and reached round to re attach them, only I couldn't; they were half an inch away from connecting round my chest and the one at my hips rode up. My head fell smack dab into the palm of my hand as Ashley turned the corner. making final adjustments to his vest, he set his glasses back on his nose.

"Something wrong Fitz?"

"No."

"Okay then, hurry up."

"I am!"

He kept his eyes fixed on me. My cheeks burned as I pulled on the strap around my chest and desperately tried to reach.

"Does it not fit?" he asked

"No! Shut up!"

"Want me to get you a larger size?"

"They have those?" I laughed.

"Yeah Fitz, they have those." He said after he cleared his throat.

"Please." I answered with a sigh of defeat. I handed him my armor, refusing to look him in the eye. He left without a word, and I breathed a sigh of relief. I looked round the corner to find his clothes all neatly folded in a locker with a red slip poking out of his back pocket. I moved forwards to inspect it without thinking. It was a menu for a place called, Maggie's. I rushed back as I heard footsteps, and he returned with the larger hard vest.

"Hurry up. Not gonna wait forever," he said. I pulled on my armor as fast as I could, and tried to exit the changing rooms like I hadn't been rushing. Coach Flat just pointed to the center of the room and Veronica came forwards with some paper rolled up in her hands. She took me by the shoulder, and steered me away for a moment.

"Hey there Friday, now we'd like get a shot of you and Ashley sparring, can you do that for me?" Veronica sung.

"I guess, I mean that's why we're here right?" I gained laughter.

"Yeah yeah, but I mean after what happened a couple of days ago, the fans feel like you have some unresolved issues."

"What? What are you talking about?"

"When Ashley detached the live camera in the detention room. Normally we wouldn't have noticed, but a fan pointed out one of the cameras was down," she said as she took out her phone and showed me the rankings, I'd gone up a few spaces. "Our viewers want to get a sense for what went on in there, and since there's no footage, we thought we'd film this. Okay? Great, get to it." She slapped me on the back and shoved me back towards Ashley and Coach Flat.

"Get your fists up kid," said the Coach and I moved my hands up in front of me. "First you have to know how to take a punch."

"I thought I was supposed to learn how to fight?"

"A large part of that is staying alive, kid, so put you arms up like this."

He lifted his fist to rest just above his forehead like a boxers block and I copied the motion trying to soak up as much as I could.

"Bend your knees, make sure you've got good footing, " he said as he moved round to kick my legs and make sure my stance was steady. I stumbled back and he shook his head. "Get your stance right. Ashley, make sure she gets it."

When Coach Flat moved onto the next group only Ashley was left to frown at me. The camera moved in and Veronica motioned with her rolled up paper, trying to get us to talk for the cameras.

"Okay, how would you throw a punch?" Ashley asked.

I had thrown a punch before, hell that was what landed me in Hero High, but I couldn't say that in front of the camera so I threw a strange slow-mo punch like I was trying to delicately scratch my opponent. I played it off like I had no idea what I was doing.

"A punch landed you in Hero High? How did that happen?" I ask, setting aside my coffee.

"I hadn't slept in two days, and I'd had a fight with my dad the night before. So I just, hit one of the investors when he was rude."

"Was it harder to get business after that?" I ask.

"After hitting an investor? You could say so, yes," she says with a wry smile. "People weren't flocking to the company and my dad suddenly seemed very concerned with my life." Friday sighs, and leans back. It's not a pleasant memory.

"Do you think your dad sent you to Hero High for your benefit, or his own?" I ask and wonder if perhaps I've crossed the line.

She pauses, and chews the inside of her cheek, until, she finally replies. "Yes."

———

"This is gonna take a long time." Veronica mused.

I tried to mimic Ashley as best as I could; I threw punches, blocked a few, and Coach Flat came round regularly to kick my legs and make sure I stayed upright. Veronica took me aside a few times telling me to talk more, or throw a real punch but Ashley never spoke up or got even close to acting the way he had during detention. He knew very well what they wanted, and the fact that he wasn't willing to play made me smile. Veronica gave up eventually and moved on, leaving a spare cameraman behind in case. I waved to him, getting no reply.

"Don't bother talking to the cameramen, they never reply." Ashley added.

"Why not?" I turned to the camera man. "Why not?"

He didn't reply.

I shrugged, noting the glasses in his front pocket as I turned back to Ashley. There were blasts and hisses from the other students, some of their powers were easy to see; they lit up the gym in fiery oranges, and mystical blues, but others showed nothing and Veronica voiced her disappointment wondering what sort of special effects they could get when the episode aired. It was like a swirl of magic surrounded me; sure, it wasn't magic *so to speak*, but I felt like I'd brought my fists to a wizard fight. Aya and David had very different *looking* powers, but it appeared they had similar effects. They practiced in front of me, David could look at one thing and then another, and transfer their heat properties. I wasn't sure how helpful that was until Veronica handed him a visor and a cup exploded. The lenses she'd given him were super heated, so all he had to do was focus on his visor and then something else, and boom. Veronica tapped her bottom lip, and turned to her camera crew.

"How about the name, Red Hot, David?" The crew all nodded in agreement, and she tapped her lip again. David shrugged, and she scribbled the name down. Aya's power allowed her to disappear into objects as she threw them, catching them and appearing somewhere else. Veronica looked puzzled for a moment, perhaps a little disappointed, but then she snapped her fingers and scribbled down Aya's superhero name. She looked at me for a moment, and I waited for her to name me but instead she shook her head. "I'll just call you Fitz," she said, "it's easy to remember."

I sighed and turned back to Ashley as he readied to throw a few more mock punches but his eyes widened and he yelled "Fitz look out!"

I spun. Ashley lunged, pushed me to the floor. A bolt flew over my head.

I looked up to say thank-you just as Mary's hand slashed through the air. A trail of something bright pulled me to her. Everyone screamed, I slammed into bleak black nothingness as Mary's power sealed behind me.

Falling.

Falling through the darkness.

And then…

I was hurtling to the ground. My back smashed onto something slanted. Biting rain pushed onto the side of my face. Hair stuck to my skin and. Thunder blared like the trumpets in an orchestra. A gray cloud swirled with the busy lights below. Each drop of rain pattering against my ear like white noise.

I was on a skyscraper!

My hand reached out for anything. It only found slippery glass.

Falling.

I couldn't breathe or stay upright.

I was falling.

My hands and feet plated against the glass. I ripped the velcro of my vest apart, and saw the blue armor hurtle downwards.

The falling stopped. I squeaked against the glass. My clothes had soaked up all the moisture. My toes hung to the narrow metal edge. The thunder laughed. The sky lit up in stormy white and blurs of neon.

I didn't dare look down. The needle of the building blinked with a red light.

My fingers were like ice. Should I stay here? There was a thin band of metal that lined the glass installations. My right hand reached for it. It was think enough to hold onto. I pulled myself up a few feet, until I could reach for the antenna. I wrapped my body around it.

The rain chilled me to the bone and I had never been so terrified in my life. I hated heights, I couldn't stand to look down from a two story window, or go up a ladder. It was too cold, cold enough to kill. I had to figure something out. I looked down, my teeth chattering, and spied a ladder leading down. Someone had to come up here for maintenance, right? It was thin and insubstantial but my only way.

I reached out from where I sat. Hands wet as the clouds rumbled again. I took hold with one hand. The ladder snapped.

And the broken metal bar puffed through the clouds.

There was balcony below. It looked like it was covered in gravel. Maybe a maintenance area. It didn't look like it was for patrons assuming I was on a hotel. I couldn't stay here.

A fall like that though, It was going to hurt. It might have been two stories down.

I took a deep breath.

I braced myself. I looked at graveled are below one more time. The cloud was reforming, covering it up. There was no way I could stay on the slanted roof of a skyscraper. Or wrapped around it's antenna. But on the other hand if I was surviving here for at least a few minutes, maybe I could just tough it out. Not risk a change of scenery.

I readjusted myself around the blinking needle. It was too slippery, too cold. I had to take this risk.

I nodded to myself. Closed my eyes.

And let go.

I was falling again, sliding, like I was a rain droplet. My feet left the slanted roof. Now nothing but air held me.

I slammed against the floor of the balcony. My scream joined the thunder. The rain seemed louder and heavier. The gavel dug into my sides.

I only felt pain. Not in any specific place. Rolling over I opened my eyes. My body was intact; head, legs and arms, check. My head lulled back. Everything hurt, but I'd be okay. Above me was a sea of thunder and lightning. Rain trickled into my eyes. My teeth started to chatter as pushed myself up. There had to be a door around here somewhere.

I limped round the graveled area. Pieces of scrap metal and wires lay abandoned. No one but technicians were ever supposed to come up here. Weeds had started growing through the stones.

Then I saw the door. All glass, big handle, stairs inside, and, and…

With a big honking keypad.

My forehead slammed against the door. I tried to suck in any tears. I pulled at the handle, just in case. The door wouldn't budge. I stood back and shook my head. I wasn't giving up. I looked for something large and heavy I could use to break the glass. Wrapping my arms around myself, I wandered along the path. The clouds were in turmoil. As they swirled I caught sight of the Parisian style town houses in the center of Icon City; I knew I hadn't gone far.

I pulled over a large metal girder. I could only lift if for a few seconds, there was no way I could throw it at the door.

I wrapped my arms around my self again, wracking my brain for a solution. My eyes searched the sky for someone, *anyone*…

It was cold. So cold.

"Need some help?"

I spun to the sound. A voice I didn't recognize. A man, dressed in full superhero gear, stood beside me. His domino mask glowed an icy blue. His suit, a cat burglar's dream.

I couldn't quite see him through the veil of rain. There was something familiar about the suit. Like I'd seen him on TV before. He didn't look as high-tech as some other heroes I'd seen, no super skeleton, only simple gadgets hanging from his belt. It was the man from the fire, the one with the yellow hair…

The one who'd been watching.

"Who are you?" I asked, holding myself tighter.

"There's no time for that," he observed, "you're going to freeze to death."

"So? Why do you care?" I said, teeth chattering.

"Your lips are going blue," he replied taking two steps forwards while I took two steps back. "There's no need to run. Do you know who I am?"

There was a note of surprise in his voice. I peered closer as he stepped out of the rain and into the space under the slim concrete roof of the floor above us. I knew that mask.

It was Dr. Dangerous!

Or rather, some weirdo wannabe.

I knew The Captain inside and out, so of course I knew who his nemesis was. I'd kept up with theories among fans as to why there was such a feud between The Captain and the Dr., but this was *not* Dr. Dangerous.

Dr. Dangerous was dead.

And even if he was somehow alive, he'd be in his forties. The guy in front of me wasn't old enough; he was a boy pretending to be something he wasn't. "You're not Dr. Dangerous," I said.

His lips twitched up at one side. "No? I have the outfit," he pointed out.

"No! Dr. Dangerous' suit had red lines, and there were red eyes on his mask!" I'd once had pictures of the Dr. above my desk next to my picture of The Captain.

"The red faded, and blue's easier to see in," he replied. I backed up, pressing myself against the wall. "Stop backing away, you have no-where to go." He drawled. Walking slowly he took a few steps closer, paying no attention to the rain that rippled down his suit. With a side step, I put more distance between us, still shaking from the cold. "Really?" he said with a sigh.

"What?" I said, "What are you gonna do about it? Faker."

"I'm not a fake," he told me.

"You're not The Dr," I reaffirmed.

"No?" he asked.

"Then, what did Dr. Dangerous do during the 1984 attack?" I jutted, trying to forget about the rain.

"Are you quizzing me?"

"Are you backing out?" I laughed.

"No."

"Then what did he do!?" I shouted.

"He set a bomb on an elevated highway-"

"Ha! You said, *he*!" I screamed in triumph.

In the blink of an eye he was in front of me. He wasn't fast, he wasn't stealthy, he was instantaneous. It was as though he could simply move from one place to another whenever he wanted. My shout was lost, all I could hear now filled up my ear. The cold tickled at my nose.

"A talent of mine." For the first time, I noted the weird echo in his voice, it was edited with reverb, making it vibrate and purr.

"How did you get up here?" I asked, through chattering teeth. I didn't mind his closeness, it was too cold to mind the closeness. He pointed to something high tech on his low hanging belt.

"Then *why* are you up here?" I questioned.

"To make sure you don't die," he breathed.

"Why?"

"I was told to. I could just let you die I suppose," he said with a shrug. He leaned back, looking me up and down.

"If you're here to make sure I don't die, why don't you take me down the same way?"

"My line can't carry two people. And I only have one."

"What about that teleport thing you did?" I huffed sliding down the wall. I wanted to curl into a ball, maybe that was the best was to preserve heat. For a moment he didn't answer.

"It's not teleporting," he replied, crouching down to my level.

"What is it then?" I huffed.

"I'm not telling you."

"Then why don't you get help?" I grunted. He radiated heat. I was just close enough to sense it, but too far away for it to do me any good. Every inch of my body was drenched in icy water; so was he, only he didn't seem to care. The water seemed to rise off him in a mist.

"I did, I'm only here to make sure you don't die." He leaned in, trying to glimpse my hidden face.

"You're too close!" I insisted and pushed him. He looked surprised for a second, and then scowled, pulling his hand back.

"I'm not going to hurt you," he said with a sigh.

"I don't know who you are!" I scowled.

"Stop being so stubborn, and let me help," he growled.

"How?" I said.

"Wonder why the rain isn't bothering me?" He smiled.

"No! Maybe?" I cried.

"My suit keeps me warm." He said, settling next to

me against the wall. He was big, much bigger than me. If we'd been anyone else we might have looked like two friends watching the storm.

"So?" I swallowed.

"So stay still. I'm trying to help." he said again. He looked down at me and sighed as he extended his arm above me and wrapped it round my shoulders. His warmth was like settling into a bath. Warm, but sudden. He pulled me in slowly, giving me time to get used to the heat. Until my cheek lay against the dark smooth fabric of his suit.

He was so warm. Part of me shrugged and cuddled closer. "You, are, weird." He hummed. The reverb thick. I pulled back. He was looking down at me. His eyes flickered all over my face. Then he leaned down.

What was he doing? Was he going to…

I wasn't ready!

I didn't even know him!

Then his nose traced along the edge of my ear. "What are you doing?" I felt my cheeks go red in spite of the cold. My voice like a whimper or a gasp. My ears were sensitive, *too* sensitive. I grabbed the front of his suit. His mouth opened around my ear, and he pulled it in, nipping the flesh between his lips.

I fell backwards onto the gravel with a squeak. A red hot flush ran through my *whole* body.

His lips were pressed against each other. He was trying not to laugh, that ass!

I pushed up and knocked him in the chest. He was so much bigger he barely wobbled. With a clearing of his throat he tried to draw me back into his arms.

"Stop moving, and let me help." He rumbled. I pulled him off and turned round. I pushed my back up against his chest instead, and folded my arms in compromise.

The heat sent thrilling shivers through me. As he put his arms around me from behind. He moved a strand of hair from my forehead.

"And your name is?" he asked. I only grumbled in response. "Scared?" wondered. This was not a man to be trusted, and as long as I knew that, I was fairly certain I'd be safe. "Tell me," he insisted. "It's only fair." He said, nesting his chin on the top of my head.

"Friday. My name's Friday." I mumbled.

"Interesting name." He pulled me closer again. Something outside rumbled and buzzed. Not lightning or thunder, more like a car. I looked into the stormy sky.

I glanced over at the keypad again, trying to recall anything useful. Dad had keypad locks in the garage, he always used the same code, and after a while he wore down the numbers.

"Let me look at the keypad." I said. He let go, and stood with me. His shadow settled behind me as I inspected the keys. The average sequence was three to five numbers. The most worn pads were, two, five, seven, and nine. People like combinations that sound good because they're easier to remember. For example, five seven nine, doesn't sound as snappy as nine seven five, so I tried that one first. It flashed red. I tried two seven nine, red again.

"What are you doing?" His voice wobbled.

"These numbers are the most worn," I told him. He peered over my shoulder.

"So you're just guessing?" He asked.

"Basically," I replied. He leaned closer, his breath tickling my ear. Who the hell was this guy anyway?

"What if it's personal?" he suggested.

"Like a date?" I wondered. He nodded and I looked at the pad again. Two, five, seven, nine. Nine two five? Was the combination a joke? The Dr. pushed closer, looking over my shoulder.

"Get an idea?" he asked.

"Nine two five? Like nine, to five?" I shrugged, tried it and-

The lock pinged green. A smile took over my face. I spun round to show him what I'd done.

But the Dr. was gone.

Like he'd never been there, all I saw was the storm and a puddle where he'd been.

A chill ran through me.

I shook it off and dashed inside the stairwell. I left rain water on the floor as I scurried out. A door took mt to a much nicer hallway. It smelled like expensive hotel, which for reference I guess smells like jasmine and spice.

I shook in the elevator while a very tall woman tilted her head at me. "Shower head's on the fritz." I shrugged. The doors pinged on the lobby. Would you look at that. It had been a hotel. I ran past the Ikebana arrangements, that were so tall they touched the ceiling. My shoes squeaked against the marble floors, and few people shouted to me as I passed by.

I was out on the street. The sky still roared. I stopped at every awning and restaurant umbrella until someone yelled at me to buy something or leave.

I'd been at the chrysanthemum hotel. The most expensive hotel in the city. It was a block or two until I saw the outline of the superstructure in the storm.

I relaxed, everyone would be in there and I could make it. I stumbled into the Super Structure's court yard. Filled with flowers statues and a big fountain. The Captain's personal bus was parked in the street. Honestly I wanted to seem him, and I seemed weird to just go back to my room, so I tried to step on board.

"You're not allowed in here," said an assistant, popping his head round the door.

"I'm a student," I told him, "I need to talk to The Captain. I go-"

"Friday! Is that you?" asked The Captain as he came round the corner, out into the rain.

"Are you okay? We didn't know where you'd gone," said The Captain flinging a blanket around my shoulders.

"I was on top of a skyscraper," I told him.

"In this storm? Do you need an ambulance?" he asked.

"No, I think I'm fine."

He nodded, and steered me inside. it was warm but I couldn't relax until The Captain closed the door on both Veronica and the cameras. He rubbed my shoulders like my dad did. An assistant brought over a blanket to wrap me up in. This bus was different from the others, better furnished. On one side was a poster of The Captain, making it clear this was *his* bus. His *personal* bus.

I collapsed onto the sofa and he did the same as we started to move back to Hero High.

"You okay?" The Captain asked and I nodded, sipping my soup as I wondered why it felt slightly awkward to sit next to him saying nothing, so I looked round the room, and then realized, I didn't know his name. I knew his superhero name, but not his real one.

"What's your name? I mean your *real* name," I asked, setting the mug down. He raised a single eyebrow at the question. I expected him to tell me it was secret, or just not for students to know.

Instead, he said, "Adam. My name's Adam." He smiled.

I sat back in my seat as he watched the news, and mouthed, 'perfect'.

Adam was a perfect name for him wasn't it? I mean, come on. How much more special and amazing does a person get? He was super nice, super kind, super smart, super pretty, and super powered. I was a fool for superheroes, I always had been, or maybe it was just him. Something caught my eye on the screen, I almost snatched the remote from The Captain. *Almost*.

"Turn it up," I asked. As the bar on the screen scaled forwards I caught the end of the anchor woman saying, 'The Figure In The Flames.' I leaned forwards. Adam's lips pursed, and his knuckles grew white. Suddenly *that* was more interesting to me than The Figure walking out of a burning building. "What's wrong, Sir?"

"Nothing," he said as he leaned back into the sofa,

covering whatever tense feeling he'd had only moment ago. "Call me Adam. No. Wait, I guess I am your principal," he said with a sigh. He wasn't big on the formalities. "Better call me… Principal Armstrong."

"Adam Armstrong?"

He nodded, and smiled faintly. I knew his name! My inner ten year old was screaming. "But Sir, Principal Armstrong, I've seen this man before."

"Where," he asked, setting his mug off coffee on the table, "where have you seen him before? Or her," he corrected.

"Tell me what you know," I suggested, "and I'll tell you what I know."

He pursed his lips again, and I saw the twitch of muscle behind his cheek as he clenched his jaw. "Alright Ms. Fitz, you have a deal."

"You first." I said.

"There have been rumors, circulating with the other heroes," he said, looking me in the eye. "There might be some drug on the streets, something that affects superpowers."

"What?" I blurted.

"Now. Your turn," he replied.

"Right, yeah. I saw him at the car fire a week ago. I don't think a lot of other people saw him, but I did. It's the same guy."

"Or girl," he corrected again.

"Right," I agreed.

"Friday, please, even though I've told you this, it's not an invitation to go looking for trouble."

"What makes you think I will?" I asked him.

"A lot of the kids at this school have a strong sense of justice, and that's what we want, but, don't let it make you stupid."

I nodded and settled back into the sofa, trying to forget about The Figure and enjoy the ride back to Hero High. I didn't plan to ignore The Captain's warnings, but still, something told me I'd get myself involved somehow.

The bus slowed. I sighed throwing off the blanket. The Captain and I walked to the exit wordlessly. I stepped outside into the dripping rain. Mist covered the road, and the rain had dropped to a drizzle. The Captain raised his hand to me as I turned back. I waved as I ran into the gardens in between the two buildings of the Super Structure. My phone buzzed with light and sound.

"Where were you!" yelled Jake. "Are you okay? Day? Talk to me!"

"I'm fine, meet me in the computer room," I said and slammed the phone shut to slide it across the lock for the elevator doors. It was here, finally! The frustration that shook my bones was gone, replaced with excitement. There was a mystery to solve! Finally I could be useful, I could *do* something. The elevator pinged at floor forty three. The lights down here were a lot dimmer than the rest of the Super Structure. Rows upon rows of people sitting at computers. Screens lighting up the massive room like a bug zapper. The place buzzed with electricity.

The elevator next to me pinged and Jake wandered out.

"'Day, what the hell?" he said, staring at me. "You're dripping with water."

"No time to explain," I said sitting down at the nearest computer. Jake pulled up a chair and I opened the browser.

"What are we doing?" he asked.

"Looking for answers." I typed in the name 'Dr. Dangerous', and received a list of reports about a 'new' Dr., who'd been spotted at the sight of the car crash on the elevated highway. The pictures were blurry, but news outlets seemed sure. Everyone knew he was back now, or at least a different version of him. I searched for older reports, ones from twenty years ago. The man in the pictures looked at lot like the one I'd seen, same blonde hair, and cat suit, but the 'new' one, *my* one was not thirty plus years old. He couldn't have been beyond his twenties. What was going on here? Jake scoffed from behind me.

"What?" I said, "What is it? Jake?"

"Nothing," Jake replied, "he just looks like a real poser."

I bit the inside of my cheek. There were no reports on what his real name was, when he was born, or if his power stopped the aging process. This guy was not the *real* Dr. I hadn't brought any of my superhero pictures with me to Hero High, so I clicked on one last photo and had it printed out for future reference.

"You're printing a picture? Why?"

"I might need to remember what the original Dr. looks like for future reference," I said and cleared out the search bar and this time looked for news reports made within the last hour. At the top of the page was the report of The Figure.

I read a few articles, but every reporter referred to him exactly the same way, a mysterious, super powered loner.

Jake groaned from behind me.

"Day, are you done yet? School's already over and I'm hungry."

"In a minute, I'm almost done." I didn't matter how high res the picture was, I could never make out his face. I sighed.

"What did you find? Are we on some sort of case?"

"Case?" I asked, unsure of what Jake meant.

"Yeah, you know, like an investigation. Solving crimes."

"Probably not, no I just wanted to be safe."

"Can I see it?" Jake asked.

"Nah, it's not important, and besides, his face is always blurry. You said you were hungry?"

"Yeah. And since you made me wait so long, you're buying."

As I pushed the seat back, turned the computer off and stood up, something metallic clattered to the ground.

"What was that?" Jake asked.

"I don't know," I replied and looked down to where a small silver disk with a faint blinking red light lay on the floor.

"What is it?" Jake took my hand and pulled it closer, squinting at the details. "It's a tracking device," he said, looking looking me up and down, "I think it was stuck to your top." He sucked in a breath. "And Friday?"

"Yeah?"

"It's not Hero High issue."

———

BEAT OF MY HEART

I'D TUCKED AWAY THE tracking device somewhere safe.

My best guess was that it was the Dr's.

The outside sparkled with neon, blocking out the stars. I yawned into my hand and tightened the last bolt on the junker bike, I'd bought with what was left of my Hero High allowance. Most of it had gone home to my dad and my sister. The bike was a little too loud as it rattled into life; I tried to shhh it as I turned it off, as though that was something you could do with a bike. As soon as it stopped I shook my head and clapped my hands together: ten at night, and I was leaving. I was leaving to do *real* work after several weeks of taking maths classes, and watching the Hero High cameras follow kids around. I needed to do *something*. This was my chance, to do what I'd really come here for.

Finding that tracking device had forced me into action.

I'd jotted down the name of the house The Figure had blown to pieces, and was ready to 'investigate'. Every time I saw The Figure, it seemed like he wasn't *trying* to hurt anyone, and no matter what I did I couldn't shake the feeling that someone was lying. Something was going on and I wanted to find out what, even after The Captain's warnings.

I pursed my lips and purged the face of Dr. Dangerous from my mind before throwing on my jacket and gloves and pushing the bike towards the exit. I'd bought it from a junkyard, Lisa insisted I needed one.

I pulled out into busy streets where the night life of the city was in full swing.

The traffic lights glowed against the road. Gangs of friends wandered the streets, with shopping bags or beer, sometimes both. The smell was overwhelmingly of cigarettes and fuel. My hands curved over the rubber handle of my bike, feet sturdy on the stirrups. Sounds of construction and cars honking mixed with all the music pumping out from the department stores. I could make out sections of loud stories from construction sites or a balcony above as I moved past. The wind my bike created was thrilling. All the noise and activity could have been exciting, but nerves still bubbled in my stomach.

"Friday!"

Huh? I looked around for the voice as I stopped at a red light. Had someone said my name?

"Friday!" I turned my head to the sidewalk full of people, and shrugged. "Friday!" I looked again. Pushing through the crowds was Jake, and he looked very, *very* angry with me.

"What do you think you're doing!?" I shouted, worried he would run into the path of a car. I bounced up and down on my seat willing the light to turn green, but it was useless; he didn't seem to care that he was wandering straight into the road. "Come on! Go green!" His hand came down on my shoulder. I'd never seen him so angry. The light pinged green, and I revved.

"Oh no you don't!" he snarled.

I revved again, but something heavy hit my back. I allowed myself to turn and found Jake had climbed on the bike and was holding on to it for dear life. "Idiot, don't hold on to the bike, hold onto me!"

"No! Pull over! It's way past curfew," he cried.

"There is no curfew!" I roared.

"Fine! It's past a moral curfew!"

"No!"

"Then I'm not going!" he insisted.

I rode on, my face an icy glare. I felt Jake wobble, and heard him panic. He felt around, and finally lunged forward wrapping his arms around my waist for support. About time. "Got there eventually!" I complained.

"Where are we going?" Jake asked.

"You're coming *with* me?" I replied, trying not to look back.

"If you're not going back, yes!"

"Fine!" I couldn't help but tingle at the wondrous sensation that was riding through the city on my bike. It wasn't at all the same as walking though the crowds; this had a strange sense of privacy. I dipped into a part of the city slightly lower than the rest, and finally brought the bike to a halt.

Jake jumped off, straightened his jacket, and sighed. "Where are we?" he grumbled.

"This is the house The Figure blew up." We walked down the alleyway at the side of the house and every now and again I stole a glance back at my bike, worried it wouldn't be there when I got back. The sign at the front of the house boasted a rebuilding courtesy of the city. Some of the area had already been covered with tarp and covered up with duct tape to keep the bare wood protected from the city's regular rainfall.

"So. What're we looking for?" Jake asked.

"Anything. There has to be more to The Figure, I feel it." I scanned the ground meticulously and found it surprisingly clean. Something glistened behind the dumpster that caught my eye just like the picture I'd printed out. I pulled the piece of paper out of my pocket and lined it up. It was a wonder no one had found it.

"Help me move it." I ordered. Jake and I pushed as hard as we could. It only moved a fraction of an inch, but it was enough. My head tilted as I scratched a place above my ear. I was looking at a gold plastic syringe. A syringe? I picked it up and tucked it away in my bag. It was tacky, but it was definitely a syringe.

"What are you gonna do with that?"

"I don't know yet." I said with a shrug.

"What are you thinking?"

"I'm not sure. The Figure is a bad guy. I know he's caused some serious disasters, but I don't think he meant to."

"You mean he's a superhero?"

"No, I don't think so, but maybe he's trying to be. I think he was *trying* to help.

"If he's trying to help, shouldn't he be enrolled at the school?" Jake asked.

"I don't know about that," I told him.

"Why not?"

"His power's a bit destructive don't you think?"

"I mean, maybe, but if he is, like you said, trying to help, shouldn't we give him the benefit of the doubt?" I looked the building up and down once more and sighed while Jake ushered me back to the bike.

"Can I drive?" he asked.

"No. You can't," I said.

"Oh come on." he pleaded.

"You haven't got a license!"

"It's weird seeing a guy on the back of a bike."

"I don't care," I told him and he rolled his eyes, but smiled anyway.

"You know, this is cool, Friday."

"How so?"

"This! We're solving a mystery," he said and I chuckled. "You're like... The 'D' detective."

I paused as he wrapped his arms around me. "Why am I a 'D' detective?"

"Your boobs."

"That's not funny Jake." He sighed, his head nestling in the crook of my neck.

"I'm sorry," he mumbled against my skin.

I shook my head and started the bike. "Maybe just, regular detective."

He nodded. The ride was short, Jake got off as soon as he could and trotted off to the handlers dorms, but not before giving me a goodnight hug. It was true, there was no curfew. The show would get more bang for its buck if they let the kids out in the middle of the night, but still, the term *moral* curfew was right; my father wouldn't allow me out alone at ten in the evening, not in a big city.

I wandered the halls without any light, hoping no one would see me as I sneaked back to my dorm. The halls were lit only by city lights from the windows. I heard a scuffle and a couple of groans. Maybe someone else was up? I turned a corner and smashed right into a camera crew and two students who pushed away from their make-out session.

"Ew!" I shouted as the cameraman told me to quiet down, and the producer shoved me back.

"Get out of here, we're filming for next week's episode."

"Ew," I said again and jogged back down the hall, slamming right into someone's chest, and staring straight into a flashlight. "Ow! Jeez!"

"What the hell? Fitz, what are you doing sneaking around?" asked Ashley, looking as blank as always.

"None of your business," I told him. "There aren't any rules against it."

"You went to see your handler friend didn't you?"

"No. Maybe. Shut up," I told him.

"Stop telling people to shut up."

"No." Could I have been more dumb?

"So you're just going to be rude then?" he asked, settling the flashlight on my face.

"Yes."

"Fine," he said, crossing his arms.

"Fine!" I replied, leaning forward.

"Good."

"Good!" I agreed and stood on tip toe, trying to match his height.

"Great," he said leaning down.

"Great!" I agreed and pushed forward 'til my nose was nearly touching his. He didn't move.

"Fitz."

"What!"

"Stop shouting," The same amused smile I'd seen at gym practice began to spread across his face.

"No." I replied.

"I sure am surprised that you said that," now his smile was clear.

"Shut up!" I said, but it came out all wrong, probably because I was smiling too. I ducked back, my nose tickled, ready to explode. I covered it just in time with the inside of my elbow, ready to keep on talking but two more sneezes came out in quick succession.

"Do you have a cold?" he asked.

"I was stuck up a skyscraper in the middle of the storm. So yeah, I think so, but it's not super bad."

"You need to be resting, not running around at midnight," he scolded.

"It's a cold, I'm barely sick." His large hands took me by the shoulder and started steering me towards my dorm. "What are you doing, Ang?"

"Taking you back to your room," he said.

"You're not the prefect, or the school police, " I told him and swerving out of his loose grip, I turned to face him. "You're not in charge of me. I can get back there myself."

"It's my fault you're sick," he said with a sigh.

"What? No it isn't."

"I pushed you back into Mary's power, that's why you ended up there. So please," he said, leaning down, only inches away in the torchlight, "let me walk you back." I pursed my lips and thought it over, I could see him resisting the urge to roll his eyes.

"Don't make me carry you." Like he would. Wait, he wouldn't, right?

"Fine," I snapped.

"Fine," he replied. We walked down the hall side by side. I opened the door, and he strode right in, judging the walls, and furniture as though it were a museum.

"What? Is your place that different?"

"It's a lot more… expensive."

"Well, I think this was the last dorm house they had."

"I didn't mean that as an insult; I like your place better than mine. It's not intimidating like the gold team's."

I moved into the center of the room, and held my arms up, as though to show I was fine. "I'm here, you can go now."

"Do you have any chicken stock?"

"What? No!" I told him, "this is the bit where you leave."

"Have you had dinner?" He mumbled.

My lips pursed together, and my eyes rolled round the room. I'd had a sandwich but nothing else. "No."

"Then I'll make you soup," he told me, "and then send you off to bed."

"I'm not a kid," I said, not sure how to react.

"I didn't say you were. Sit down, and I'll make you some supper," Ashley said.

"Are you serious?"

"Yes! As I said, it's my fault you ended up in the middle of a storm."

He looked down at me, and I could see the regret in his eyes. I bit the inside of my check and hummed in agreement. "If you're going to do that, let me take a look at your watch while you cook." Confused for a moment, Ashley remembered the conversation we'd had when we first met and unbuckled his watch, handing it to me before pulling out the pots, pans and kitchen utensils he needed. I ran into my room and dropped the watch onto my desk before pulling out my set of watch tools, unscrewing the back and placing each nano machine sized screw in a careful line. It was just as I'd thought; the hairspring had become so coiled up, it overlapped itself. I prodded it back into place, the thin piece of metal loosened and I screwed the back on. By the time I'd put my tools away and returned to the living room, Ashley was pouring warm soup into a bowl.

"Fixed it," I said as we exchanged objects.

I hadn't realized until then, but no one had cooked for me in years, not since we'd had to let my sister's Nanny go, and even so, it was a job, not something they did for me, personally. I bit the inside of my cheek.

"Eat it all, don't let it get cold, and then go straight to bed, you'll probably be all better in the morning."

I nodded and he nodded back, looked the room up and down as though he was inspecting for structural weaknesses, checked me once more, and left without a word while I sipped the soup. It was good. Really good. He was weird. But nice. Well, not really nice, *superfi-*

cially nice. I carried the soup into my room, gripped the syringe tight in my fist and stored it nice and safe under a floor board, the same way I hid things back home.

Just in case.

———

It was one of those special days, when the sun it out, and it's warm, but unless you're not directly in it's light, you still cold as balls. I pulled the blanket over my head with a sigh. My phone dancing with the same jingle it did every morning. The sound was starting to become maddening. I slammed my head into the pillow a few times. My bed warm, and the outside still obviously cold. I didn't;t want to get up, let alone face the fact that I'd been 'investigating' for nearly a week now. Every night I tried to sleep I lay awake anxiety thrashing through me. Until all I can do is get out my laptop and try not to think about it. There had been no new reports of The Figure. No sightings of the Dr. No other syringe's.

"Rise and shine kiddo!" Lisa's voice cheered. I pushed the sheets off my face, the lights forcing me to squint.

"What are you doing here?" I croaked.

"I'm here to teach you how to be a hero." She

smiled, both fists on her hips. "Get up get, get dressed, meet me in the kitchen. Lot's of work today kid." She gave me a quick thumbs up. I sighed and pushed my sheets off to show here I was doing it. Lisa turned closed the door behind her, and I hurried on my clothes.

Lisa threw me a slice of toast as I stumbled out. She clapped me on the back, tucking away a bottle of orange juice in her bag. I pattered into the elevator as Lisa tried not to laugh. "Not a morning person huh kid?" I shook my head and rubbed my eyes. The door pinged just a few floors down. Jake yawned into my face as he joined us.

"Hey 'Day," he said.

"Hey, what time is it?" I asked.

"Eight." I groaned, but it wasn't early enough for me to complain. Lisa pushed us out in a single file line. Apparently she wasn't one for skipping the mall at the bottom of the building. I'd been at Hero High for over a month, but I hadn't been down there since my first day, although if I kept getting the same lousy allowance, I'd have to get a job as a café server to pay for life at the school as well as back home. Lisa charged through the crowds of people buying mugs, book marks, and weird towels with our faces on them.

Jake was in utter awe as he looked at the shops. One of the giant three story high banners hanging from a higher floor had changed. It was now a huge mishmash of all the new students, and right in the back was my giant face. Well, giant in comparison to my actual size, but small compared to everyone else on the banner. The picture of me was set next to no one in particular, and it looked as though they'd decided that my best picture was the one where I'd glared at the photographer as he tried to get me to smile. Jake stopped dead in his tracks in front of the year one store.

"'Day!" Jake was pointing straight at the key ring rack. He ran in, and Lisa and I had little choice. We followed. "It's you!" he said, staring down at the plastic key chain in his hand.

One rectangle had my picture on the front along with my name, and a similar plastic square had my team color. A small piece of paper wrapped its self around the ring and showed the price; eight dollars. I squinted at it, the price seemed a little high for a key ring. Not to mention I wasn't sure how much money *I* was getting for this, though considering my popularity, I was probably getting next to nothing.

A few of the other students had been pulled out of class in the past few weeks to have photographs taken for what everyone thought was more merchandise. Which now, I could see was true. Aya had a pillow of herself smiling sweetly, she looked like a tween idol.

David had signed pictures of himself with his visor on, though the moment I rubbed my finger over the supposed ink, I could tell it was printed on, David never actually signed them. I wondered if he knew? On the wall above those was a poster of sorts, it said 'First Year Gold Team Photobook, Coming Soon'. Despite the fact that Ashley was The Captain's mentee, he only had one more piece of merch more than me. As Jake noticed, his brow furrowed.

"Come on kids, we haven't got all day." We both hurried after Lisa, and no one in the crowd really noticed that we were on the show that they were so adamant about. The sun was hot and, I almost, *almost* regretted wearing my letterman jacket.

"This way," said Lisa, leading the way, but all Jake and I could do was stare in awe at the skyscrapers. I couldn't decide what I liked most about Icon City; was it the rain, the misty mornings, vibrant nighttimes, or the blazing hot days?

Lisa knocked on the side of another two story bus, with the names, Sense and Barney taped to the outside. I was glad to get out from under the heat of the sun, and into the cool interior. The inside wasn't as nice as Captain Fantastic's bus had been, but it was still pretty great.

The team in Lisa's bus was considerably smaller,

The Captain had at least three handlers for various different jobs, Lisa had only one, and he seemed to be ignoring us completely. I only noticed her new partner Barney when I saw the sharp expression on Lisa's face. Barney was even more handsome in person; he had a nose so straight it could have been sculpted out of marble.

His eyes were sharp, and a bright crystal blue. He clearly took great pride in his hair since it seemed to be quaffed and gently curled into golden perfection. In person he wore reading glasses and they made him look a little older, more like someone's dad than in the pictures, but most of all they made him look less intimidating.

"Partner Kisaragi, I'm glad you could make it."

I could hear the faintest grunt of disapproval from Lisa when she saw him. "Ugh," Lisa replied as she dumped herself into one of the chairs next to the mini fridge and various hot drinks. "Kids, get yourselves something to eat, can't have you moping *all* day." Lisa pulled her sunglasses down to rest over her eyes, and leaned back to catch a few Z's. Barney halted, not quite understanding he'd been ignored, then he turned to us.

"So… Are you Lisa's mentee?" He asked. His tone was calm, and confident.

I wasn't sure which one of us he was talking to so I

put up my hand as though I was in the middle of class. "Yes sir."

He nearly choked on his espresso. "Please," he coughed, and set the cup down. "Call me Barney. I've never been called Sir before. You guys, think I'm old?"

"No sir, crap, I mean, Barney," I said.

Jake leaned in to whisper like someone giving their sibling crap for being scolded. "You're screwing it up, Friday," said Jake.

"No *you're* screwing it," I growled.

"I'm not even talking to him." Jake blurted.

"Shut up! He can hear us." I grumbled back.

Barney's chest rose up in a sputtering laugh, he held back. "Kids think I'm old, and she thinks I'm too young."

He had such a youthful face, and painfully trendy clothes, but he held himself like someone much older. He sat straight backed, legs crossed, gently sipping his tasteful espresso. This was not a man that had been born poor.

Jake inched towards the snack tray like a thief trying to hug the wall.

"Jake? You know we can see you?" I pointed out, "also, get me one too."

"Oh-kay!"

I took my place on the sofa next to Barney and the

sleeping Lisa as Jake handed me a sandwich. "I don't think Lisa thinks you're young, just youn*ger*," I told him.

"Why would that matter?" Barney asked, setting aside his book and his reading glasses to give me his full attention.

"I'd say, but it's not really my place," I told him, "she is my mentor after all."

"Fair enough. And… Friday, since Lisa is your mentor, and Lisa is my partner, consider me your mentor too. And Abe over there, you could learn a lot from him."

The man in the corner, fixated on the computer screen, grunted in response. His eyes darted around the screen, as though there was something very important he was working on.

The lights in the van started to flash red, and Lisa shot up. Abe, the man at the desk, spun round throwing Lisa and Barney their ear buds. "Downtown bomb threat, the new Dr. Dangerous has been spotted." Abe told us.

"Suit up, kid, let's boogie," said Lisa throwing me the same kit I'd worn with her before.

Barney leaned over to me, and said in a whisper. "I love it when she says 'let's boogie'." He clamped his lips together as we both stifled a laugh.

"Jake, kid, you're staying here with Abe, he'll show you the ropes of how to be a good handler. He's the best."

Jake hurried to his chair, and then turned back. "Doesn't The Captain have the best handlers?"

Lisa smirked, and slapped him on the back. "No. Why do you think he needs three?"

Lisa laughed, and with Barney, pulled on her suit. Jake made sure I could hear him, but the moment I stepped out the hot sun came crushing down on me. Lisa looked at me as she mounted her bike, and Barney did the same.

"Did you not bring yours?" Lisa asked.

"No, sorry."

"Don't worry today," she replied, "but try to remember in future."

I climbed on behind Lisa, and the bike jolted forwards as though it had *started* at max speed. Lisa was the only hero who regularly picked up bomb threats.

———

"Was that her specialty? Bomb threats?"
"Basically. You remember the highway collapse of '84?" Friday asks.

I nod.

"She got to the bomb under the highway, and realized she didn't know a thing about bomb disposal."

"So, she started learning?" I ask.

"She took bomb disposal very seriously, made every effort to keep up to date with the latest technology."

"Because she didn't know what to do on the bridge?"

Friday nods again, smiling. "Exactly. So, by this point, she was the most qualified hero for the job."

———

Once on Lisa's bike, I held on as tightly as I could while the engine propelled us like a bullet through the city streets.

"Is this the normal speed?" I asked Lisa.

"When there's a bomb threat it is!"

My ear buzzed, and Jake started talking. "Abe says he gets updates from people on the scene, so here goes. The place has been evacuated, so chances are it's not a false alarm. There're hostages inside, as far as we know the kidnappers haven't made any demands yet." There was a pause, like he was checking with Abe, and then he came back. "Day, I think this is a real, *building*, collapsing bomb. You could die."

I swallowed, hard, and held onto Lisa tighter. She'd

know what to do, and I wasn't going to run. This was now my job.

I took a deep breath, as the bike skidded to a halt. The building was a hotel, a big one, not as large as the Super Structure, but still a city skyscraper. The area was sectioned off by police, holding curious bystanders back. Lisa squared her shoulders, and looked over at me. "You don't have to come kid. I won't blame you. If this goes wrong-"

"I'm coming." Barney looked surprised, but Lisa just nodded.

"'Day, no!" yelled Jake in my ear. "Come on! It's dangerous in there, you could die!"

Lisa turned round and placed her hand on my shoulder. "You sure about this kid?"

I nodded. "Let's do this."

The policemen on duty looked at us with weary eyes, they didn't expect this to go well. Veronica came up behind us lugging a huge camera over her shoulder.

"If you want something done right, you gotta do it yourself," she muttered.

"Veronica? You are not going in there with us!"

"Stop me," she said pulling her hair up into a tight bun, while she readied the camera. The woman was crazy, seriously.

Was I really going to follow? This was crazy!

I launched in after her.

The hotel's lobby was huge, decorated in bridal white, every inch glittering as though it were a diamond. The stairs that led from one small level to another were the most opulent and theatrical thing I'd ever seen; it was the kind of place you could yell your name and hear it call back to you. Barney, Lisa and Veronica all pulled ahead of me as I gawked. Trying to catch up I dashed past a map of the floor bolted to the wall in the hallway. Lisa's ear piece rung and she pulled out her phone. "Day, this video just came through," said Jake in my ear.

Abe's face appeared for a brief moment, and then flickered to a large bomb set against a white wall. Dr. Dangerous tuned in, he shook the camera, and stated calmly that he would blow everything sky high. The video then cut away to footage of the bomb in what my gut told me was a completely different room. There were twenty minutes on the timer. The lighting was darker, the color of the walls were more beige than white. The moment the video stopped, I saw Lisa panic. It didn't make any sense, there weren't any people left in the building, why would he blow it up? Even so, what did he get out of blowing the building up? He hadn't made any demands, mentioned money, or motive. It didn't seem right, but it wasn't the time to quibble, not when a bomb was ticking, so I set the thought aside.

"Abe, play the video again! Maybe if we each isolate a different sound, we can figure out where it is." We all nodded and closed ours eyes to listen.

"Just the hum of electricity," said Barney.

"With the bomb...Rushing water maybe, and something else..." said Lisa finishing his sentence.

I grabbed her by the shoulders, nearly shaking her. "Not the specific noise, what did it remind you of!?"

"Hotel rooms, not a buzz exactly, something else..."

"A ceiling fan?" shouted Barney.

"Yes!"

I blinked, and the world had stopped. I was once again, inside my head. They heard running water, and a fan. Running water could be a fountain, or it could be a faucet. No, that didn't make any sense, why would the tap be left running? Maybe it was the pipes, perhaps it was a toilet. And a ceiling fan. How many toilets in the building had ceiling fans? No. How many toilets were big enough to provide a blank background for the videos, *and* have ceiling fans. I opened my eyes again just as Lisa reassumed her shouting. I whistled to get their attention, and pointed to the map of the building.

"We're looking for a large bathroom."

"You sure kid?"

I took a deep breath; I could have nodded, could have said yes, it was the first thing that crossed my mind, but instead I said, "No. But it's the best I've got."

"Wait, kid. I've got an idea." Lisa crouched, and swung her fist at the floor. She stared at the world like she could see so much more. "There are seven large bathrooms. But only two of them have something out of place."

Barney stared at her wide eyed. "How'd you do that?"

"Kinetic energy, If I can create any sort of movement, it's almost like radar." Lisa turned to the map and pointed at two different locations. "Baxter, go south, Friday and I will go to the top floor."

We split up as fast as we could, Lisa hot on my heels. Veronica wasted no time; she chased after Barney, after all he was the one the public knew best. I breathed carefully in and out, trying not to vomit, especially not in a wedding fantasy hotel. I was determined to keep it together. I got off the stairs at floor ten, and found a toilet sign to the right. I goosed it down the hall nearly stumbling into the men's bathroom and there it was. My body froze as I took in the scene, the flashing red numbers, and the RGB wires.

A shiver ran through me as I inched ever closer.

Lisa cried from behind me, and I spun round to see Dr. Dangerous rendering Lisa unconscious with one of his gadgets.

"Usually I like to get the drop on someone," he said, "but that gets harder with two people."

"What have you done to her?" I asked.

"She's fine." He sighed. I rushed forwards ready to fight. He reached out the same device, and I ducked left, running round him, making for the door, maybe I could get help. He swayed, making a grab for me, pulling me back. My back hit him, and I pressed my hand up, pushing against his chin. The Dr. stumbled, and I swung my fist. He gripped my arm, and pulled me again. I struggled, but couldn't break free. He pressed the device to my back, and everything from the neck down went limp against my will, as though I was gracefully falling asleep.

As my legs gave way, he scooped me up into his arms.

I couldn't move a limb, every inch was held in place. My eyes drifted up to his face, and I saw his blue eyed domino mask. I felt like one of those limp damsels being carried away by a B-movie monster.

He kicked in a door across the hall taking me far away from the bomb as I tried to gather my bearings, and he spoke to someone through an ear piece. I needed to get out, out of his arms and out of the building. He continued down the white halls, and then up a set of red carpeted marble steps.

The room above was all white, a penthouse suite. Guess he liked to pretend to be a high roller. The only source of light came from the monitors he'd brought in and the small jazz club light fixture. It reminded me of a rooftop observatory the way the sunlight shone through the balcony window. He set me down on the bed, softly laying my head down last, almost as if he was worried he'd ruin my hair. He stood just at the edge of the balcony, checking his watch before he spoke to me. "Hello Friday. Lovely to see you again." I tried to move my fingers, but all they did was twitch. "There's no point in trying to move," he said wiggling the gadget he's pressed to my neck. The huge room was filled with cameras and monitors he inspected idly like a bored security guard. "How powerful exactly are you, Friday?"

"I'm not telling you."

He smiled at me, turning away from the screens only for a moment. His face was almost completely shrouded in darkness. His fingers danced on the keyboard of a computer, and his eyes scanned the screens. "I looked you up. Funny we should meet again. You're not supposed to be here."

I tried to turn my body, but my limbs still wouldn't budge. His fingers stopped on the keyboard for a moment, but he didn't turn.

"Why are you doing this?" I asked.

"Doing what?"

"The bomb."

"Oh, don't worry about that, it won't go off... *If* they get here in time."

He was waiting for someone? Was he waiting for someone to defuse the bomb, but not us?

"Who are you?"

"I like that name. *Friday*. The Hero High website seems to call you Fitz?"

"Most people make fun of me for it," I grumbled.

"I could see that." He pushed away the keyboard, and clapped his hands together, checking his watch once more. "Looks like we're out of time. You just can't find good help these days." My fingers twitched as he towered over me. "I'll see you again soon Friday. I would call you Fitz like everyone else but-" He leaned down, his face only inches from mine, "-I like knowing I'm the only one using your real name." His canine smile flashed in the shadow his body set over me, sending a pleasant shiver through me. I thrashed my head to the other side to hide my face. But when I looked back, he was gone.

My body twitched, and my legs moved upwards, but only a little. Where was he? How had he done that? I didn't hear him leave. Another one of his gadgets? I looked at the clock trying to figure out just how much time I had left as feeling returned completely. My stomach nearly flipped, I could have sworn I'd lost at least five minutes. I pulled my leg out from under me, and ran as fast as I could, back down the stairs, through the hall through the door that had been kicked open, and back into the men's bathroom.

Lisa was still on the floor, tossing and turning. I slapped her hard across the face, and she jerked upwards.

"Where's the bomb?" she asked.

I pointed to the mess of wires. "Jake? I found it. Help." I heard a scuffle from the other end of the communicator and Veronica's voice came through the ear piece.

"Barney and I are on our way. How much time is left?"

"Five minutes," I replied, my voice breaking as I tried to stop myself crying, vomiting, or both. "Jake, help!"

Barney nearly bashed into me. Only a few seconds later Veronica was catching it all on camera.

"You're filming this! Really, Veronica?"

"Just save everyone, Lisa."

Lisa's hands hovered over the device as Veronica's camera came painfully close. "How many wires does it have? Eight, okay. Three blue, two red, and three green. Okay. I know this model." Lisa closed her eyes much like I did when I used my power. Her fingers wobbled in place as she thought. "Hold down the button, and pull the second red wire from the center."

Barney laid a hand on her shoulder. For a moment her eyes flickered to his hand, but seemed all the calmer for it. As the timer counted down from five, she plucked up the courage to pull the red wire, but stopped. My fingers clenched around her shoulder, no air finding it's way into my lungs. At the last second, her hand twitched, and she pulled the blue. We all gasped. It went dark.

There was no noise from the bomb, no message, no weird sound effect, nothing.

The display just turned off like we'd pulled the plug on the microwave.

But outside the building there was a roar of applause. People were cheering. I looked round to Veronica's camera; the red light was still on. Everything we'd just done was live. I was *live*. I rushed over to the large window, and sure enough there was a timed delay of my face on the jumbo screen in the city.

Men and women in head gear jogged up the stairs and into the bathroom just as others walked out as though they couldn't believe they'd made it out alive. Veronica's hand hit me hard in the back as she tried to give me an encouraging slap. "Good going. We should talk about your prospects sometime." I stood there stunned as Lisa tried to maneuver me down the steps and out the door.

Crowds of people were holding out paper and pens and snapping pictures. I waved to the crowd and clambered back into the bus. Jake wrapped his arms around me out of relief. My mind went blank as I collapsed on the small sofa. I could not believe what had just happened. I'd found a bomb, watched someone defuse it with five seconds to spare, and survived to tell the tale.

"I want to go home now," I said and Lisa, who'd collapsed on the floor right next to me, agreed.

"I'm with you there kid."

———

"It must have been about a week after the bomb,"
Friday says, "I wanted to focus on the 'investigation',
but I needed to send more money home, and since

second jobs were prohibited by Hero High, I was serving in the Super Structure's café."

"What was it like? Was it nice?" I ask.

"It looked much like our cafeteria, for the fans and all. It was fine, the only problem was the uniform." I nod, and she sighs, as though recalling a mixture of troubling, and fond memories. "It was frustrating, but I still didn't have any leads on the Golden Syringe, The Figure In The Flames, or the new Dr. Dangerous. I was the worst crime solver ever."

———

"Here's your uniform," said my new boss, Ms. Fletcher, dropping a plastic bag in front of me.

"My what?"

"You can change in the back," she groaned.

The Hero High cafe was where most of the students who wanted to earn some extra cash went. It was pink, retro, and it's menu was 3D. Everything we made there had a clay model on display behind the counter. The place wasn't huge though, it only needed about two servers at a time. One for the section at the front with all the tables, and one for the section at the back for the sofa's and booths.

The cafe always smelled of cherry blossom and

bamboo, which is to say it smelled fresh and floral. The pink in there was muted, more grey that it was Barbie. The sound of cooking never made it onto the cafe floor. If you were at a table you only ever heard soft music or the sound of the TV in the back playing hero high. And at the very back wall was ceiling to floor candy for patrons to buy and eat while watching the show.

I'd managed to get myself the pre-lunch shift with Aya Asimov. I moved into the back, pulled open the locker that now had my name on it. Inside was a note.

Coach Flat told me you had some issues with your uniform, so we had this made from your measurements. We will now be tailoring all your clothes.

-Veronica

I sighed and closed my eyes while the urge to vomit crawled up my throat. I pulled the plastic apart and there was my new uniform. The sleeves of the top were long, that was good, the collar and cuffs were a sharp white. The cuff turned up in a stiff classic roll up like a vintage dress, and the collar was pointed, purely for decoration since there were no buttons on it.

I nodded slowly, dreading the next layer and of course as I pulled out the next piece I found a box pleated skirt in my hands. At the very bottom of the pile was an apron with a tie so thick that it stopped right under what was supposed to be my bust. My forehead slammed against the shelf of my locker, and my hands held the back of my head.

"Hurry up in there!" screamed Ms. Fletcher.

"Yes Ma'am."

I pulled off my sensible clothes, checking the door every few seconds, and pulled it all on. At least they didn't have uniform shoes. Luckily no one was in the café when I walked out and took my place next to Aya in the same uniform. I leaned over to her, and whispered. "I've never been a waitress before."

"You've never had a job before this?"

"I have, but it involved drawing blueprints, and talking to old men in suits."

"Well, Ms. Fletcher can be a bit tough, so just ask me if you have any questions," she said. "You watched the video right?"

"Yeah."

"Then you'll be fine," she told me.

A family walked through the door giving a short, polite bow to the manager. I gripped Aya by the arm before she could walk away, the new customers setting me on edge.

"I hate this uniform, I feel completely exposed."'

"I know, I know, but it's not *that* bad-" She turned round.

"Oh. No."

"Is it that bad?"

"Considering what you wear most of the time, I can see why you feel exposed… I have just the thing, wait here." Aya ran back into the locker room and came back with a large jacket that matched the uniform. "I think it's for winter uniforms. You can have it for today. Okay?"

"Thank you so much."

"Don't mention it," she said with a smile. She left to get the drink order for the family, and just as she did, a group of boys walked in. I was petrified, but Ms. Fletcher caught me, and pushed me closer to their table. My legs felt like jelly.

"Hello, do you know what you want to drink?"

The blonde one looked up as I looked down. "Oh, I thought we were going to get Double A."

"Double A?" I asked, making sure not to look up from my pad.

"Yeah, Aya Asimov?"

"You call her Double A?"

"The website does." He pulled out his phone, scrolled down the Hero High website, and placed it in front of my face. Every one of my classmates sat on the web page ranked by popularity and year, with their name, nickname, team color, and "fun facts". Aya's nick name was indeed, Double A. Like she was a battery.

"I didn't know we had that," I said.

Another boy, a ginger, looked up from the menu with his brow raised. "What kind of a student doesn't know that?"

"This kind." I said, looking up from the first time.

"No need to get rude, lady."

"I wasn't being rude."

"Don't push it. Which one are you, anyway?" said the blonde.

"M-my name's Friday."

"Friday's not a name, it's a day for the week," said the ginger, chiming in.

"No wait, I've heard that name before," said the third boy, a brunette. He took the blonde boys phone, scrolled down a long way, and showed the others my picture. "They call her Fitz, she has some boring power."

"I'm right here," I growled.

The brunette leaned over to the other two as he looked me up and down, and whispered something in their ears that made them snicker.

"Are you going to order any drinks or not?"

All three pairs of eyes, without shame, stared straight at my chest. "Where do you think your looking!?" I pulled the jacket over my chest, and turned to leave.

"We want cola!"

"Fine!"

I gave them their drinks, and waited for their orders, glaring at them every time they dared to glance any lower than my face. It was only then I realized what the point of the uniforms was, and why I'd been given one that actually fit. The realization made my skin crawl.

The bell on the door rang about an hour later. Jake pushed past me and sat down at one of the tables that hadn't been cleared yet, popping a left over french fry into his mouth.

"What are you doing in here?"

"It's time for Hero High," he answered between chews of whatever was left on the plate.

"Want me to get you something?"

"I can't afford it, I'll just eat the left overs."

I'd been so concerned with work I'd completely forgotten about the airing schedule. The opening was almost half way through when he turned on the flat screen that hung over the bar. My picture that popped on the screen for half a second had changed as I greeted someone coming through the door. The café was starting to fill up, people filing in to watch the new episode.

The opening used the picture of me glaring at the camera. Someone snapped a picture behind me and Ms. Fletcher pointed to the sign saying no flash photography. The episode started with a brief musical montage, the end of school bell ringing in the background, and the usual establishing shots of the tower and mall shops.

The camera first focused on the most popular teams, and added to the already escalating romantic drama between Cassandra, the shy over achiever, and Donnie, the high school jock from team Mint. The problem? They were clearly only friends. I just wished they'd stop pushing Cassandra and Donnie.

Eventually they left the dull romantic sub plot and wandered over to the gold team's lunch table, and lingered on a photoshoot Aya had been to. Unlike the previous two episodes, the camera chose to feature Ashley and me as we sparred half heartedly. The footage was interspersed with what they had left of the detention I'd spent with him, they were trying to infer we were seconds away from killing each other, which... seemed a *little* exaggerated. Jake's eyes twitched, and he turned away. I couldn't help but laugh a little.

"What? You don't like him?" he sneered in reply.

"Yeah, I kinda hate him too."

"Yeah, right," he mumbled.

"What's that supposed to mean?"

"Nothing."

The episode broke for ads, starting with Captain Fantastic toys based on all of his various gadgets. Another quick ad for the upcoming Power League championship rolled across the screen, showing the teams and their most famous players. My eyes fastened on Grey London as she stepped out of the Power League stadium and waved at the camera. Something gold glinted in her bag. It couldn't be a syringe, she wouldn't be so blatant. It had to be jewelry she'd removed before the match. Just to be safe, I took out my phone, and did a quick search for a better picture.

"Day, your lunch box!" yelled Jake and I looked up in time to see the ad for Hero High lunch boxes. Every single student's face appeared on the screen with their own designs and colors decorating the surface. Customers were waiting, so I resolved to look at pictures later. I rang up the purchase of a tea-set and collectors plate, so I didn't catch a glimpse of my lunch box on TV. The rest of the episode was what they had of the next day, other romantic entanglements, various sob stories, and more of Cassandra and Donnie. Most of the plot of this episode had been about the school play. Against all the odds Cassandra had been given a leading role where she was required to kiss this douche bag kid in her class called Joey. Cassandra had let slip that she'd never kissed anyone, and Joey seemed to have been teasing her about it the entire week, making weird kissy faces and sticking his tongue out like a bad French kiss.

The weird thing was that by the last ten minutes Mr. Nott had told him to stop, and he did. Joey just *stopped* making fun of her. One minute he'd dragged the two of them away to have a talk, and then the next it was all over. The whole on-stage kiss with douche bag Joey didn't bother Cassandra any more. It was entirely too weird. And it just *ended*. The credits played over another pep filled pop song sung by one of the various Hero High graduates. I was clearing a table when I heard the much more mature theme of Real Heroes, start to play before fading into an interview with Lisa and Barney, with trumpets and drums, as opposed to the sparkling synths of Hero High's opening.

The leather of the chair creaked as Jake sat up. I handed out a bag of jelly beans, and moved round the candy bar to join him. This must have been what Lisa and Barney were doing before she picked me up. Wait - This was the episode I was in. Oh no!

The camera barged into my room catching a moment of my bed hair. The show didn't bother showing anything of my waking up, eating, or changing. It filled in the spare spaces with confessionals from

Lisa and Barney, with small spots for a class run by The Lightning Kid teaching a group of other superheroes. Soon though, it returned to Lisa and Barney, only rarely showing me and never showing Jake. Veronica clearly liked the relationship Barney and Lisa had going on, regardless of the fact that it didn't seem like a good one.

The alarms in the bus rang, and the show immediately cut to Veronica's camera as the three of us figured out how to find the bomb. All the rest was Veronica's commentary as Barney dropped to his knees next to me on screen, cutting out the fact that she'd followed the wrong team member. Lisa defused the bomb as the camera focused on the short look that passed between her and Barney, and the machine turned off. I found myself releasing a tense breath all over again. My phone rang. The blue cover flashed like an alarm. I flipped it open to see Veronica's name.

"Ms. Fitzsimmons? I assume you're watching the latest episode?"

"I'm actually at work, but yeah… Why?"

"I just had a conversation with the other producers, we'd like to expand your merchandise."

"W-what? Really?"

"It's nothing special Ms. Fitzsimmons, just some sneakers, a T-shirt, maybe a phone cover. Just something in case your popularity goes up."

"Why would it?" Just as I'd said it, I saw the moment Veronica's camera caught the crowd outside once the bomb had been disarmed, and then after, Barney, Lisa and I all standing side by side.

"You were just in two back to back episodes. The cameras will be required to try and make you more interesting."

"But, I can't," I said, "I wanted to be background."

"If you want to be an extra Ms. Fitzsimmons, don't run into buildings to defuse bombs."

"But, I wasn't! I, that's what I'm meant to do!" I protested.

"And you're also meant to be a celebrity," Veronica pointed out.

"But I don't-"

The line cut. It was Veronica's way of making sure I had no way of arguing.

"Day?"

"I-I... Veronica just, they want more merchandise."

"What?" Jake jumped up. "That's awesome!" Jake pulled me into a crushing hug, to only push me away a second later. He started running around the café like a mad thing, disturbing everyone, and pulling something out of his school bag. "I was saving this for later, but now couldn't be better!"

In his hand he held a large piece of white board, and positioned himself firmly in front of me. "Okay, ta da!"

He flipped the board, with several pictures of me on the other side. Each picture of me was photoshopped in various different outfits, with the heading at the top of the board reading, 'super suit ideas'. It would have been a nice gesture if it weren't so… weird. The first picture was a swimsuit in the vein of Mistress Widow, accompanied by a cape so short that it might as well have been a scarf. The second was *technically* more covering, but painfully skin tight, with no innovation, special details, cape, or gloves. It was just a blue latex suit. Jake had even gone so far as to photoshop my face on to a completely different body. The third and final picture was so sparse and strange I had trouble telling where the suit began, and my skin ended. All three of these pictures seemed like wishful thinking, plastering my face onto those bodies.

"I'm not wearing any of those, Jake."

"What? Why not?"

"Because they're dumb, and lame." I said turning away.

"They're awesome!" Jake insisted.

"They're stupid and sparse," I told him. "I'm not wearing underwear into battle."

"It's not underwear! It's armor."

"How is that armor? How is that realistically helpful?"

"You're a superhero, you're not realistic."

"Oh really, I'm not real then am I?"

"Oh my God, 'Day, cool it. All I'm saying is, stuff like this is part of the superhero culture."

"Read my lips. I'm. Not. Wearing. Those."

He scoffed at me, and shook his head as though I'd just refused to give a kidney. I couldn't help but feel like I'd done something wrong. Maybe he was right? I wanted to be a superhero, and that was how they dressed. But I didn't understand why I had to look a certain way to be worth someone's time. It felt like paying rent.

I heard a loud stomping, and then Lisa's hurried voice as she raced in and took the controller from Jake. For a moment I thought she was here to warn me about something, but instead she collapsed onto the café's sofa as the Hero Channel switched over to a special. Jake made himself comfortable next to her.

"What's happening?" I asked.

"They're broadcasting a special about Baxter and me. I found out a few seconds ago from my agent. Yours was the nearest TV I could borrow. Sorry kid."

A few people in the café tried to sneak pictures of her, mumbling about who she was. My brow scrunched as Lisa came into view. It was a recorded segment called the latest duo. I handed someone a milkshake and turned the volume up. Lisa waited outside the tower for Barney, standing next to a red car.

It didn't look fake, but then I reasoned that this was a prop the show had given them since they didn't want a superhero duo driving around in a mini van. Barney finally showed up and got in the drivers seat. The show cut away to black screen confessionals. The woman behind the camera asked both of them what they'd thought of each other when they'd first met. Lisa sat up straight on the coach and pointed at the TV.

"I'll tell you what I thought! The first time I met him I had to watch him have his photo taken. I had to wait hours. I thought, wow I *hate* this kid."

I patted her shoulder to try and calm her as the heads in the café turned round. Then on the recording Lisa spoke.

"He seemed pretty quiet, smart, well adjusted." There was a small frown on her face as she continued to obviously read off a cue card. "I'd like my son to grow to be like him someday." The *present* Lisa groaned.

"I mean what was that line about? Are they trying to imply that I'm old enough to be his mother? Because I'm not. I'd have to have had him at ten! This is ridiculous! I'm not that old!"

I tried to usher in new customers but they left as soon as they noticed the angry woman on the sofa. The camera cut to the very first time they'd met, and it was indeed as Lisa had said, a photoshoot. The only thing was that Barney seemed to be in his underwear and Lisa was frowning at the camera. It was too funny watching her glare directly at the camera as Barney posed in the background, I couldn't help but laugh.

"It's not funny!" said Lisa.

"It's hilarious!" Jake held out his hand for a high five, and I took it. As I looked round the exact same expression was on her face now as she grumbled under her breath. The show didn't seem to answer the question of what Barney had thought of her, it just seemed to move onto showcasing his talents and then having Lisa congratulate him as though she was his sixty year old grade school teacher.

"What is this?" Lisa grumbled.

"I think, maybe, just maybe," I started, "they're trying to play you off as a mother figure."

"Why? I'm not that old!"

"I know, I know, but I think they're doing it so no one thinks of you as a couple."

She paused, as though the thought had never once occurred to her. "He's just a kid."

"He's twenty six," I pointed out.

"Like I said, he's a kid."

Jake and I sighed at each other, and I continued my analysis. "It probably also means that they have someone in mind for him. They always do this with the newer ones, try and set them up."

"They never did that for me," said Lisa.

"You were married." I blurted. I felt the urge to slap my hand over my mouth the moment I said it. I had never wanted to bring up her husband. I was *sure* he was dead, but she still wore her ring... I didn't want to dig up that painful memory if she was happy forgetting it. Lisa placed her hand on my shoulder sensing the panic in my posture.

"It's okay kid, it's been a decade since he passed."

I turned the volume down and Jake frowned. My attention was all on Lisa. "How did he die?" I asked.

She fiddled with her ring for a second, and then looked up at me. "Brain tumor. It got him real fast. Kids were two at the time, they don't even remember him."

I held back for a second and wondered if I should go on, but I had to know. "Why did you never re-marry?"

She shrugged. Her nose twitched as she took a sharp inhale of air. "Never wanted to. It didn't seem right, after everything. I loved him, still do. I don't think it's fair to put that kind of baggage on another guy." She looked me straight in the eye, I'd never seen her so serious. "I'm sorry for going all sappy on you but, I just don't think it's right to be with someone unless you're fully committed to them, and I don't think that's something I can do."

I could tell she wanted to go on, but tears were tipping off the edges of her eyes.

"It's okay, I get it. Don't worry."

She nodded and wiped her eyes even though she hadn't shed a tear.

"Hey friend!" Aya said, running over to David as he poked his head out from behind the café doors.

"I asked Ashley if he wanted to come, but he was busy." David explained.

"No biggie, a team doesn't have to do everything together," she said.

"But you're always with David," I said setting down a jug of soda.

"That's because they're dating!" shouted Jake from the couch.

Aya slapped David on the back who gave a sheepish smile. "What can I say? The cameras really love us together."

David didn't seem to meet Aya's bright smile, and instead preferred to look at the ceiling. "Actually Friday there was something we wanted to talk to you about. We, uh… Is that Sense?"

Lisa turned round on the couch and waved. "Hi kids."

"She's my mentor," I explained and they nodded.

"We know, I mean we all saw you with the bomb and then… You know. But, she hangs out here?'

"She just barged in really."

"Sorry about that!" Lisa waved the remote in the air as she continued her viewing of the TV special.

"Okay, right, well. We uh, wanted to ask you, Aya?" David prompted.

"Would you be interested in joining the gold team!?" Aya asked, jumping up and down.

Jake's body spun round like the head on an owl as I replied. "What, like, transfer?" I asked and Aya nodded.

"Do it Day! Do it! Just do it!" urged Jake.

"Alright, alright, calm down." I said.

"He's right kid," said Lisa, "that's a good idea. You're moving up, it might do you some good to have some team mates."

"Really?"

"I'll still be your mentor if you change teams," she told me, "but I think it would get you more practice."

"Why me?"

"Honestly?" said Aya leaning forwards as she

spoke, "Veronica wanted us to get a new member before Christmas. We all agreed you were a good choice, you're a no nonsense type, you've got a great mentor, and I think you and I would be great friends!"

For a moment I considered telling them I'd think about it. I still wasn't used to the idea of being a super-hero even though I'd had a power for years. I didn't have to tell them I'd think about it. I blinked, and spent what seemed like twenty minutes debating what I should do. I'd come to the conclusion that I needed more practice as a hero, that I needed to push myself, and maybe living and working with other people was a way to push myself out of my comfort zone, and get something out of it. I opened my eyes again, seemingly no time had passed, and I said, "I'll take you up on that offer."

"That's amazing!" Aya threw her hands up into the air, and Lisa cheered from the sofa.

Jake came running round with an ecstatic look on his face. "We should celebrate!" Jake announced sloshing a drink as he waved his arms.

"Be careful with that." I said. Aya chuckled and David nodded.

Jake nudged me in the side and spilled pop on my top. "Oh, sorry 'Day."

I took a deep breath as Aya hummed with sympathy

for me, and I held my hand up. "It's fine, my shift was almost over anyway. I'll just go put a different top on." I walked back to my dorm room, setting my apron and jug of water aside. If I was going to switch teams, I'd have to move into their dorm. As I slipped the new top over my head I stopped and remembered the gold syringe. I took my phone out, searching for the picture of Grey London but at higher resolution. It wasn't difficult to find. I zoomed in, the picture wasn't perfect, but the object was there. It wasn't jewelry, but it could have been a pen. I cleared a space, pulled out my suitcase and bent down to pry open the floor board. I could compare it to the photo. I couldn't see anything at first so I put my hand down to search more carefully, but couldn't find a thing. I set the floor board aside and wondered, had I opened the wrong one? I checked each floor board carefully, but this was the only one that budged and I'd been sure this was where I'd put it.

Which meant… the gold syringe was gone.

———

CAST AWAY

THE NEXT DAY WAS a late lazy afternoon. The cold had let up some what, and the storms had too. I felt warm and cozy, I didn't want total to anyone, I just wanted to curl up in bed.

The hallways were mostly empty, barren even as I trotted through them. Veronica had texted me before I'd even made it to the elevator after school. I was needed in the photography room.

I rubbed my eyes, and swung open the glass doors to the photo room before throwing my bag into the corner. Aya waved over the shoulder of the makeup artist, it was about time for the new group pictures of the gold team to be taken and I was dreading it.

Ashley looked at me out of the corner of his eye, but ignored me anyway. The rest of the team was slurping down various hot soups and quick snacks which meant they weren't going to get a chance to eat later, there must be somewhere we had to go *after* the pictures.

Veronica threw the doors open, the sound of her practical boots slamming against the floor was reminiscent of a sergeant major. Aya passed me an energy bar, and pulled me into a quick hug.

"How's my number one freshman team?" Veronica asked and we all hummed in reply, "We're going to take some pictures," she told us, clapping her hands, "Liddy Dhonage will be interviewing you. Friday, could you go get changed, please?"

I nodded, and two women set me behind a screen and handed me some clothes. My hands started to sweat as I slipped the top over my head, there were too many people in the room for comfort. I took a deep breath, tried to ignore the shaking in my chest, and stepped out. My other team mates were already sitting on this strange wooden crate like something out of a movie, the backdrop was plain white, and everyone was waiting as I went to take my place.

"I'm going to look like an idiot," I said, throwing my hands up in the air. "Veronica please, I'm not made for the camera, I'll go all awkward. Come on, look at me!" I swiveled in place, displaying the strangest faces I could make.

"See! This is a bad idea!" I said as Veronica winced. Aya bit her lip and sighed, I got the feeling she didn't like having her picture taken either.

"Just let me think, Ms. Fitzsimmons, I'll come up with something," Veronica said.

"The only picture you have of me is one where I'm frowning! Apparently it was the best one!" I frowned. Ashley snorted. "Shut up Ang," I said and pointed an accusing finger. He bit his lip, and looked away.

"Calm down," insisted Veronica.

"I *am* calm!" I said and collapsed on the floor in a single movement, crossing my legs and arms. Veronica stepped away and lifted up a book entitled 'Gold Team, freshman year: Draft, Do Not Distribute' and flipped slowly through it, nodding as the pages turned.

"Aya, David, you take better pictures just the two of you. Ashley, you're shooting with Friday."

"What?" I grumbled.

"Friday, you'll get used to the camera, I guarantee it, so until then, we'll work up. But we do need a picture of you."

She was right, I couldn't just sit this out because I was nervous.

"Why Friday and me?" Ashley asked as he pushed up his glasses.

Veronica shrugged, and waved him out of the way as the photographer started snapping pictures of Aya and David. They really did seem comfortable with each other; Veronica kept stepping in and draping them over each other, telling them to look more in love, whatever that meant. Standing between Ashley and me she whispered advice like; stick your chin out, stand as straight as you can, if you can't smile think of a joke. Finally she leaned in and said, "Know your good side Friday, it's your right. Stick with it."

I'd run a marathon before but this was exhausting. If the picture doesn't come out good enough, that's on you and your face. I can't change my face. Unless Veronica recommends me for extensive plastic surgery and liposuction. Which incidentally I would just like to say plastic surgeons do some genuinely great things, and seem to get a bad rap. Anyway... just imagine, flashing lights, camera man *constantly* staring at you. Production assistants, Veronica, the water boy, interns, all *looking*. And while they're doing that you have to be as beautiful as you ever have. I guess I never realized the pressure of being a model. How do those amazonian girls handle all the looks, the attention? I hope all models are extroverts. I could tell I looked stupid in every picture. However I was learning that the key was to, one, not look at them afterwards, and two, throw up when I'm done.

David and Aya finished and gave me a thumbs up. Aya stayed by the side gulping down a bottle of apple juice while David played on his phone. Veronica sat the woman from deco magazine in front of Ashley and me for a few questions.

She'd questioned us all throughout the shoot; simple things like why we were here, what did we like about each other and so on. She'd left me out and since I was new it seemed right. I wasn't as familiar with my new team as the others were. Finally, though she turned to me. I'd expected something easy, something about why I'd joined, but no.

"So Ms. Fitzsimmons, do you ever feel inadequate now you've joined the most popular team in the freshman year?"

"I don't know what you mean. Because you think I have less practice? You might be right I guess."

"No," Ms Dhonage said, "I mean, before you, Aya was the sole woman on the team. Do you ever feel like you have to keep up?"

My eyes slowly narrowed, and I heard the snaps of the camera slow in rhythm as the room got quieter. "What?"

Ms. Dhonage adjusted her position, and cleared her throat. "It's just, Aya is already so popular, especially with the young men. Don't you feel like, you know-"

"Actually, I *don't* know," I replied, my voice just a whisper below a shout.

"I just mean you must feel a little bit as though you're in her shadow. She's so beautiful, how do you cope with that?"

My fists clenched, and my body shook. Ashley's hand reached out to my fist, and his fingers curled around it, sending a wave of calm through me. "We're not competing, she's my friend." I said.

"I wasn't saying that. I just meant that-"

"I cope with it by trying not to define myself by the way *other* people look." I snapped.

"Ms. Dhonage," Veronica started her best false smile on, "thank you so much for coming by, we'll be in touch with Deco." said Veronica indicating the way to the exit. Ms. Dhonage returned the same false smile, and packed up her things. I think we'd left her a little short of content, but she didn't care, she wanted to leave as much as I wanted her to go. The door to the photo room closed behind her.

"Did I do the wrong thing?" I asked.

"No. You didn't do the wrong thing," said Veronica, "I'd say you handled it well. No violent outbursts for one." Veronica drawled. Aya smiled at me. Before Ashley let go of my hand the photographer snapped another picture. Veronica put down her clipboard and took her place behind the photographer, checking all the pictures that came through. She peered at the latest one.

"This is your best picture yet, front page worthy even." She turned it round for us to see and I puffed up my cheeks to hide my expression; the picture looked like I was seconds away from leaping into action, and Ashley was the only thing holding me back. His hand had dropped from mine a split second before the picture was taken, so only our fingers brushed.

"That's a good one kids," Veronica sighed and rested her chin in her hand. "Lets try and get some more."

I nodded, and stepped back to Ashley's side.

"Okay kids, look at each other."

"What?" I replied.

"Friday, look at Ashley." she dictated without looking up from the monitor.

"I'd rather not."

Ashley grabbed my shoulder and spun me round. "Just do it," he groaned.

"Fine. I'm looking at him, I'm feeling anger."

"That's all you ever feel," Ashley added.

"He's not wrong. But I swear to God, one of these days, Ang-"

I waggled my finger in front of his face to issue a warning, but the quirk of his brow made my face go all red. The camera flashed and Veronica practically gasped.

"I'm gonna use that one all over the place."

I blew a raspberry and settled in on the wooden crate. Veronica loved pictures of me frowning while Ashley smiled so we took several more. Aya finished her dinner and decided to tell me some jokes earning a genuine smile or two for her efforts. Soon Veronica had everyone back in the frame, Aya wrapped an arm around me, and rested her head on my shoulder. The next thing I knew a laugh escaped my lips and everyone was so surprised they all broke out into smiles. I knew we'd got a good group picture.

"Alright kids! That's a wrap, good work today!" Veronica gave us all a quick shake of the shoulder, and everyone started putting away their stuff as we shuffled out of the room, one by one.

"Everything okay, Friday?" Aya asked, setting a hand on my shoulder.

"Yeah, it's just I've been meaning to buy tickets for the championship power league game."

David frowned and dipped his hands into his pockets. "The Championship game sold out months ago," he told me.

Aya saw the disappointment on my face, and slapped David on the back. "Maybe Veronica could get us some tickets?" she chirped.

"Would she?" I asked.

"Sure, they probably have some spare tickets for Hero High kids. They usually do."

"That's great!"

Aya beamed, glad she'd cheered me up, and hung onto David's arm as the lighting crew walked past us. "I'll go ask her right now. It's on Saturday, I'll find you before the game, okay?"

"Do I need anything?" I asked, worried, now I was part of the gold team.

"I'll take care of that, just keep your phone on and I'll call you, okay?"

"Sure, thanks Aya."

"No biggie," she said with a shrug for emphasis, and left with David.

I checked down the hall both ways expecting to see Ashley, but it seemed he'd already left. Oh well.

Not that I cared.

———

Saturday came, and I wandered down the slanted cobbled streets, refusing to look at my reflection in the tempered glass of the buildings. I hated having to walk through the streets alone. The butterflies in my stomach were more acutely aware of how many people were around me now than ever before; it was ridiculous. I had to push through like my father taught me, I had to *live* in Icon City, but as I walked my heart sped up and with each step it became harder to breathe. I knew I had to find somewhere safe. My stomach rumbled. I also needed something to eat. I walked past most of the café's, coffee shops, and bars because they seemed too crowded, ideal for a person that thrived in the big city. Right then, I was anything *but* that. From the corner of my eye I caught a glimpse of something in a dark, burnt red, and found a squat restaurant. The sign read 'Maggie's'. I recognized it from Ashley's menu, maybe he came here often? I needed to get away from all the people on the street, I couldn't handle feeling like millions of eyes were watching me and judging. I gripped my bag like it was my life line, or maybe I just needed something to hold, and decided to try it out.

The moment the door of Maggie's closed behind me I breathed a sigh of relief. It wasn't perfect, but it was better. Here I could sit without feeling I was going to have a heart attack, but still, it didn't wash away the sense of vulnerability. I had no choice. I'd have to keep trying to go out and see if I could lessen the anxiety, only I wasn't sure if that was how to fix it or even whether it *could* be fixed. The hostess showed me to a booth in the corner of the room and handed me a menu. I'd chosen the spot so I could watch the door. I lay my bag next to me hoping I could watch something on the web while I ate. When the waiter came to ask me what I wanted my eyes bulged at the sight; Ashley in an apron.

"Fitz?"

My confusion was over in an instant, and now I had a one way ticket to frustration station. Ashley wasn't wearing his usual clothes, they weren't old, or freshly pressed, his hair hadn't been pruned or combed back with just the right amount of gel. Instead he looked like someone who worked for a living, and he'd switched out his horn rimmed glasses for contacts.

"What can I get you?" he asked grudgingly.

I raised the menu up to cover my face, as though I could make him forget it was me. "Can I have shrimp?"

"This is a restaurant, so, yes." he replied.

"There's no need to be snappy," I told him.

"I'm not being snappy," he said, clicking his pen rapidly.

"Yes you are."

"No I'm not," he said leaning forwards on the table, trying to use his size against me.

"Fine, then that's what I want!".

"Fine," he said and stopped clicking his pen.

"Good!"

"Good." He left, chewing the inside of his cheek.

My phone rang, the picture on the inside displaying Aya's face. "David and I just got done with some interview, we've got a couple of hours until Power League, tell us where you are so we can pick you up." Aya's tone reminded me of a woman happily looking through the racks of clothing.

"I'm sitting in a place called Maggie's."

There was brief silence, and then a grunt from the other side. "Oh yeah, okay. On our way! What ya doing?"

"Just, eating here really," I told her.

"That's all? You know they pay us right?" She laughed.

"I send a lot of it home," I explained.

"Oh, that's so nice of you!" said Aya, "but is that really all you've done today?"

"Well… I don't know," my voice trailed off, I didn't exactly want to tell her I had a panic attack from walking through the streets.

"Is there something wrong?" Aya asked.

"No, I just got nervous, I guess," I said and twiddled the cutlery with my fingers, wanting something to distract my over active mind. "There were so many people, I just, I guess I felt a little crowded. It's hard to explain."

"If you have a problem with crowds, that's totally normal," said Aya, "it'll get easier."

"I know, I know. But whoever heard of a superhero that suffers from anxiety?" I pulled the phone from my ear, Aya's voice trailing off slightly, when I realized Ashley had been standing there for a while, ready to pour my drink. "How much of that did you hear?" I asked him.

"Most of it."

I clenched my jaw, and set the phone back to my ear. "I'll talk to you later," I said and snapped the phone shut. I turned to Ashley. It didn't matter, he wasn't going to use it against me. After all he hadn't mentioned the chest plate, boob fiasco. I wasn't ashamed of people knowing I had some social problems, I was ashamed of not living up to expectation, and not being able to handle it myself. I wasn't afraid of what other people thought, I was afraid of what *I* thought.

"I guess that makes sense," he said as he poured my cola.

"What makes sense?"

"You having anxiety," he said, like it was obvious. "It makes sense you'd be nervous in a big city like this. Just take deep breaths, try to focus on something."

Was he being nice again? "What would you know about it?" I asked.

"My Nana used to get panic attacks after she moved here."

An old woman hobbled down the aisle of booths and waved to Ashley. "Xiao-Ley stop talking to your friends, I need help in the kitchen," she hollered.

"Coming Nana!" he yelled back.

Before he could leave, I grabbed his sleeve, "Xiao-Ley?" I asked

"Xiao means little, Ley is short for Ashley." A few other employees passed her some papers, and whispered things to her.

"Is this your grandma's restaurant?" I asked.

He nodded cautiously.

"So that's how you learnt how to cook?"

"Yes, Fitz, that's how I learnt how to cook. How did you learn to fix things?"

"Fix things? You mean like you're watch?" I asked. Ashley nodded, settling against the wood of the booth as we spoke. "My dad's a designer and an engineer.

When I was growing up the house was always full of old junk."

"You learn by watching?"

"By doing, eventually I had to join him, make stuff. After um, well," I swallowed, "my mom was a designer too, his partner." I smiled. This was always the worst part. Ashley stood straighter. "She passed away." I said with a nod. Ashley's face dropped, the jug in his hand lowered.

"I'm so sorry, Friday." He said with pursed lips. I looked up and shrugged. "I lost my father just before I was born." Ashley said with a nod.

"I didn't know that, I'm sorry." I stared at him, and he looked right back. At least we had *something* in common. Sucks that it had to be dead parents. I almost wanted to laugh. "Is that why you-"

"Live with my Grandmother?" He finished for me. I nodded. "Yeah, she practically raised me, my mom wasn't too interested. She used to say looking at me reminded her of my dad."

"My dad says the same thing about me." I scoffed.

The silence stung.

Ashley's grandmother came hobbling down the aisle. "Xiao-Ley, stop talking to your girlfriend and help me."

"She's not my girlfriend," he said, but his grandmother grabbed my hand and shook it without giving me an option.

"You're the spunky one he talks about, yes?" she asked, "Friday?" I nodded quickly. "Good to meet you. Maggie, Meili, Ang," she said pointing to herself as she let go of my hand.

"I'll just let you finish then," Ashley said, backing away.

"Now you want to help me?" she smiled and pulled him along to the kitchen, which was honestly, unbearably sweet. The image of an old woman dragging her six foot five grandson was cute.

The food at Maggie's was some of the best I'd ever had. Ashley happily informed me after my compliment he'd been the one to cook my meal, which shut me up, and forced a rarely seen smile onto his face warmed my heart. As I was about to finish the very last of my meal and Ashley was refilling my glass, the bell on the front door rang. The moment Ashley saw the new customers, he dashed under my table, his head banging against the bottom.

"What are you doing?" I asked as he grabbed my leg and held a finger to his mouth.

"What in hell do you think I'm doing?" he whispered, "I'm hiding. Don't let them see me."

"What?" The idea struck me as ridiculous, "you're too big."

"No turning back now," he told me.

Aya and David turned the corner as the hostess pointed towards my table, and they waved. "Hey Friday," they said.

"Hi guys." Ashley's hand around my thigh tightened in warning.

"Ready to go to Power League?"

———

"Power League was the serious version of Hero Colosseum," Friday tells me.

"Hero Colosseum?"

"Sort of like a game show where superheroes fought with foam swords, and sparred using their powers. Power League was an actual sport, one I knew inside and out."

"I've seen that!"

"Yes, it's still popular today, I played once," she says.

"It was a lot of fun!"

"I don't know much about it."

Friday waves her hand in dismissal and smiles. "Don't worry about it."

"My husband watches," I tell her, "but I don't understand how it works."

Friday sucks in a breath ready to explain, though I haven't asked. "A team member is assigned to each area of the court and confined to their space, but, they also have to shadow the member of the other team that shares their position." She takes a deep breath and continues. "You score differently depending on the goal. There are five in total, each getting smaller the further they get from the center. Three members on each team are allowed to score by getting the disk into one of the goals."

"A disk?"

"Disk's are easier to move with powers than a ball, more aero dynamic. Some people are excluded from using their hands. It's crazy."

"Why is it so complicated?"

Friday shrugs.

"It's quite an event," Aya said, "there are thousand dollar gift bags, big name celebrities, and it's a chance to wear something super pretty." Aya was almost squealing as her sentence came to an end, and David accompanied it with a gentle smile.

"You had me at thousand dollar gift bag," I told them, "no, wait, you had me at just gift bag." I saw Ashley roll his eyes under the table, and gave him a kick.

"Everything okay, Friday?" David asked.

"Everything's fine! So, is Ashley going with you?" I asked and earned another glare from Ashley.

"He might be," replied David, "he said he had some errands to run before or something, so we'll see."

"Okay, cool."

"So, you ready?" Aya asked.

"Sure." I replied.

"Do you have anything to wear? We need to get you something."

"Aya loves shopping for people," said David.

"Isn't it just a stadium?" I asked. "I was thinking pop culture T-shirts that say stuff like, 'who farted'."

"Well, I guess," said Aya, "the guys usually wear shirts and stuff…"

"But not the women?"

"God no! Why pass up a chance to wear a couture dress? It's a big event!"

She had a point.

"I'd love to get a dress for you Friday," said Aya.

"You don't have to," I told her, "besides I'd feel like a chump next to the guys wearing T-shirts and jeans."

"But, D'Fwan is the best," she said with a giddy smile.

"Well, I'd love to come with you, after all, we are team mates now," I said, trying to get the whole idea of being part of a team.

"Exactly! So," said Aya, "see you outside in a minute?"

"I'll be there, just let me pay." Aya and David disappeared, chatting, and as soon as they were gone Ashley tumbled out from under the table.

"What are you thinking?" He asked me. "Your anxiety's so bad it sends you running through the streets, and you're going to a power league game?"

"How did you know I was running?"

"I saw you come in," he said.

"Look, I can't let my anxiety dictate what I do, and besides I couldn't say no," I replied. "I have to go."

"Why?" he asked.

"The investigation."

He shook his head at me. "Fine, whatever."

"Are you coming?" I asked him.

"To the games? No, I have a job." I nodded, laid out the money I owed on the table and picked up my stuff.

Ashley slammed his hand down on the table blocking my path. "Oh, and Fitz, don't tell them I work here. Second jobs are prohibited by Hero High."

"So I hear. Why is that?"

"Because they want you to earn money by working in the cafe, and selling autographs," he explained. "It's all about making you sell yourself."

"Oh. I work in the Cafe."

He paused. "They make you wear the uniform?"

"Yeah, why?" I prodded. He cleared his throat.

"No reason. Just, don't tell anyone I work here." He finished, starting to turn away.

"I won't," I snapped.

"Good," he said.

"Right," I agreed.

"Fine," he added.

"Fine," I agreed as we shot each other another glare, and I left.

As soon as I stepped out, Aya turned round on her heel and took me by the arm, leading me over to a company van. The inside was smaller than Lisa's or The Captain's, but still big. It was nicely furnished with accents in gold, the team's color. On the wall hung a portrait of each member. Aya clambered into the front, and tapped the driver on the shoulder.

"Can you drive us to Duff's?

"Certainly Ma'am."

Aya smiled to me from the other side, and proceeded to show me all the other things she had bought today. My phone twinkled with light, and I opened to a text from Veronica, that said.

Heard you're going to Power League, wear a dress, don't embarrass the team.

I sighed.

"Don't worry you'll be in great hands!" Aya squealed.

The van stopped after a twenty minute ride, and Aya threw open the doors. Outside was a large department store with the name, 'Duffs' overhead. Thin posters hung from the inside of good looking people fake laughing at each other. My stomach twisted, maybe Ashley had been right, maybe this was a mistake, but I didn't want to disappoint Aya. I stepped out, and let her and David escort me in.

The store looked like the kind of place where a T-shirt sold for a hundred dollars or more. I was wearing a jumper with a picture of a cat in a space helmet. Personally I loved the jumper, the cat, the helmet, in fact, the whole thing, but something told me people here wouldn't feel the same way. An elegant slender woman danced over to us in what must have been one of the store's gowns, and turned to Aya. "Can I help you today Miss?"

"Yes, we're from Hero High. My friend is looking for a dress to wear to the game tonight."

"Right this way." The woman placed her hand on my back and steered me towards a changing room. She closed the door behind me and waved over a man with filed nails and baby smooth skin. "Get her measurements please, D'fwan."

"Of course, sugar."

"And I'll go pick out something for you, Miss?"

"Fitzsimmons," said Aya, "Ms. Fitzsimmons."

"I'll be right back, Ms. Fitzsimmons."

D'fawn measured my shoulders, chest, waist, and finally hips. He looked up at me from the floor with pursed lips. "Girl, you are short." I shrugged and he smiled. "So am I. Own it."

"D'fwan?" I asked, not sure if I'd heard the name correctly.

"Yes sugar?"

"Are the Power League Games very formal?" I asked.

"They're not black tie, more cocktail."

I stared at the wall for a long time, not thinking to use my power to waste less of these people's time.

Eventually D'fwan interrupted. "Do you wear formal often?"

"Frilly dresses when I was a kid," I replied honestly. "Since then, not so much."

He chuckled to himself, and flung his tape measure over his shoulder. "Don't worry, we've got you." D'fwan snapped his fingers and someone rushed out to get me a drink, and he turned me to face the mirrors. "I saw you on TV, well, on the jumbo screen anyway. What you did was real brave."

"Thank you," I said, surprised to be recognized, "I was terrified."

"I'm not sure the blonde one, and uh, the lady. I'm not sure they would have found that bomb if it weren't for you." I smiled at him, and he nodded my way.

The woman returned with several short dresses that nearly made my eyes pop at the length. Carol and D'fwan looked me up and down, deciding if I needed anything else.

"Are you wearing anything under your sweater?" said Carol.

"A vest. Why?" I asked.

"Can we see it?"

"I suppose." I pulled my sweater off in the least awkward way I could muster, and left myself in my vest.

"Turn, sugar." I turned as D'fwan asked me.

"She won't fit into the…" even though he didn't finish his sentence Carol nodded before doing the same thing.

"We should get the ones with the…" D'fwan nodded to her, like they could read each others minds. Carol left, taking away some of the dresses she'd already brought in, and D'Fwan pulled in some nice shoes. In a few minutes Carol returned with three new dresses.

D'fwan shoved everything into my arms as someone set a drink on the table in front of me, and D'fwan told me to change. The first one was cream, embroidered with beads of a slightly lighter shade, and accented with blue ribbon. It looked very regal and proper, its puffy skirt hitting a little below the knee. Carol and D'Fwan said they both liked it, but it looked more garden party than city social event, so I took it off. The second one was black, with thin sparkling lines that reminded me of the silhouette of a tree. This looked like the shortest, because it had two layers. It made the bottom look like it faded from clear to opaque, only covering the very top of me. Carol and D'Fwan loved it, but eventually sighed, saying it was too nightlife. Carol handed me the last dress, and a pair of pointed toe heels that made me nervous.

"The trick to those shoes is holding onto someone," Carol said as she handed them off. The last dress was a royal blue and stark white, vertically striped on the skirt, and then moving diagonally up the front. It didn't scream attention, and it wasn't beaded, so it wasn't as showy as the others, but it was perfect for the occasion, or at least that's what Carol and D'Fwan said. The only thing that made me nervous was the triangular hole in the back.

"Why does there have to be a hole?"

D'fwan sighed as he tipped his hip. "It's not a hole, it's an open back. If you don't wear an open back, none of these dresses are gonna look right."

I nodded, and looked down at my shoes. "And what about these?"

"Pointed toe looks expensive, never wear round toe. Like Carol said, hold onto someone."

"Can I hold onto you until I get out?"

"Course you can." D'fwan waved his hand at me as though it was nothing, and Carol mussed up my hair the best she could. I stepped out, with my hand on D'fwan's shoulder to Aya and David in a heated conversation. Aya had already picked out a dusty pink dress, and David looked like he was going to be one of the few men who wore a suit for the occasion. The two looked me up and down and nodded.

"Looks good. Not very you, and I would fix that if we had time."

"It's okay, but, it's kind of cold, can I have a jacket?"

Carol wandered off, and brought back a powder blue jacket that I put on quickly.

"You're wearing a suit, David?"

"Sure," David said with a smile, "it'd look a bit odd if my girlfriend showed up dressed to the nines and I didn't."

Aya pulled out a gold card bearing the words 'Hero High', and used it to pay.

"You come back now!" said D'fwan and I waved, hoping they'd remember me if I returned another time.

The sun was starting to set, and the air was getting colder. Jake joined us soon enough, in his idea of formal attire. Which meant, all his regular clothes with a suit jacket on top. The jacket was the formal part. Car started to honk, and the chatter of people outside are louder as everyone tarted arriving.

I dragged myself out of the bus into a massive crowd of couture clothing. Photographers tried to get as many pictures as possible as the herd of celebrities thinned out on the carpet.

Just as Aya had said, only the women and a few select men, had put on formal attire for the big game.

Aya linked her arm with mine as though she were my date. She had no idea how grateful I felt until I wondered, was she using me for balance. Her dress looked like she was *wearing* a peony. Jake pried us apart and wrapped an arm around each of us.

"Two beautiful ladies on my arm, sorry, *arms*," he said, looking smug. It took only a second for David to appear, and unwind Jake's arm from Aya, acting as her escort instead. The carpet for this event was golden, though not metallic, that would screw up the pictures. So, I mean really it was yellow. We all walked the stretch of cameras as fast as we could, and scurried through the thick glass doors of the stadium.

The walls were covered in posters, illuminated by a rainbow of lights, while moving walkways helped patrons from one side of the stadium to the other. Men and women dressed as old and new superheroes littered the halls handing out gift bags. The place smelled like a cauldron of strong perfume. If you turned your head there was another fruity musky scent to greet you. Posters hung a few stories above us, dedicated to specific players on the championship teams. Trays of champagne passed through the crowd while a bartender mixed drinks with just the right amount of flare. The noise was loud but cultured. Like the buzz before a play. There was a wind indoors from the air conditioning, and juicy color of the lights that played super league adverts and old matches above us.

The call for seats started. Other heroes and celebrities had reserved booths, and fans who had paid for their tickets a year or more in advance were sitting in the bleachers.

"You go ahead Aya, I have to go to the bathroom," I said and watched David and Aya move to one of the booths reserved for Hero High students. I turned down the hallway looking for a sign as the very last of the crowd shuffled their way to their seats. Most of the super athletes would be in the stadium by now, so I could use the time to search for Grey London's bag. The only problem was, I wasn't sure where to go. I wandered down the hall, only to see Grey London waiting for something, rubbing her hands on her thighs like she was moments away from a blind date. I hid behind a pillar, the tension surrounding her was too much to ignore. She should be changing right now, what was so important she couldn't be on the field?

I stayed there, waiting and no more than a minute later someone walked up and handed her something wrapped in plastic. I couldn't see who it was, the other person wore a hood, but I saw Grey London take something, quickly wapping it in her jacket and handing the man in the hood some money. He pushed it away and shook his head. Was Grey London using drugs? I tip toed forwards.

Or was that a syringe?

I had to know.

"Friday?" said Jake pulling me back by the hand, "where are you going?"

"I think one of the heroes is on drugs, look," I pulled Jake round the corner, but Grey London had gone. Which one was her dressing room?

"What? What are you talking about? You've been watching too many dramas," he said yanking me back into the hall.

"Jake slow down, I can't move that fast in these shoes," I told him. He was moving along far too quickly, but he didn't listen so I tried to pull back and stop him and lost my balance. Two hands caught me from behind, strong and precise, unmistakably Ashley's.

I was set back on my feet. He stepped round, and held out his arm to help me up the stairs. Ashley was another of the few men wearing a suit. After seeing him at Ang's, the contrast was stark, and it *definitely* worked for him. For the first time, I felt a little nervous around Ashley Ang. Maybe it was my dress, or his suit, but being around him sent butterflies through me. For the first time, I thought he was handsome, still strange looking, but just for a moment, I thought he looked striking.

Jake took my other arm, a little too forcefully, and Ashley rolled his eyes. I pushed away from both of them, and walked up the stairs myself. Aya held the door to the booth open, and closed it behind us. I could find proof later.

"Ashley! You changed your mind?" Aya asked.

"My Nana didn't want me to miss out."

The booth was littered with snacks and flat screen TV's that showed the field and the commentators, but I didn't care. I hadn't imagined it, I'd seen a member of the team taking something from someone. Maybe I was paranoid and all they were exchanging was a newly sized ring, and the person had simply been too kind to accept money?

Yeah, that was it. Jake sat me down next to Aya, and left to get popcorn. The game stopped and started three times until half time was called and Jean-Claude Nakata came running onto the field. A few of the other kids got up and walked out to talk to the athletes during half time, or get something else to eat and drink.

"Friday, I was gonna go backstage and see if I could get an autograph for my sister, want to come?" Aya asked and I nodded, maybe I could sneak a glance at

Grey London's bag, or whatever she'd had wrapped in plastic.

Aya knocked on a door in a sea of people exchanging logo printed cups and towels, looking at trading cards, and meeting their heroes. The door swung open to a large broad shouldered man in the middle eating some cookies out of care package he'd received from a fan. "Hi, I'm Aya Asimov a-"

"Oh my God! I know who you are!" The large man took her hand and shook it vigorously, his hand making hers look dainty. He beamed at her.

"Oh, well thank you," said Aya with a smile. "I was wondering if you could sign this for my sister?"

"Of course!" Clearly surprised at how well things had gone, she handed him a kids jersey, and he set it against the wall to sign it.

I saw Grey London move though the crowd and into her own dressing room. Instinct told me to follow her and forget about Aya. Over the crowd of excited fans no one could hear me as I pushed open the door to her dressing room ever so slightly, and peered in just as she pushed something against her arm, and sighed with relief. She was in the bathroom in seconds, breaking out in a cold sweat, so I moved in to get a better look.

My gaze found the syringe, it was gold just like the one I'd found in the alley way. Something told me it wasn't legal in Super League. My hand reached for it. Finally proof.

The bathroom door moved. crap!

I dated for closet. The door slammed at the same time the lock on the bathroom clicked. I look deep breath. Her footsteps sounded behind the closet doors, and breathed a sigh of relief. My eyes adjusted to the light. Soothing was wrong with my foot…

My shoe, my shoe had fallen off! The footsteps stopped. I covered my mouth, and waited. She might not see it, maybe she would think it was hers?

Could I announce she was cheating? Could I chase her down? I couldn't take this. With my hand still over my mouth, I peered through the key hole. I spied on her putting the gold syringe away.

Silence again. Ws she looking at my lost shoe?,

The turn of a knob. And then the door closing. I spired thought he keyhole again, just to make sure she hadn't caught on. I saw no sign of her.

I rushed out of the closet. The room was clear.

I ran over to her bag, and opened it. I didn't have much time. I felt something long and smooth. I pulled at it. A golden syringe. The same as the one I'd found before.

What did it mean? Did she have more? It wasn't normal, I would have known. I fumbled around for somewhere to stash it. I wrapped the syringe in a napkin on her table. Found my shoe in the corner, and got out fo there.

I returned to the booth, offering smiles to everyone, starting to wonder; just how far did all this go?

———

SLEDGEHAMMER

THE BLUE DORM HAD been homey, with its warm, exposed brick and small cosy bedrooms, but the gold dorm was extravagant. The sofa was low, comfortable, expensive. At first I couldn't even find the TV until I saw it come down from the ceiling. The table wasn't round, it wasn't part of the kitchen; instead they had a dining room, with a long wooden table to match.

My new bedroom was a square, my bed a large double, draped in gossamer. At home my bedroom had a single bed that sat on a box platform, a computer next to the window, and a desk where I could sketch. But this was the kind of room where you'd wake up at night and wonder where the serial killer was hiding. In the walk in closet? In the other walk in closet? The powder room?

I had an hour to wake up and get to Lisa for our appearance on Super Variety Hour. Apparently it was a mentor, mentee special. The prize of super variety hour was a dinner with your hero of choice. And I wanted Grey London, I wanted answers.

The sky was a little pink, and rain from the night before still lived in the wind. I covered myself in a blanket as I stumbled out to the smell of bacon. Ashley shoved a half eaten bar of chocolate into my hands as he cooked, and grunted some advice about remembering to eat. "Aya?" I yawned. She spun around from the living room sofa, ears open.

"You're up! Ready for the special? I can't wait, it's my third time!" she said, her legs waving in the air.

"Yeah, actually, since you've done this before, can you help me? I have a closet with stuff I'm supposed to wear, and-"

"I'm there!" Aya cut me off, and jogged into my room, and threw open my closet. It was filled with the outfits picked out for me by the team's stylist. I yawned in the doorway as she sifted through the clothes, pulled back, and rubbed her chin. "They haven't given you a lot that's loose." She pulled out the paper I'd received on the first day, and skimmed it. "Oh, I see, it's tailored to your body type. Okay, so…" She read through it instantly, nodding as though taking notes. Once that was done she started pulling out some different things, but eventually returned to the clothes labelled seven and shoved one of those thousand dollar trench coats into my arms. It's collar was like a mountain of fabric, and the sleeves were etched in leather. It was the sort of jacket that had it's own presence and made you feel important just to wear it. "The jackets best for you, it'll make you feel more covered." She nodded at it all, and left to let me change. The front of my phone danced with light; I flipped it open as I bit into a bar of chocolate, and sent a text to Jake to wake him up.

I picked up my backpack, and stumbled out the door with a simple goodbye to Aya, David and Ashley, and flipped open my phone again as I waited for the elevator. I dialed Jake as fast as I could. It took him a few rings, but he answered, voice groggy.

"What, what is it?"

"I'm doing Super Variety Hour with Lisa today, you need to be ready."

"Oh, yeah. Whatever."

"Whatever? What does that me-"

He hung up before I could finish; he'd never been so rude to me before. I got in the elevator and got off at the bottom floor before plodding out across the early morning plaza bathed in the grey pinks of the rain sputtering sky. Even early in the morning there were people eating by the fountain, they didn't think they needed umbrellas, but judging by the big solid grey cloud coming our way, they were going to get wet soon.

The two buildings didn't have much distance between them, there was just enough space for a small park with a couple of benches, and a tall, dramatic fountain.

As I walked into the part of the building reserved for *real* heroes I was struck by the lighting; dim, but somehow expensive, like the lobby of an hotel. The elevators were a bit different, all glass rather than gold. This wasn't a place for the cameras, the building for *real* heroes was much more business casual. If the two buildings had been people, my building would have been a flamboyant, lovable drag queen, while the other was a sexy but conservatively dressed business woman. One wasn't better than the other; they were simply too different to compare.

I hit the button for the offices that sat at the same level as the Hero High garden no one ever went to. Even then I had no idea what the gardens really looked like. I stood in the elevator all by myself. Clearly not many superheroes came to work on Saturdays. The office floor was a lot more crisp and white, like the

offices of a fashion magazine, they even had a recep-
tionist to match. I leaned over her white desk and she
covered the receiver on her ear piece.

"Can I help you?" She hurried in a hushed tone.

"I'm looking for Lisa Kisaragi." I replied. The
woman shook her head at me as though I'd spoken
gibberish. "I mean, Sense."

"Take a right, then a left, you'll find her in the door
at the end." She nodded to me, and brought the phone
to her ear again.

"Thank you." I whispered.

She waved me away down the hall without even so
much as looking. Slowly and carefully, I read the name
on each door, all names of superheroes, their handlers,
support heroes. Some had customized their doors with
different fonts, gold etchings, bright colors, but one was
just a sheet of gold, like, it looked like *real* gold. The
knob was gold, the door was gold, the name plate was
gold, the name etched into the plate, also gold.

The plate said Disco, a hero known for the full face
mask he never took off, and the rumor that disco played
constantly in his helmet. I never believed that rumor
until then, but I could have sworn I heard the pounding
sound of a disco track playing inside. My best guess
was The Bee Gees. I was tempted to turn the handle,
but decided against it.

When eventually I came to the door at the end of the hall, I noticed it read 'Barney' while underneath, in smaller letters, it said Sense.

I sighed and swung the door open.

"Are you serious?" Lisa demanded, glaring directly towards her partner.

"Well you can just forget about the picture then!" said Barney cracking a wolflike smile, as he slid a head shot of himself down what looked like Lisa's desk. "It's okay to admit you're a fan."

"I am not one of your fans!"

"Then what about the interview? 'I'd like my son to grow to be like him someday' That's what you said, right?"

"They told me to say that!" Lisa told him, "you're not old enough to-"

"I'm barely younger than you," said Barney, interrupting, "I mean we're closer to being a couple than-"

Lisa slammed her hand down on the desk, and stood up, not *quite* meeting his height. "It's for my daughter, she's the fan! Please sign the damn thing."

Silence hung for a moment as Barney looked the picture up and down. "Really? I'd think you wouldn't bother, we've been arguing about this for ten minutes."

"I told my kid I'd get her a signed picture, so that's

what I'm going to do! Now are you going to sign it or not?" Lisa growled as Barney flashed her a closed mouth smile that would have made anyone else's heart skip a beat.

"Stop shouting and I'll think about it," he said, as Lisa bared her teeth. "Alright, alright. I was just kidding. I'll sign it." He leaned over, picked up a pen and Lisa relaxed.

"Lisa?" I called, deciding now was the best time to announce myself.

"Kid. I was wondering when you'd get here. How much of that did you hear?"

"I think I walked in on, 'are you serious'." I threw up my hands to enhance my impression.

"Oh jeez." Lisa reached up to rub her face as though she'd made a grave mistake. Barney finished his autograph off with a flourish, and handed it to Lisa before turning to me.

"Nothing to worry about, Momma Bear's just trying to do her job."

"Shut up, Baxter," Lisa said, snatching the picture and stuffing it into her weathered handbag. It really looked like she needed a new one. One she could rely on, but Lisa wasn't the type to spend money on things like that. As Barney sat back down at the desk that stood directly opposite Lisa's, I noticed she had on a white suit. She moved towards me, and pulled me into a hug.

"You okay kiddo?"

"Sure, but what are you wearing?"

"What do you think? They're giving me a super skeleton like Baxter over there, and this is what goes under it."

It was a skin tight white suit, with impeccably tailored red panels as opposed to Barney's green. It was nice, it fitted her beautifully without seeming to cling like a wet suit, well fitted with reinforced shoulders, elbows and knees. Her shoes though were her usual firetruck red sneakers. She faced the mirrors and fiddled with the collar.

"I like it," I told her, "it's very nice."

"I just got it back from the seamstress, she said I could wear it out today."

"So you're using a super skeleton today?" I asked.

"Not today, we've got a game show to do. Although I have been getting training from Baxter for a few weeks now."

"My name is Barney."

Lisa shrugged him off and smiled at her reflection in the mirror. At least he was raising her profile. She'd have her very own Super Skeleton now, she'd be on even footing with superheroes laden with gadgets, able to lift things too heavy for most, run faster, and be safer.

I opened my mouth to try and say something to him, but stopped as I turned round, trying to figure out what Barney was looking at. For a moment I was confused, what *was* he looking at so low down, maybe something on Lisa's desk, a hole in the wall? Did he really not have anything better to do than stare into space? Then I realized he was eyeballing Lisa's ass.

I had to slap a hand over my mouth to hold back the giggles, but I was laughing on the inside. Barney sat there for a good five minutes appraising Lisa and her new, well tailored suit.

"Are we ready to go?" I asked, "we're supposed to be on set in ten minutes."

"Really? I'm sorry kid. Let's boogie." Lisa straightened her collar once more, nodded to her reflection, and led me out without so much as a word to Barney.

The halls of the Real Heroes building were busy with interns and ringing phones. Lisa held onto my shoulder as we walked. We shoved ourselves into an elevator. We rushed out of the sweaty stressed crowd the moment the doors opened. Lisa pulling on my shirt to speed me up. We wandered onto the set. This floor of the building had no walls to speak of, it was just a huge open space, but in the middle of that space was a well lit yellow background with five desks and buzzers.

I'd seen this room so many times on the Hero Channel, I'd never thought of it as a set, but of course it was. Carey Fry sat in one of those tall chairs you see on movie sets. He was skimming the cue cards he always carried, rolling his eyes as Veronica wagged her finger at him.

A man with a headset grabbed us, and plonked us down in the chairs next to Carey. He didn't seem to notice, he was too focused on his lines. A woman came round and looked me up and down, just the same as on my first day.

The makeup artist pushed through a large makeup back, product rustling against each other. I closed my eyes, and let them work. It was right after they sprayed something on my face, that I was pushed out of the chair.

As I got up, Lisa was still being done over. She looked like she was made of plastic. But something told me it wouldn't look out of place on camera. If I'd learned anything since coming to Hero High, it was that Make up was very different for TV. Lisa blew a stray strand of hair out of her face, and looked as me as though she knew exactly what I was thinking. This was weird.

Together we were ushered onto set, and placed behind the blue desk. Our names sat on plaques in front of us and beside us were Aya and her mentor, Black Magic. Aya waved, I waved back and she tried to hold back her squeal of delight. The players rotated week to week, and finally it was my turn. On the other side was the boy I'd met on the first day who'd brought far too many clothes, and his mentor, Disco. Despite being someone's mentor, Disco still insisted on wearing a helmet wherever he went. I wondered if even his mentee knew what he looked like.

"Disco's a weird one, but he's a nice guy." Lisa told me.

"Huh?"

She leaned over and started whispering. "They say what power you get depends on what you're thinking when you have your near death experience, it's just a myth."

"And what, he was thinking about Disco?" I asked.

"I guess. I've only seen his power in action once or twice. His skin glows, and every hole he has pumps out music, it's great for stunning an enemy, and good fun at a party."

Carey stepped on set, still scanning his cards, and took his place behind the orange podium. The heavy, wheeled cameras started to move and my mind kicked into action. This was really happening. My hands clenched the fabric of my jacket under the table, and my teeth ground into each other. I wasn't ready for this! There would be millions behind that camera! Possibly billions! Sure I'd been on TV before, but that was while doing a job, while I was learning. This time I had to be entertaining! I couldn't just try to be a superhero, I had to be a celebrity! Could I leave, could I try to be ignored? I placed my hand over my heart, and took a deep breath. It would be fine, there wasn't even an audience, it'd just be like Carey and me playing a board game, right? Wrong. There wasn't an audience, but there was still a crowd, and the crowd was waiting to see which one of us would fall flat on our faces so they could decide who would make a good superhero.

"Kid, relax," said Lisa and her smile calmed me down. There was no getting out of this.

A man with a headset walked up and stood next to the cameras, Carey had to finally put down his cards, the man held up his hand and counted down from five. The red light on the cameras went on and Carey burst into life.

"Welcome, welcome, welcome! It's seven o'clock on Saturday morning, which means you're at home ready to start the day, and it's time for another episode of Super Variety Hour!"

A small jingle played through the set, and the crowd of assistants, technicians, and producers whooped and hollered. I wasn't sure if it was for show, or if they were genuinely happy until I noticed several had pulled up seats and handed out snacks to the others. Super Variety Hour wasn't a reality show, so the producers didn't have to step in every five seconds to well, produce. So maybe this was like a vacation for them?

"This week we finally get to meet the last of our new class! So let's meet the teams!" The secondary camera's light turned red, and focused on the boy from my first day. A technician held up a card with the word, 'wave' on it. "Our first team is Peter from Ohio, he likes Fashion, music, and his power is called Fungal Reproduction. His mentor is Disco, the faceless, name-less, hero of style! Remember folks, Disco never dies."

Peter winked at the camera, and Disco did nothing, Disco never did. He just stood there, like a terminator. The crowd of technicians clapped. The next camera lit up, and cut to Aya.

"Our second, and returning team is Aya Asimov, she likes her fans, cartoons, and cute things, her power is called Temporary Object Transportation and with her is her mentor, Black Magic."

Aya blew a kiss to the camera, and Black Magic nodded in a military fashion. The crowd clapped again.

My stomach flipped as the light on the camera facing me went on.

"And last but not least, Friday Fitzsimmons, also known as Fitz. Her power's called, Hyper Synaptic Activity. And with her, the Legacy Hero, Sense!" Lisa smiled, but didn't wave, and I did nothing, still frozen in place. The crowd of technicians clapped once more as the roll call finished.

"And I'm Carey Fry, let's have some fun!" Carey pointed to the screen that sat between us, and it sparked into life. "Now, you all know how this game works. I ask a few questions, whoever gets the most right gets a head start on the other teams in our main event, the scavenger hunt." Super Variety Hour always went the same way, the teams answered a few questions and then sent half the teams out into the city to run a scavenger hunt.

"Tonight's prize is a one on one dinner with a member of your choice from the recently crowned championship Power League team." Tense and twinkling music sounded throughout the set as the lights were lowered. The number *one*, flashed up, and then flipped to a question. Carey smiled, and picked up a card, reading it out loud. There was a tablet in front of me along with a pen to write with, I took it, and readied my hand.

"Who was immortalized in marble in the Rosemary City park?" Carey asked. I didn't have to think about that. The answer was Captain Fantastic, I scribbled it down, Lisa gave me a quick thumbs up. "Number two, what was the first Hero Channel toy to go on sale?" Lisa took the pen from me, and wrote something down quickly. "Number three, when was the Bo Bridge built?" The Bo Bridge had been built by Stronghold. He'd built it back when Icon city was still being constructed, and carved a hard edged woman into the side of it. The Bo Bridge was the largest bridge in the city, so I scribbled that down too. Lisa took the pen, and wrote beneath my answer, 'and to honor a young girl called Bo.'

"Is that who's in the carvings?" I asked. She nodded in response.

"Question four, and we're getting near the end now folks. What does the gold statue on the banks of the river depict?" I knew this one well, the city had unveiled it all across the world. It was the second largest statue in the city, it stood as high as Cleopatra's needle. It was a statue of Captain Fantastic and Dr. Dangerous. I remembered there'd been an outcry when the statue was erected, it didn't show the Dr. being killed, beaten, or defeated in any way. The statue was an honest representation of the long struggle between the two. So that's what I wrote, not that it depicted a fight, because it didn't, it depicted a painfully long rivalry, and sat as a tribute to its end.

"Final question, solve this equation!" Carey shouted. Everyone's head shot up to the screen and on the inside, I fist pumped. Carey looked ready to laugh and so did the crew as they exchanged high fives. This happened on the show every now and again, they loved to throw out word puzzles or math to the contestants to throw them off. Frankly I'd been counting on it. Most of my superhero knowledge was thanks to this show, and an equation was perfect. I did algebra for fun. The only problem was, the equation didn't make sense as I looked at it. It took me a moment to decide the equation was badly formatted rather than just hard. A bell rang, and Carey straightened his cards with a big grin.

"Let's look at the teams answers." Carey cycled through each question, and each screen in front of a desk lit up with a big red cross, or a big green tick. Lisa and I received green ticks for every one, the same as all the others, save for the very last. "Now, could everyone figure this one out?"

Aya and Peter looked shaky, but I was confident. Aya said the answer was 2, she received a red cross and loud buzz to reinforce the point that she was wrong. Peter said nine, and received the same. Carey turned to

Lisa and I, and repeated the question. "Do you girls know the answer?"

I sucked in a breath to clear my nerves, and answered as confidently as I could. "Okay, first of all this is not a proper equation, once you're out of middle school you don't write multiplied like that because it makes the structure of the equation un-clear. Second of all, this was clearly written by someone who is not a mathematician, third of all, the answer is ten." The crew cheered again, slapping each other on their back, happy I'd pulled their equation apart, as the screen on the front of my desk pinged green.

"And there you have it. Let's look at the scores. Aya and Black magic are tied with Peter and Disco for second place, with Sense and Friday in the lead!" I was one step closer to winning that dinner.

"You know what that means, they have the five minute head start in the scavenger hunt, so stay tuned, and we'll be right back."

The lights fell, and the light on the camera turned off. Another man stepped up to Lisa and I with a clip board in hand. "Ms. Fitzsimmons, are you ready for the scavenger hunt?"

I nodded and followed him off set, they placed in an elevator with Peter and Aya. I slammed my back against the wall of the elevator as we sped down. The doors opened onto wet streets and rain, I'd been right about the storm. Veronica didn't shove the usual colored armor into our arms, instead she handed us pins and checked our outfits up and down. She nodded to Aya, but criticized her shoes and advised her to wear more "womanly" clothing. She then straightened Peter's tie and told him to wear a size down and avoid the color yellow. She then stopped in front of me, pulled at the jacket to make sure I hadn't stained it. "I'd like to see some shorter skirts in the future, Fitz." I was about to open my mouth and say something I'd regret when the camera blinked into life and I heard Lisa's voice joined by Jake's in my ear. Carey sat on a table as he read out instructions.

"You kids have got three check points, whoever gets all three first, wins." The image of him cut out, and Veronica produced an umbrella for herself as we were forced out of cover and into the pounding rain. Lisa and Jake's voice's came in through my ear piece as they repeated what Carey told them. "Okay, everyone, here's the first clue."

"In a historic corner, people consume a heroic food."

Veronica held up a tiny flag, and yelled ready. I

braced myself forwards. She brought down the flag and I ran forwards with my five minute head start. We had to find where the riddle was pointing us.

"Theories guys?" I asked Lisa and Jake. I ran down the streets, hoping something would spark my memory, but to be honest I was too distracted by the man carrying the camera following me. Glasses hung out of his front pocket, bobbing as he ran, he was the same cameraman I tried to speak to the day I'd ended up on that skyscraper. "You're Kevin?" I asked, noting the name tag on his rain coat. He nodded and stepped backwards to get me from the right angle. I tried not to run in case he tripped or hurt himself, which probably made my head start pointless.

"Historic corner?" mused Lisa.

"Heroic Food?" chimed Jake.

I could hear Lisa snap her fingers over the coms. "Heroic food, I think it means food named after heroes, Barney recently had a sandwich named after him. I don't have a sandwich named after me..." she grumbled.

I stopped on the sidewalk to catch my breath. "So you're thinking the place that named a sandwich after Barney?"

In an instant I heard Jake's nimble fingers working over the keyboard. "There's a place downtown, a few blocks from here called Allie's, apparently it's been around since the city was first built, and it names its dishes after heroes and villains. According to this, it's a big tourist attraction." said Jake.

"That's the name! Good work." I started running again as Jake directed me down the right streets, I skidded to a halt as the small restaurant came into view. Just as I saw it, Aya came down the other side of the street, and we dashed inside. She pushed in first, and I was a close second. The man behind the deli counter handed both of us a card, and our respective cameramen zoomed in. It was another riddle.

"Where will he go, what will he be?"

Aya and I both stared at it blankly. I heard Lisa inhale across the ear piece. "I know those words, I've heard them before." I ran out of the deli and down the street, leaving Aya behind. Kevin now seemed content to run behind me which seemed safer for him, and faster for me. I'd heard those words before as well, but I couldn't think, not in this cold. The rain was starting to get to me, it nearly made my fingers numb. I looked up, my face was briefly on the jumbo screen that hung high on a department store skyscraper, and then Peter's took its place as he arrived at the Deli. The whole city was watching us run around from place to place, *live*, as their morning entertainment. It was bizarre.

"Guys I can't think in this cold."

I heard Jake's finger slide across the keys of his computer again, and firmly hit enter. "*Where will he go, what will he be,* is a quote from Dr. Dangerous."

Dr. Dangerous? Was it the statue of him and The Captain, was that it? I heard Lisa's hand slam down on the desk as she chimed in. "Those were his last words before he died, "where will he go, what will he be? It has to be the statue of him and The Captain, it was built after he died!" said Lisa.

I looked up to see my face on the jumbo screen again, either I was the first to figure it out, or my idea was hilariously wrong. I ran along the streets, and through a city park until I came across the statue of The Captain and Dr. Dangerous that stood tall and in gold on the banks of the river. On one side was Dr. Dangerous standing tall, on the other side, with his back against his opponent, was a younger Captain Fantastic. The Captain wasn't posing, he just stood there in his double breasted uniform and knee high boots, strong and proud. It was a simple statue standing as tribute to those two men. It wasn't crude in how it chose to remember a well known villain, and I think that had been how The Captain wanted it.

A flash of something black flickered and blinked away in an instant under the statue, but I couldn't be sure of what I'd seen for all the rain. My cameraman almost fell over in surprise.

Then it happened again.

The figure blinked back, and stopped; silhouetted against the bright lights and the storm. It was Dr. Dangerous again, or whoever was pretending to be him.

"Lisa! It's Dr. Dangerous! It's the man from the bombing!"

"What!? Where are you? Kid, get out of there!"

I hadn't told anyone about my encounters with the Dr, so of course no one would know. Why was he here? Had he come to convince me again? Or was he trying to stop me from winning? I heard scrambling from the other side of the coms, and Jake readjusting his position. I grabbed Kevin by the shoulders and forced his eye away from the viewfinder. "Run!"

He took a few steps back, but hesitated. "Please! I'll be fine!"

Conflict written all over his face, Kevin paused and then ran with everyone else, evacuating the park. In this city people know what to do when a figure clad all in back appears out of nowhere; run like hell. Super-villains were like the city's own Godzilla, an everyday nuisance. I think I even saw one woman trying to finish her donut as she goosed it.

"'Day don't engage!" Jake yelled into my ear.

"I have to!" I needed this, I could ask him questions, I could figure something out, he was coming to me.

The Dr. walked towards me, slowly but surely decreasing the distance between us.

I clutched at my shirt, my heart was pounding in my ears like a sledgehammer.

A panic attack. Again.

He was after *me*, not the civilians.

I was going to stay *right* here.

I straightened my back, and looked him in the eye.

The Bay Side Park was beautiful, even in pouring rain. The tulips swayed in a wind that pushed my hair across my face in thin strands, while icy raindrops shook my body bringing my skin out in goose bumps, or was that Dr. Dangerous himself?

"What are you doing here!? Is there another bomb?" I yelled, but received no reply. I stood there, watching the drops of rain follow the silhouette of his suit before they fell to the ground. Just like the first time, he didn't seem to care. "What do you want?" I asked again.

Water streamed down his face as he took one last

step towards me. "You." He said as he wrapped an arm around me and pulled me as close as he could.

"'Day what's happening?" Jake demanded.

A loud clap echoed through the air, but it wasn't thunder, it was The Captain! Dr. Dangerous grunted. I hit him as hard as I could, but from so close it was pointless.

"Let me go!" I yelled. He yanked me even harder against him as he pulled out the same device he had the day of the bomb. I struggled in his grip, but my only power wasn't going to help in a show of strength. He was too big, too strong, and I was far too small.

I fell limp in his arms once again, as he pressed the same cold metal device to my neck. Just as I heard a crash on the ground, and The Captain's voice, Dr. Dangerous hoisted me into his arms, carrying me like he had before.

What?

Where was I?

My chest was warm, panic gone.

It felt like, like, waking up from a really good nights sleep. Warm, and lazy.

The rain was gone. So was The Captain. All I heard was a low hum of power. All I saw was the blue glow of the Dr's eyes, in almost *utter* darkness.

My eyes got no chance to acclimatize.

A bright light winked on. I winced as I looked around. Somehow I was somewhere else, in a greenhouse of sorts. He'd taken me away from The Captain in the blink of an eye. I tried to move, but realized I didn't know where to go.

Dr. Dangerous stood in the shadows right in front of me. I took steady and slow breaths, just like Ashley had told me. My chest no longer hurt, the anxiety was less, even though his eyes bore into me. My back was against a marble fountain, the blasts of lightning only looked like flashing light bulbs behind the frosted glass.

"It's nice to get this time, for just the two of us alone."

I tried to leap forwards and rip the smile from his face, but he simply grabbed me, and pulled me against him.

"Don't be like that," he said, his words were teasing and carefree.

"Who are you?" I asked, "you're not Dr. Dangerous," I told him pushing against his chest like before.

"I am Dr. Dangerous, new and improved. And so are you, Captain."

For once, I had no clue what he meant, "What are you talking about?"

He leaned towards me, cutting off the cold wind

that rustled through the flora. "I'm the Dr, you're The Captain. 2.0."

"I'm nothing like The Captain. I'm just, *me*. And besides, The Captain already has a mentee."

"That doesn't matter, Friday." I pushed against him again and he gave me a little more room, but not enough to get away. The trees above us waved their leaves, and the thunder boomed from far away. Only the occasional lightning strike lit up the room, and showed me the edges of his face.

"What do you know about a gold syringe," I asked. His lips tightened, but he said nothing. He knew *of* them, but perhaps not *about* them. "You know what I'm talking about."

"I'm afraid I don't," he said.

"So you're in on it then? Whatever this is."

He suppressed a growl, like he really didn't want me to continue.

"If I found that syringe near the burning building, chances are it was The Figure's. So then I find a regular super hero using one. Okay fine, that's one thing, but you know about them?"

He shook his head. "Stop, Friday."

"No. You were watching The Figure. You know him. Was it The Figure you were waiting for in the hotel?"

"Friday," he said in warning.

"Tell me what's going on!" I yelled.

"Why do you insist on being a superhero?" He gritted.

I took a breath, trying to decide if I should speak, and eventually let my voice out in a gentle whisper. "Because I want to be good."

"Who says you can't be good if you help me?" he cooed.

"What? What do you mean?"

"Join me, my boss, and my colleagues. One way or another we're taking over the city, the only decision you have to make is what side you're on."

"So you do know what I'm talking about," I said.

"What side are you on?" he asked again.

"Not yours," I told him.

"Why not? I could say you'd make a better villain, but you wouldn't. Not really."

"No," I said, and it was true, if he'd known the truth. He looked at me startled, perhaps he hadn't expected my answer. The lines around his mouth softened.

"What you've got," he whispered, "is self loathing, but I don't know why."

"Because I could be a better person. I *will* be a better person." I said.

"Would you die for someone?" He asked, the most serious I'd ever heard him.

"Yes," I answered without thinking, like it was a knee jerk reaction.

"If I gave you a choice between your life, and someone else's, what would you do?" he asked.

"I'd sacrifice myself, obviously." I felt it was true, I wanted it to be true.

He laughed gently, as though I'd told him a cheesy joke, then he pulled me closer with one arm and used the other to run a finger through my hair. The frosted glass wall grew colder in the chill of the storm and my body curled into him instinctively.

I *hoped* I would sacrifice myself, it was my job. Sure my sister, father, all his employees wouldn't have the same kind of money if I died, but sacrificing myself was what I'd signed up for.

"Friday, you're not making any sense. You're a superhero, think of all the other people you could save if you were still alive. You might as well be killing hundreds just to save one."

"That's the stupidest thing I've ever heard," I told him. "I'm not the *only* superhero. If I die someone else takes my place. Those lives will still be saved."

I said it like I could win. His eyes scanned me up and down and settled on my face while I tried to ignore the temptation to hold him, settle there, stop fighting.

"You really would give up your life for someone else?" he spoke softly, searching my eyes for the echo of a lie.

"Of course I would. I want to help," my voice was pleading, hoping, that *maybe* he'd agree. My bones were shaking from the cold as I tried to ignore the shivers of warmth his body sent through me. "I want to be useful, and if that means giving up my life, I'll do it."

A whisper of a wistful smile grew on his face. "You really mean that don't you?" he asked trailing his finger across the back of my neck.

"Of course I do." My voice came out in a whisper, my chest was heaving.

He leaned closer and the warmth of his hands sent a chill right through me. I must have looked like a deer in the headlights, I had no idea what to do. "I mean, I just, I want-" I cleared my throat to keep speaking, but he drew closer as I spoke. Everything in me pounded with his proximity. "I want to be good."

The edge of his lips twitched upwards as I spoke and right then and there, like I was his next breath, he kissed me. The thunder roared as my chest rose in surprise. I'd only ever kissed Jake, and that had been a peck when we were kids. This was completely different. His fingers were warm and gentle on the back of my neck, but his breath was hot and avid. I tried to stay still, but couldn't help myself; my head tilted back, I wanted to touch his hair, feel the heat of his skin beneath my fingers.

As the thought crossed my mind I felt stupid, but when he tipped my chin and tasted more of me, my mind went blank and I kissed him back. His lips teased me into a sigh and he smiled into it, as though he'd won something from me. I snapped right back and as his lower lip slipped between mine, I bit it, hard. He flinched, grinding his teeth as he released me, then his lips pulled up into that dangerous smile again as the shock of the bite wore off.

"Your lips are all swollen," he told me, as though it was proof I'd really done what I'd done. I was too embarrassed, too ashamed, so I let *him* have the last word. "You can still join me, Friday."

"Never gonna happen." I spun him round, shoved him into the fountain and ran for what I thought was the door. I was in the middle of a courtyard, there were maps on posts describing the garden.

"Friday!"

I kept running, nearly colliding with the nearest map as I looked for an exit. The top right-hand corner said, 'Hero High'. I was in the Super Structure, these were the gardens. He caught my look as the realization hit me. One moment he was there, the next he was gone. I saw short flashes of him walking out the door, like he was in a room with a single light, flickering on and off, and then nothing.

I kept running along the paths, and into the halls of Hero High. I rushed outside into the storm and found The Captain's bus pulling up to the school. I didn't wait for permission, I just dashed through the door and found The Captain resting, his head on his wife's lap. The last time I'd seen her was their televised wedding.They hadn't noticed me, they were wrapped up in each other. Adam's eyes were closed, as if focusing on his wife's touch. His wife, Katherine, wasn't what I'd remembered, her suit was impeccably tailored but her hair was a mess, like she'd run all the way.

"I don't know what to do, Kate," said The Captain, his voice breaking.

She hummed above him as his eyes knit tight, fighting tears and I backed out quietly, resting my head on the pole outside.

———

"The Captain was crying?" I ask, inching forward.

"I stood outside the bus, trying to figure out why, and realized it was the Dr," Friday tells me as she nods and leans back.

I cover my mouth, as if holding back a breath.

"The Dr's ghost, or his son, whatever you wanted to call the new Dr. Dangerous, it was killing The Captain." Friday takes a deep breath, and then another long sip. "I'd never seen him so, human."

———

I shook my head, and took a step back. "Captain!" I yelled before running in, like I should have.

The Captain was already moving forwards when I stepped in. "Friday!" Captain Fantastic, every inch the hero, wrapped me in a hug. It was the first time I'd seen him in uniform.

Had he been meaning to come for me?

Had *everyone* been looking for me? "Are you all right, Friday?" he asked. His eyes were sick with worry as he kneeled to grip my face in calloused hands.

"I'm fine, Adam," I replied, brushing it off and hoping he'd no idea what I'd just done. His name just slipped out. I'd run to him, because now I had questions, serious ones.

Katherine, put a hand on his shoulder as she tip toed up to kiss her husband, she wasn't too tall herself. She stepped outside as a sports car pulled up, and the man driving it opened the door for her. "Don't be late for dinner, Adam." She warned as she closed the door.

"I won't." The Captain waved his wife goodbye, and then directed me to climb to the upper deck where it was just the two of us.

"What aren't you telling me?" I asked.

"What?" He looked at me in feigned surprise, so I asked him again.

"What aren't you telling me, Adam?"

"I don't know what you're talking about."

"That's not Dr. Dangerous and you know it. Dr. Dangerous is dead. If I'm ever going to be a hero you need to trust me. Tell me!" He hung his head and I regretted the words just as soon as they came out of my mouth. "Or maybe, am I over stepping my bounds?"

He shook his head, and sat up properly, "No, you're not over stepping your bounds."

"Then tell me." I said.

He patted the seat next to him, and I sat down refusing to take my eyes off his. "Do you know why I started the hero program?"

"No." I told him.

"Because, in the eighties, I knew a super villain

called Dr. Dangerous. I was only a kid at the time." He sighed.

"What happened?" I sat forward.

"He went too far, or *I* thought he did, and people, the public I mean, they called for an end to him. People spent months convincing me to *Kill* him."

———

"What happened?" I ask.

"Between Captain Fantastic and The Dr.?"

I nod.

"The Captain hadn't decided to kill him, he just knew he had to do something. The Dr. and The Captain met each other at the river bank and the Dr. ripped into him, so…" her body shakes as she sucks in a breath.

"Why?" I ask. "What did Captain Fantastic do that made The Dr. hate him so much?" Friday nods slowly at the floor, and then looks up, determined to say what she has to. "He let the Dr.'s parents die. The Captain had a choice, his parents, or the Dr.'s. Back in those days, the Dr. And The Captain were close, the Dr. was The Captain's tech guy, he made all his gadgets."

She takes another quick breath and I use the opportunity to ask a question. "Why did he have to choose?"

"An old super villain, from the war, he'd infiltrated
Icon City, trying to ruin The International Heroes
Group's credibility. The Captain and the Dr, they were
both very young, the villain engineered a situation
where Captain Fantastic had to choose who to save. He
chose his own parents and the Dr's parents died."

"And that was what made The Dr.?"
She nods. "The Dr's first real act of villainy was the
highway collapse of '84."

"He didn't mean for there to be a school bus?" I
finished for her.

"No. The road was new, it hadn't been opened. All he
wanted was to lure The Captain out. The school bus
was never meant to be there. That was what made the
Dr. a villain."

"But still, The Captain killed him?"
"The Dr. wouldn't stop fighting, saying one of them
needed to die. In the end they were both injured but
Captain Fantastic received better care. The Dr. died of
his injuries, in hospital, a few days later."

———

"And?" I asked, sitting forwards.

"I did. I killed, I, I killed him, and I've never regretted anything more in my entire life." his voice broke as he sped through the sentence, as though saying it faster would make it hurt less.

"So, why The Hero Channel?" I whispered.

"I wanted to raise you kids right, I wanted to put you somewhere where you were safe, surrounded by other people like you. I didn't want people treating you like gods, or trying to make you believe everything was up to you to fix. Remember that."

"I will." I nodded.

"I didn't want you to be strangers to the cameras or the fans, or the media, I wanted you to be so used to it, it wouldn't affect you or your decisions."

"You're trying to acclimatize us so we can adjust before we become superheroes?" I asked.

"Exactly." He smiled.

"You still haven't answered my question." I frowned.

Adam sighed, and swallowed. He looked me right in the eyes, and pushed through the pain of what he'd done. "Before I killed him, he said, "Where will he go, what will he be?" He was talking about his son. I considered adopting him, but, I didn't know how to find him."

"So, you think-"

"I don't think, I *know*. *This* Dr. Dangerous, is his son."

———

FLESH WITHOUT BLOOD

"**I**'M AFRAID YOU WON, Ms. Fitz. Who would you like to have dinner with from the Championship Power League team?"

"Grey London," I answered in a rush. Despite not quite finishing the treasure hunt, Lisa and I still had the highest points, and had just squeaked in a victory. The man with the clipboard nodded and left. I texted Lisa and Jake to make the date and told them who we were eating with. Lisa replied quickly with an apology, she was busy with something at her kid's school. I asked her what, and she simply replied. 'Baking'. I shrugged and ran to get changed for the dinner.

I picked out one of the pre planned outfits laid out in my closet. I packed the syringe into my bag, and hurried out into the hall as Jake arrived. He pulled everyone into a hug they didn't ask for. I squeezed him, and he pulled on my hand dragging me down the hall. We took the students elevator down and Jake held onto my hand the whole way down. The doors opened onto the lot behind the buildings. A producer I'd never met tapped his pen on his clip board. I held my bag tighter as Jake and I stepped onto the Hero High bus. Most of the busses had numbers on the front, so producers could keep track of which students were where. We started to move, I'd never noticed before, but people in the streets would wave at the bus and take pictures as we passed by. There were three other students with us who got stopped off at the Super League stadium.

The restaurant, the Verde Foglia Café, wasn't too far from the center of town. As soon as we arrived, a producer trudged over, and tapped his watch at Grey London.

"Does that mean there's a time limit?" I asked sitting down.

"There's always a time limit," Grey London replied as Jake took his seat beside me.

My legs bobbed under the table with anticipation and nerves, what would she say? Would it turn out all of this was normal? Had I found something everyone knew about except me? Did the syringe actually have nothing to do with The Figure?

"So, you're Lisa's mentee?" Grey London asked.

"Yes, yes! That's right, she couldn't be here, something about school."

Grey London nodded and our food arrived. My hand reached down, my fingers grazing the syringe. "Lisa's great, you couldn't have asked for a better mentor." Should I just slam it on the table and demand answers?

"Except for you, right?" Jake added with a laugh.

I'd have to do it some time, I had to stop procrastinating, I needed to push myself. "Exactly!" she replied with a swish of her fork.

"What is this, and what are you doing with it?" I said and threw the syringe on the table where it collided with a fork. Grey London's eyes went wide and Jake nearly choked on his chicken. "I won't tell anyone I swear," I said, leaning forward. "I just need to know what this is, why you have one, and why The Figure In The Flames has one," I whispered.

Grey London's eyes darted round the room, fixing on me for a moment and then on Jake, as though she were worried about bystanders. "Like I said, there's always a time limit," she hissed, her eyes going back to Jake as he took a long drink.

"What do you mean? What does that mean?"

"I can't tell you! Who do you think you are anyway? You're just some random first year," she growled.

"I'm a superhero in training," I told her, "and I demand to know what's going on."

She started wiping her palms off on her thighs, just like she did in the stadium.

"Shut up, shut, up! You're going to ruin this for me!" Heads turned and she raised her hand in reply. The other diners settled down. She got up from her chair, and started walking. I pushed my seat aside, and ran after her.

"Where do you think you're going?" I whispered. "We're not done here."

"Oh yes we are." She spun me round and pulled me into a dark corner. "Let this go, kid, the syringe ain't bad," she said, her eyes wide, checking the corner.

"Then why are you so scared?" I asked.

Her head turned, as though she'd only just now realized she was terrified. "You have to go, he'll kill you," she said, tripping over her words as they rushed out of her mouth.

"Who? Who'll kill me?"

"I can't tell you, he'll find you, kid. So shut-"

A flash of black.

London's face froze.

And then, gone.

Not even a second. She was

She was gone. The Dr. had taken her. I ran back to the table, pushing a server out of the way. If the Dr. Was here the syringe would be next.

I grabbed at me bag. "Day what's wrong?" Jake rushed. I didn't reply. Pulling open my bag I couldn't see it. Why could I see it!

I emptied the bag over the floor. No syringe.

"Friday?" I turned. It was London. Jake's hand reached up for me.

"'Day are you okay?" He asked. I shook him off, as London moved closer.

"W-what happened? Are you okay? Did he hurt you?" I asked, looking her up and down.

"I don't know what you're talking about," she replied with a frown.

"Dr. Dangerous, he took you, he, he-" I stuttered. She started blankly at me, refusing to admit what had happened. Jake peered at me from behind. "What about Dr. Dangerous? 'Day? Did you see him?"

Grey London narrowed her eyes at me, and I sighed. "No, no. It was nothing."

"I think this dinner's over. Go home, Friday," she said and sighed taking her bag from the table. Jake moved over to me, pulling me into a hug.

"I think maybe I'm just tired," I said. Jake nodded, and pulled away. He wrapped an arm around my shoulders as we walked.

————

Half an hour later my rusted old bike had delivered me safely to Lisa's home. The sky was pitch black in the residential area. The far away hassle of the city giving life to the soft rosy umbers of the street lights. I left the bike in the drive, rapped on the door and sighed with relief when Lisa ushered me in.

"Is everything okay, Friday?" she asked. Barney sat on the sofa, the ghost of a smile on his face. They'd been laughing. Together.

"I didn't mean to interrupt, I can go if-"

Lisa's cleared her throat, and shook her head.

"Non sense," she paused, "get it?" she said with a laugh.

Barney snorted. "I should go anyway, Lisa. It's getting late." Lisa nodded and fetched Barney's jacket while I stepped aside, inspecting the pictures that hung on her wall and trying to pretend I hadn't noticed; Lisa was smiling at Barney, Barney was smiling at Lisa, he was at her house late at night, and her kids were in bed. They mumbled to each other, Lisa trying to hide her smile while Barney let it run wild. One last adjustment of his jacket and Lisa held the door open while he gave her one last nod before leaving.

"So, what's wrong, kid?" she inquired, "is everything okay? You look worried."

"Do you know anything about a golden syringe?" I asked as we sat down together on the sofa.

"Where'd you hear about that?" she asked, leaning forwards.

"I found one, two actually." I told her with a clearing of my throat.

"You found one?" she repeated, struggling to keep her voice low.

I nodded. "But then I lost them."

"Friday, what exactly have you been doing?" She sounded like a mom.

"Please, I have to know!" I blurted.

"It's not your job to look into this kind of stuff," she told me.

"Lisa, please! I can't sit still and do nothing. What do you know?"

"Not a lot. It was a couple of months ago," she said, leaning forward once again. "Someone approached me to ask about my powers, whether they were OK, or whether I wanted some sort of upgrade. He showed me a gold syringe."

"What did you say?" I asked.

"No! Obviously." Lisa growled.

"Right. Of course."

"Now tell me, what have you been doing? What do you know about the syringe?" Lisa asked.

"Grey London, she was kidnapped." I could feel something rising in my throat, I swallowed hard. "Then she appeared outside the Super Structure and she told me I'd-" My eyes burned as I looked down at shaking hands. I was scared, so scared. Lisa said nothing, pulled me into a hug, the way my mother used to, and let my head rest on her chest.

"You need to stay safe Friday," she told me, as I fought back tears.

"I can't."

She pulled back, looking down at me, holding my shoulders. "Not everything is up to you, kid," she said, smoothing my hair, "you don't have to grow up so fast."

My mind skipped back to the syringe, The Figure, Dr. Dangerous, Grey London, the fact that the same people had approached Lisa, and even she didn't know what was happening. She wasn't asking me to ignore it, she was asking me to be safe, to take my time.

I couldn't, not when frustration and the drive to *do,* shook me to my very core. I'd lock it up, like I had at home. I would try, I would *try* to be patient. I nodded and she wrapped her arms around me again, telling me to start from the very beginning.

————

After I told Lisa what I knew, she helped me search my room for the syringe, just in case I'd missed it. I told her I'd been kidnapped by the Dr. but left out the kissing part. She said she'd keep an eye out for any other heroes using syringes, and then I knew I should have told her earlier. Why hadn't I? Was I just so used to doing things by myself? Maybe I just wanted to prove that I, alone, had done something.

On Saturday the gold team and I had to be ready for a yearly meeting called the Hero Channel's Upfronts. Aya slaved over all the clothes in my designer closet, trying to choose between two skirts. I'd almost fallen asleep watching her pick. She sighed, and threw me the tea length one with a shirt.

"You're sure?" I asked, jolting awake.

"The flap pocket it too casual. I just *really* like it."

I changed quickly as Aya rushed out to finish her hair. David and Ashley were waiting by the door, playing rock paper scissors. I almost giggled when I realized David had matched the color of his jacket to Aya's dress. Ashley wore the same suit I'd seen him in last time, it still sent flutters through my stomach. Did I like him? I wasn't really sure.

I slipped my phone into my pocket just as Aya rushed out and David took her arm. As soon as the bus pulled up outside the tower, Veronica slid the door open and looked us up and down as though checking we were dressed well enough. She paused when she got to me, but didn't say anything. As soon as I sat down and the bus started up, I leaned forwards.

"What exactly is it we're doing?" I asked her.

"Going to a restaurant. I would have told you earlier, but I didn't know the shareholders wanted the gold team, most of you are freshman, usually they leave them out of the Upfronts." She said this all while texting on her phone. I was genuinely impressed. "All you kids have to do is make simple chit chat and enjoy the meal while the cameras make the rounds, and some people make some announcements." The others seemed to nod as though that sounded pretty simple, but I couldn't make simple chit chat. I resolved very quickly to hide behind one of my team mates. No one would want to talk to me, I had the least media coverage of anyone in the gold team. Aya already had a deal with a clothing line, David had been on two magazine covers, and Ashley had an endorsement deal with Strawberry Tarts, a product title I had mis-read as 'Strawberry Farts' on *multiple* occasions.

The bus pulled up to a tall restaurant painted emerald all over and just for once there were no paparazzi outside, nor any reporters in sight. A large gold sign atop the entrance said 'Émeraude'. Two men opened the front doors in tandem, their hands splayed on the horizontal gold bars that made up the handles. Aya stood on my right, whispering in my ear about how she'd never been here, and Ashley on the other side sighed. As the doors opened, I held back a whistle.

The restaurant was ginormous! Symmetrical steps on either side led up to a balcony dining room across from the large glittering chandelier that hung in the center of the restaurant.

We moved through crowds of servers and customers to the hostess. I recognized almost all the faces as several camera crews weaved through the tables picking up conversation. A small stage and podium sat atop a balcony for addressing the whole restaurant. The walls were the same shade of green as the outside, but so were the chairs, and the tables. Veronica waved her hand at the hostess, urging her to go faster and soon we were on the balcony, seated at a long table that sat at the same level as the shower of diamonds that hung in the room. It seemed as though million dollar dresses and designer tuxedos were the regular dress code.

"Ah Veronica, darling!" Veronica embraced a portly old man with rosy cheeks and kissed him twice on each side.

"And this must be the freshman team. Come, come, sit down, children." Four seats lay spare, so we each took one. I ended up on the very end next to Ashley as everyone resumed their conversations. Veronica took a seat next to the portly man and started discussing us with her neighbors. Captain Fantastic nodded at me from the other head of the table. I forgot to hold the kind of smile I reserved only for him, goofy and child-ish. Ashley's knee tapped mine, so I jolted back, and glared at him. "What was that for?" I growled.

He leaned over to whisper, "try not to swoon at the sight of him."

"I wasn't swooning," I insisted.

"Looked like you were."

I huffed as Ashley took a swig of his drink. The cameras focused on a man standing behind the podium talking about the next wave of hero high toys.

"Eh, Veronica, I know it's unusual for me to ask for the freshman team, but I felt it was necessary this year."

"I understand, Sir."

"But uh, why are there four of them? I thought it was a three man team?"

"Ms. Fitzsimmons over there joined recently at the invitation of the other members." Veronica's voice was soft, she sounded much more timid around this man and I wasn't sure if it was because she was cautious, or because she was hiding just how ruthless she could be.

"Ms. Fitzsimmons is it?"

I jumped and hiccuped. My team laughed. "Yes, Sir."

"Your first name?"

"Friday, Sir."

"Good strong name. My grandmother was called Friday. And what have you done, girl?"

"I was featured on an episode of Real Heroes with Sense and Barney, and then-"

"I remember you, the tiny little thing Dr. Dangerous went after. Well isn't that interesting." His gaze returned to Veronica, and he continued to speak as though my team and I weren't there. "It's a shame really, with four of them we'll have to re think the love triangle."

Veronica nodded knowingly and took a sip from her

glass. I looked past Ashley to see Aya and David holding back groans. Love triangle? With Ashley? Aya saw my knitted brow and leaned over Ashley to whisper.

"They like to pair us up, though if you're wondering if they wanted Ashley and me to be a thing, the answer is no. They never even considered it."

She sat back and accepted a menu from the waitress as Ashley continued the explanation. "They wanted another girl in the team for the love triangle, they were about to hold auditions, but Aya decided she liked you, so we made the decision before they could."

"So then, I'm not part of this, right?" I said.

Ashley sighed, and set his cutlery down. For once it didn't feel like he was sighing because of me, it felt like he was sighing because he had to explain to me what was essentially multiple seasons worth of a soap opera. "It looks like even though they have another girl on the team, now they're not going to go through with the new team member being the last piece of the triangle."

"Okay? Then what were you supposed to be?"

He chewed the inside of his cheek. "David's boring best friend."

I looked up from my menu in time to catch his smile. He did not think of himself as *anyone's* boring best friend. I couldn't help but laugh a little as I turned my head away.

"Don't laugh, I'm not boring," he whispered.

"I'm sorry," I said and giggled once again. I looked around the table and saw Matt from Hero High. He was on Real Heroes now, he'd graduated this year. Cassandra and Donnie sat next to each other; they were an important couple the show was trying to push. It looked as though Lisa hadn't been invited, but Barney was. He sat to the right of The Captain wearing something a bit more modern than the rest of the men. He was already *gulping* down the wine.

Eventually we all ordered, and I didn't have to worry about filling my mouth with words when instead I could fill it with chicken. I had a hard time convincing myself I wanted to eat. The food wasn't bad by any means, but I'd ruined my pallet on too many chicken nuggets and was forced to face the truth: I was no longer refined enough to appreciate food that wasn't deep fried or coated in breadcrumbs.

Trudging on through the night, I tried to finish as much of the food as I could. The rosey cheeked man stopped speaking to his producer friends every now and again, and looked over at one of the students. At one point in the dinner a young man with dark hair walked over to the rosey cheeked man and shook his hand. I looked at the badge on his jacket, and realized he was the Mayor, Thomas February, the third member of the February family to be elected as mayor. The Mayor smiled as the cameras caught him, and then waved as he left. The rosey cheeked man started to talk about this year's teams, and what they were doing on the show.

The Plum team had three members, they'd stayed the same since their first day, they were all sophomores. The man was worried about their appeal since the team was all female. He suggested a more mature concept for them, which everyone knew meant he wanted them scantily clad. Veronica rolled her eyes, and then nodded.

The Olive team were two boys, one sophomore, one senior. They'd been a two man team for a while, so no one dared add a new member to the team this year for fear of fan outrage, though the producers and the rose cheeked man did discuss adding a girl to the group so they could start a romance arc in their last year.

As the dessert arrived they moved onto the fuchsia team which had five members, all seniors. Five was enough. No-one even considered adding new team mates this year. All eyes were going to be on them this season, the most pressure was always on the seniors. All they seemed to say was that their merch wasn't selling as well as it could and no one could work out why. They'd doubled up on couples this season, and prepared merchandise for it, what they didn't seem to know was they'd forced a couple pairing that no one liked. Everyone could tell Maya liked Lucas, and Lucas liked Maya, but they insisted on Lucas liking Riley, when we all knew she was completely in love with Farkle.

Cassandra and Donnie sat without the rest of their team. The Mint team was one of the larger teams on the show, but the cameras usually focused on the core group which meant Cassandra and Donnie, a couple on show, but a couple with no chemistry. It was all a *complete* mess with *old*, out of touch men trying to relate to the younger generation and failing to figure out what they were doing wrong. Sitting at the table was like a show of its own.

"Well we have time to figure out what to do with the new girl." My head shot up from my chocolate cake to find the man and the other producers looking me up and down. I felt like covering myself with a black bag. My team mates faces twisted uncomfortably as they tried to stay quiet. "She's not very-" one of the suited men searched for his next word carefully.

"Womanly?" finished another.

"Exactly."

I was completely taken a back, and of course I put

down my fork and forgot I'd been told to cut the gas. "I'm seventeen!" I said. Their eyes widened, and the cutlery dropped. "Of course I'm not very womanly, I'm not a woman, I'm a girl!" Their mouths hung open and the rose cheeked man glared at me like I'd killed his dog. Stupidly, I continued, I thought I might as well. Go big or go home, right? "Oh I'm sorry, was that a private conversation? Should have had it somewhere *private* then."

"I think you should leave young lady," said the rose cheeked man.

"Fine by me." I pushed back my chair, panic written on the faces of my team mates. Ashley reached for my hand. I shook him off. For the first time in the dinner The Captain looked up from his plate with a somber expression that I couldn't read. I picked up my plate and fork, I wasn't about to leave the cake behind. The cameras down below swerved round to me and moved in, still trying to keep their distance as though they could hide that they were hoping I'd freak out. The staff stared daggers at me as I left. I walked straight out into the street, eating as I went, giving them what I hoped was nothing to film.

What a bunch of old farts. I stomped down the side walk and into a city park, placed my cake beside me on a bench and picked up my phone to call Lisa.

"Hey kid, what's up?" There was a scuffle from behind the phone, Lisa shouted to her kids to keep it down.

"I got stuck walking home, can you give me a ride back? I don't know who else to call, is that okay?"

"Of course kiddo, that's what I'm here for, where are you?"

"Hilary Park." I mumbled, cheeks blazing.

"Give me ten." She uttered, and then hung up.

I closed my phone again and finished the last of my cake. I gazed at the empty plate and sighed, I'd stolen a plate from an expensive restaurant. That wasn't very superhero like of me. With a roll of my neck I got up again, I would have to give it back.

I waddled onto the sidewalk again hoping no one would see me, and nodded to the nice men who held the door of the restaurant open. I walked up to the podium only just tall enough to look over it, and set the plate down. "Sorry I took this by accident, oh, and here's the fork. Sorry."

The hostess frowned, and waved me away. I checked the balcony to make sure no one had seen me come back with my tail between my legs. The Captain looked down with a gentle, but proud smile on his face as he noticed me. I shrugged and held my hand up to him as though to say, 'what? I didn't do anything', then

283

I hurried back down the road into the park. Once there I sent a text to Aya apologizing, telling her I was fine, and that I had also returned the stolen property.

Lisa dropped me off back at the tower, and walked me to my door. I nearly told her she was going the wrong way until I remembered I lived somewhere else now. Lisa gave me a hug.

"You gonna be okay kid?"

"Absolutely, I'd just had enough." She gave me a look of understanding. "Lisa?"

"Yeah kiddo?"

"Do you think if I can't handle that stuff, should I even be here?"

"Yes." she answered without hesitation. "Heck kid, I'll admit you're not great in front of the cameras, but you've got a good heart. None of us are perfect. Hang in there."

I nodded to her and she gave me a quick kiss on the forehead before she waved good bye. She was right, I just needed to solve one problem at a time. After all that's how I'd lived my life for a long time now. Don't think for too long, just keep moving.

Opening the door to the dorm house was like a cold wind hitting after you leave a warm house. It was empty and icy with no touches of home, and far too much gold. I threw my jacket on the floor of my room, and collapsed onto the hard mattress. My back ached. Stress, most likely. My eyes felt heavy and hot, I must have dozed off, because when I looked up the alarm clock read eleven. Someone knocked on my bedroom door, I stretched my legs, and got up to open it.

Ashley stood in my doorway, his hand half-way up the frame. He looked a little different than normal. Concerned. Timid even.

"Are you okay?"

"I'm fine, tired, back pains. I just, sorry. I guess I lost it."

"It could have been worse."

"What? No lecture about being a spoiled brat?"

"You need a lecture after that? You stormed out of a three thousand dollar a plate restaurant with a slice of cake in your hand because you didn't like what the mean old man said." He laughed.

"Point taken. What are they gonna do to me?" I asked.

He shrugged. "I'm sure they'll find something. Veronica was pretty pissed."

"Hey, how come you're not at you grandmother's place?"

"What did I say about talking about that?"

"There's no one else here," I said.

"Aya and David are here, who did you think I came back with?"

"Oh, good point," I said, "sorry, sleepy brain."

"It's fine. I only go over when she needs me. I was filling in for someone that day."

I couldn't hold back a smile in the low light as I looked up at him, he was so tall, almost as tall as the faux Dr. Dangerous. This time the flicker of a thought about him looking handsome wasn't just a flicker, the thought lingered. His brown eyes were warm and his hair was silky. I shook my head and blamed it on the sleepy brain. I swore I'd been looking at him too long when he spoke up again. "You know, you never talk about what happened that day, when the Dr. took you."

My cheeks flared with red and I tried to hide it in the shadows. There was a good reason I never talked about it. How was I supposed to tell someone he tried to use some weird gadget on me, and then we made out. It was too embarrassing to think about. I tried my best to keep it out of my head on a regular basis, but no matter what I did, it kept coming back to send a wave of heat through my body.

"Nothing really happened. Duh."

Ashley nodded thoughtfully, and seemed to let the subject go. For a moment he flickered in the darkness as the lights of the city danced over the hallway. "You need some sleep," he said pointing to my bed as though it was a command.

"I'm fine, I just took a nap. I have some work I need to do anyway." I made to walk past him, but his hand hit the wall in front of me.

"Get some rest. Whatever you need to do, you can do it tomorrow." I wanted to say something else, but my bones ached, and my eyes were heavy.

"Thanks."

His brow raised. "For what?"

"Bothering." I sighed.

Neither of us said a word. The silence felt heavy, like I'd just let something inappropriate slip. The weight of the darkness and the silence didn't lift, it only pushed us closer. He leaned over me and my heart skipped a beat. I found myself pushing up as his thumb brushed over my cheek, trying to bridge the gap between us.

Was he going to kiss me?

Was I going to kiss him? I moved closer as he did the same. I *wanted* to kiss him. He was nice, and big, and-

"Ashley we're going to bed!" Aya shouted from the kitchen.

Ashley stepped back.

He cleared his throat. "Good night." He mumbled.

I said nothing, slamming my back against the wall as he disappeared. It wasn't just a flicker, or even a lingering thought.

I liked Ashley, a lot.

———

COMET

"**W**AKE UP, SLEEPY HEAD!**" Aya screamed in my ear.

I jumped up, head hitting the floor. Ashley laughed from the hall. "Ow! Come on guys, why?" I yawned.

"Ashley said you were cute half asleep, I wanted to see if he was right," said Aya.

"Ashley said that?" My cheeks went red. I looked over to the doorway where Ashley and David stood side by side. David shook his head, but his eyes were smiling.

"Come on, sleepy head, we have eggs and bacon." Aya said, bouncing.

"You cooked?" I asked.

"Ashley did."

I raised an eye brow and he shrugged.

"Come on Friday, we'll be in the kitchen!" Aya sung.

I fumbled in, wearing a hoodie I reserved for a special time of month and early mornings. Aya finished her breakfast as I settled in, and David turned on the news before passing me the paper.

In one of our first classes Coach Flat had explained why we all needed to stay up to date on the news. Ashley dropped a pancake onto my plate without a word.

"How come *she* gets your pancakes, but *I* had to cook for myself?" Aya questioned.

"Because she probably doesn't know how to cook," Ashley sighed as he poured more batter into the pan.

"No way! You can't cook Friday?" Aya dropped her knife like it was red hot, and gaped at me.

"I can cook! Just not very well. At home I always just ate fast food or *tried* to cook."

"How come?"

"I don't know, I never learnt." I mumbled. Ashley flipped the newly formed pancake. I sighed. "No one ever taught me how to cook, so, thanks for the pancake."

I hadn't sat around a table eating a breakfast

someone had made *for* me, since I was nine. And it was a *really* good pancake.

A TV news report on a cat beauty pageant gave way to a segment on last night's dinner. The story was thrown over to a panel of men and women, the women all blonde, the men all greying. I could already tell it wasn't going to go well, and just to confirm it my team mates groaned.

"So last night we saw the upfronts, they're bringing out some new stuff, including a whole new line of photo books called Couple Books." The man to the left nodded, and continued. "Yeah, apparently this is a thing now?" he said as his head retreated into his neck and he made a meme worthy face.

"Like, what's up with that?" asked the first blond

"I don't know Gloria, I really don't," replied one of the grey men.

"Oh and get this, the best moment of the night, or should I say *worst*." Pictures flashed up showing a small figure walking out of the restaurant. My team mates turned, though I wasn't sure why until I caught up and realized the picture was me. "Reporters caught a glimpse of one of the students walking out; not only that, but she stole some of the restaurants property!"

"I didn't! I returned it after I ate the cake, so shut up!"

Aya lay a hand on my shoulder, and patted my back to calm me but the men and women on TV had barely started. "So this kid is Friday Fitzsimmons, get this, she was the one with the bomb and, uh-"

"The one in the park with Dr. Dangerous?"

"Exactly, she's an up-an-comer, and she's acting like this?"

"I hate to say this, but, can I say this? I'm going to say it anyway, she was acting like a spoiled princess. There I said it!"

"Someone agrees with me for once," mumbled Ashley.

"How is that even an insult?" I demanded. "Everyone loves princesses!"

"And what about the spoiled part?" Ashley added.

"Spoil is something you do to someone you love. You *spoil* someone."

He sighed and turned off the stove.

"So all I'm hearing is, you're a princess and everybody loves you, Friday." I said.

"That's not what they're saying Fitz, and it's definitely not what I'm saying," said Ashley.

"I bet she has some serious anger issues," said a voice from the TV.

"This is bullshit," I said and slammed my knife and fork down on the table.

This time my team mates looked concerned. Aya made no attempt to reach for me this time. The greying man sitting next to the helmet hair blonde, smiled and nodded. Spoiled princess I could handle, sure I'd make a joke out of that, but I was not going to put up with being accused of 'anger issues'. My knuckles tightened and started to turn white. "Who does she think she is? How's she going to be a superhero with that sort of an attitude? I mean she doesn't even fit the profile. Look at her, she has to put a little effort into her looks, smile a little. And what's up with what she's wearing?"

The woman next to him nodded. "And it wouldn't kill her to lose some weight would it?"

My arms twitched at my side, trying to resist the urge to sweep the table, and send everything clattering down to the floor. Ashley reached for the remote and rather than switch the TV off he turned to another channel. My brows shot up and I sat back down, the weight in my stomach lifting as I returned to my food and Happy Magic Princess played. I loved that show so much I hummed the theme tune as it played. Aya sighed and patted me on the back.

"Oh my God, Happy Magic Princess, I love that show! How did you know?"

"It was on your Hero High application form. There's a box at the bottom that says, 'describe yourself'. And rather than do that, you just wrote 'Happy Magic Princess' and did a doodle of the main character. It was in your file."

"Huh? I do *not* remember doing that, but that does sound like me," I admitted.

"Now I know how to calm you down. Cook for you, and put Happy Magic Princess on."

"You're not wrong Ang, you're not wrong."

————

Coach Flat greeted us in the middle of the mall, surrounded by a camera crew. Outfits were immediately thrown into our arms, and as soon as they were on we were ushered onto one of the large busses striped with adverts and the Hero High logo. I could hear Veronica grumbling at someone below us, but couldn't make out what it was she was saying. The handlers booths were covered with snacks, drinks and various types of communicator, from ear buds colored in various tones of flesh to tracking devices.

"Hey Aya what's this?" I asked.

"Not sure. Invisible earbuds for on site extras maybe?"

The lights on the bus spun out of control the same

way they had when I'd been with Lisa and Barney and Jake's voice cut in. "Super villain downtown."

I rushed down the stairs behind my teammates, and Veronica dashed to the panels of handlers all scanning their computers for a picture of the villain in question. A shaky camera showed up on all the screen's showing a short man clad in layers of thick wool standing on top of a building.

"Short Fuse, veteran super villain. His power's referred to as Explosive Excretion." I nodded along with the rest of my team as they received the same information from their handlers. I tapped my phone, and slipped on my mask with everyone else.

Coach Flat turned to us, and straightened his shoulders. "Alright kids, get out there, don't die if you want to live."

"We're not there yet," said David.

"What did you think? We'd drive you to the front door in our big Hero bus?" replied Veronica.

I jumped out of the bus as Aya was pushed out the door by Coach Flat and it slammed in her face. I looked down to find my bike hanging under the bus.

"You have a bike?" exclaimed David.

"Of course. Don't you guys have one?" I asked, petting my junker of a bike.

"No." Aya and David sang.

"Oh, well you're gonna need one. You can ride with me." I smiled.

"You don't know how to cook, but you know how to drive?" David jutted, only to get nudged in the ribs by Aya.

"Of course I know how to-" I had to stop. Ashley slowly wheeled a bike of his own from behind the bus. His was much the same as mine, save for the stealth black paint job, the matte modern metal I suspected was carbon fiber, and the more aerodynamic appearance. He had a million dollar motor *cycle*. He looked back at the rest of us in silence. "The more fans you have Fitz, the better the equipment."

"Then why don't Aya and David have bikes?" I asked.

"They didn't ask." He said with a push of his glasses.

Aya raised a finger to protest, and then decided against it as she pressed her finger to her communicator, and mumbled something to her handler. She ran to the other side of the road, and raised her hand with something in it. "Last one there's a rotten apple!" she said as she threw a metal ball into the air and my eyes followed it like a dog. When I looked back to ask her why she'd done that, she was gone.

David waved a hand at me, signaling me to hurry up

as Ashley climbed onto his stupid stealth bike. I handed a helmet to David and he wrapped his arms around me. Unlike Jake, he didn't seem to have any qualms about letting me drive. Ashley tore away in a flash, his engine like a lion's roar, whereas my bike *clattered* into life sounding more like a toy airplane.

We were the last to get there. Aya stood at the bottom of the building, already holding the same metal ball in her hand, and readying for another throw. Ashley had stopped at the bottom of the building and I kicked my bike up onto the sidewalk just as he took off his helmet. David got off my bike so fast he knocked it over. I leaned over to pick it up while the drivers behind us yelled curse words for blocking the road. I kicked the bikes stand up just as Ashley's gadget belt stuck itself to the side of the building. Ashley was already climbing the side, Aya had just thrown her metal ball and disappeared into it and David almost slid up the glass sides with the aid of sticky boots.

"Jake?" I asked.

"Yeah?" He buzzed in my ear.

"Do I have any gadgets that help me scale buildings?" I laughed, knowing the answer.

"Nope." I could almost hear him lean back in his chair.

"Well okay then." I sighed.

I blew a stand of hair out of my eyes and walked straight through the front door of the office building. The cameraman followed me in, all excited as though he'd been told I'd come up with an ingenious way to get to the roof. Instead I called the elevator. It was *very* dramatic. I was sure the editing team would put a choir over it all, and the ping of the doors would sound like the gong before a fight to the death. The cameraman stood frozen for a moment as I turned facing outwards in the elevator; I shrugged and he shrugged back before joining me inside. The doors closed and gentle piano music played. I spied a chocolate bar in his pocket and tapped him on the shoulder.

"Hey, buddy? You gonna finish that?" I beamed.

The camera turned all of a sudden. It was much too big for the elevator.

"You get that I'm filming this, right?" he said.

"Yeah? So? I'm just asking if you're going to finish your chocolate bar. Jeez." I mumbled.

"Go ahead."

"Really?" I said, trying to hide the joy in my voice, "thanks, man." I picked the chocolate from his pocket, feeling almost guilty, so I broke off a row of squares and set it back in his shirt pocket. "Where's the other guy? The cameraman who was following me when the Dr., you know?"

"He asked for a transfer, he's filming pre planned stuff," he replied, swinging his camera round again.

"Why?"

"Don't know. Guess he felt bad for running."

I opened my mouth to reply, but the elevator doors pinged again, and the music stopped all too abruptly. Men and women still sat at their desks in the building, seemingly unfazed by the super villain above them. A few people with headsets turned to look at me as I walked down the aisles of cubicles. "Does anyone know where the stairs to the roof are!?"

A man ssh'd me from his desk, and shook his head.

"Sorry for shouting. Sorry." I whispered.

A woman silently pointed to a green sign.

"Oh, thank you! I mean, thank you. Sorry again." I back tracked to the office kitchen, and had a quick look inside their fridge for something to wash down the lingering taste of sugar. I pulled out a can of cola and left a five dollar note in its place before cracking it open. I pressed the bar to open the exit doors, and held the door open for Kevin, my cameraman. My team mates had probably got rid of Short Fuse, for all I knew they were tying him up at that very moment. There were five more flights of stairs between me and the door labeled 'exit'; I pushed it open without delay, and burst onto the roof like the cool aid man.

"I'm here! What- What did I- Ugh. What did I miss!?" I panted, resting my hands on my knees. My comms came on with Carey's voice coming through as he presented the live show. I took my place next to my team mates. A short gangly man stood in front of us, holding a woman by the collar as Carey started his announcement from the comfort of his own bus, like the entrance of a wrestler. "Who's this!? Could it really be!?" The cameraman ran along our single file line to catch all our reactions before he pointed the camera to our villain. They were so fast I didn't have time to stop yawning into the camera.

"It's Short Fuse!" Jake's voice chimed in, cutting Carey off.

"I'm looking at his file now. His power's called explosive excretion. Apparently it means he sweats explosives?"

"Sounds fun."

Carey cut in again to deliver the rest of his speech. "Short Fuse is back, and is ready to have a blast. And remember folks, when he sweats, you sweat!"

How in the hell was I supposed to beat a guy made of explosives? Maybe the trick was not to think of him as a walking bomb, but just as someone seriously sweaty? Dry shampoo always soaks up sweat... He can't force himself to sweat can he?

"Help me!" the woman yelled.

Aya ran forwards as Short Fuse raised his hand, his skin excreting explosive as his sweat solidified into off white putty. David touched the edge of his visor, forcing a tiny pang of pain into Short Fuses hand, making him drop the gob of explosive, as Aya plain old kicked him in the face.

Ashley nodded to the others and began to run around Short Fuse, distracting him from the rest of the team. Short Fuse lobbed a ball of explosive but it fizzled and popped well before reading Ashley, doing little more than making a scary noise.

I twitched in place, stopped only by a lack of understanding of what I could do to help. Aya ran in again, Short Fuse pressed the off-white substance to the woman's head, and stepped back. I heard Veronica shout something on my communicator, but she must have been far away, I couldn't make out a word.

"One step further and she gets it! How you gonna get out of this one kids?"

Aya stumbled backwards, and David lowered his hand. I had to be a part of the team I had to help…

"Jakey, what can you tell me about his power?" I whispered. The flutter of pages and desk ornaments filled my ear, until he cleared his throat.

"He's been a villain for nearly ten years, hates his

name, can detonate his explosives remotely… He uh, can't produce sweat at will, he has to build up to it."

"What are his explosives actually made of?"

"Let me see." There was another ruffling of pages, and then a slam of his finger. "It says the white stuff most closely resembles C3."

I had to do something, so I did the only thing I could, I blinked just as Short Fuse lunged forwards, and everything suspended as my mind worked in super speed. I wasn't strong, I couldn't fly, but I could think.

So think Friday, think.

I knew a little about C3. A few years back I made a blueprint for a military grade water canister, the man who bought it had told me some interesting stories over lunch, including the fact that C3 had been replaced by C4 in the 60's because the cold made C3 unusable. If I could have moved my hands, I would've snapped my fingers in triumph. I knew the powers I had at my disposal, Aya's, David's, and Ashley's. Ashley and Aya weren't helpful right now, but the great thing about David's power? He could transfer heat, and even though Veronica liked to limit him to blowing things up, his power could actually go hot or cold. I ran through the scenarios in my head, and settled on one I liked before returning to the regular motion of the world.

"David!" Short Fuse's head turned, but he didn't

panic. I lifted my cola can, still mostly ice, and nodded to David to trust me. He understood completely as he whipped off his visor and Short Fuse looked on confused.

"What are you gonna do, don't you make things explode?" the villain asked.

"Now David!" David looked at my can, closed his eyes, and opened them again looking directly at the batch of C3 on the woman's head. It frosted over and cracked. Short Fuse snapped his fingers like they were a lighter, but nothing happened. I stood straight backed, and finally relaxed.

"What did you do?" Short Fuse asked.

"Your explosive is similar to C3," I told him. "C3 goes brittle and useless if cold."

Short Fuse started yelling at the top of his lungs, Ashley rushed forwards, using his strength to force Short Fuse to the ground and bringing out small areas of heat all over his body like pins and needles as Aya appeared behind him, and cuffed him for good. David took the honors of picking the hostage up, and wiping the C3 off her shoulder. I ran to the other side of Short Fuse to help Aya keep him in line and that was when I saw something small and brown deep in his ear.

Ear buds! Why would *he* need an earbud?

It looked just like the ones I'd seen before, which meant the earbuds belonged to us.

As Aya and I dragged him to the doors of the building, I realized Short Fuse was an employee of the Hero Channel. Rage bubbled through me. Employed villains were a thing, villain school was a thing. But it was never a secret. Employed villains had their own merchandise! Short Fuse wasn't one of them, or at least. I hadn't thought he was.

I ran up the steps of the Hero High bus, fists cliched at my side. I slammed my communicator down on Jake's table and turned to face Veronica.

"What?" she said, looking confused. "What did *I* do?"

"He's an actor!" I said pointing to Short Fuse as the others followed me in. "Is he even going to Jail right now?"

"If you must know, no. We have a few 'villains' on retainer for when the weather's good and all the heroes we want are available for shooting."

Aya cringed at my side and David shook his head. "What the hell! That's not okay, I thought that woman was going to die!"

"Well of course not, I'd never do that. She was an actor too?"

"You don't seem to get it, " I said, storming closer.

Every eye on the bus turned to look at us. "I heard you shouting at him when he held her at gun point."

Veronica's face darkened. "I hadn't foreseen that."

"Bullshit! You explicitly told him *not* to do it, that is why you were shouting wasn't it!?" I turned round to the line of handlers. "Wasn't it!?" One in the corner, younger than the others nodded sheepishly.

"You can't do this!" I said turning back, throwing my armor off, smashing into the sides of the bus. Ashley leaned against the walls, watching it all play out.

"You think it's better to have real supervillains?" Veronica bit back.

"He's not that far off, after all, he did go off script!"

"I'll handle it," she said. "He won't do it again."

"How can you stand there like you're better than us!" I yelled. "All you are is fake!"

"At least I'm not dressed like a man," said Veronica giving me a condescending look, her teeth grinding against each other. "Your *mother* must be *so* proud."

"How dare you say *anything* about my mother!" I grabbed her collar. That was a low blow.

"Little baby gonna cry because she's got no mommy-"

Before she could finish I swung at her with my fist but before it could impact her smug face, Aya tugged me back, and everyone in the bus leapt up. "What the hell was that! You're *this* close to being off this team! You violent little girl."

"I'm not violent!" I screamed. Everyone around me froze, and my lunch rose in my stomach.

"Let it go, Friday," whispered Aya, "she's in the wrong, but so are you if you hit her." I knew she was right, the anger had already made me feel sick. I nodded, and she let me go.

"I *was* gonna go along with it, the whole fake supervillain thing, until I realized we could have been doing something *actually* useful. That's why I'm angry, Veronica."

Veronica pressed her finger into my chest, and loomed over me. "You don't get it, do you, little girl? You're an actor on a TV show that pays for my house, my car, and my clothes. The one thing you are *not,* is a hero."

———

The day ended late, at the point where we'd all passed being hungry, and decided that we'd just skip dinner. There wasn't enough energy in any of us to cook, and none of our teachers would ever buy heroes in training fast food, we might be seen eating it. Veronica kicked us out of the van and told us the working day was over.

Coach Flat agreed and told us to walk home, he said it would be good exercise, as though the exercise we'd already had wasn't enough.

I stowed my bike away in the parking lot basement with Ashley. Jake hadn't texted me since I'd told him it was going to be a long night. It was cold, my footsteps echoed in the parking lot. I figured he was mad that we hadn't been spending much time together and that was fine, I'd make it up to him, carve out more time, whatever it took. I wasn't willing to lose a friend, not now.

I flipped open my phone hoping to find a message from him, but the screen was blank.

"What are you doing? Looking for *more* work?" Ashley asked looking over my shoulder as we stepped into the elevator.

"Checking to see if Jake's sent me anything." I told him, scrolling through my phone's contents. Ashley scoffed. "Are you trying to tell me something?" I asked putting away my phone.

"No, no." I muttered.

"I'm not great at reading people, so if there's something wrong?" I said, raising my voice slightly.

"No. I'm fine." He said, firmly.

"Fine." I blurted.

"Fine." He blurted right back.

I sighed, and leaned against the walls. Letting my phone fall to my side.

"You okay?" he asked.

"Why wouldn't I be?" I replied, looking up.

He stood at the other side, looking me up and down with concern. "What I mean is, are you still angry?"

My eyes dropped to the floor. "I'm always angry."

The doors of the elevator opened, and we stepped out into the courtyard of houses. I could see the twinkle of the red light from one of the cameras embedded in the ceiling. There was no doubt in my mind the freshman gold team would be featured on the new episode, at least briefly. The other teams were still much more popular, they could fill entire episodes by themselves. I wasn't sure if I wanted to watch any of the episodes I was in. It always felt so strange and it struck me how strange it was to come home with someone who wasn't Jake. Standing next to Ashley as I put the key in the lock of my front door was odd to say the least. It felt like we were coming home after a long days work which, I supposed, we were.

An odd pulsing sound came from the walls and I heard calls from inside. I fumbled with the key worried something had gone wrong and Ashley pushed the door open sensing the same thing. Inside we were greeted with loud music and swaying students. Aya and David stood in front of us, mortified. I heard a crash of something in the hallway, but no one stopped dancing. I pushed through the people, catching sight of faces I knew from class. We hadn't invited them, so who had!? A family heirloom of Aya's lay smashed to smithereens on the living room floor, but no one seemed to care in the slightest.

I pushed further through the people, snatching away vases, glasses and other small ornaments until I got to my room. Figures moved behind the glass of my bedroom door. I couldn't believe someone was in there! In my room! Gross!

I swung the door open, already deciding which new sheets to buy, and walked straight in on Jake and Mary Mayberry.

He turned his head mid kiss, his hand half way up her shirt.

For a second I was frozen in place, but Ashley came up behind me and that jolted me back.

"'Day what are you doing!?" Jake shouted, reaching for his shirt.

"What are *you* doing!? This is *my* room, this is *my* dorm! Who said you could throw some sort of a bash?"

Jake pushed Mary aside, pulled his shirt on and pushed us out of the room, closing the door behind him.

Aya, David, and Ashley all stood behind me, trying not to interfere.

"Come on 'Day this is my place too," he said over the pounding music.

"It is not!" I yelled, "you have your own dorm!"

"So I'm not allowed to come here!?" He cried.

"Of course you are!" I gritted my teeth against the anger.

"Then what's the problem!?" He asked, his hand slamming against his side.

"That doesn't apply to my bedroom." I said with a stamp forward.

He shook his head, and probed his cheek with his tongue. "Look. just be honest, okay?"

"About what?" I asked, "how pissed I am right now?"

"You're jealous!" He laughed.

"You've gone insane." I was ready to slap him.

"Come on, 'Day! You and I have always had a thing going on," he said gesturing between us, "but you're just not my type, okay?"

My hands twitched at my side. Hold it together, hold it together. I stormed through the crowds, kicked over the speakers, pulled out the plugs and brought a screeching halt to what Jake called 'music'.

"You're such a bitch," said Jake, stomping towards me, "that was expensive."

"I'm a bitch!? Look at yourself! No! You know what! You don't even get to say bitch! Bitches are wonderful loyal female dogs! Get bent!"

"Here we go!" Jake yelled back. "You've been after me for years, 'Day, You even kissed me! Just admit it!"

"I was!" I screamed.

For a moment, he said nothing. Then a self satisfied smile erupted onto his face. "I knew it!" He lunged to take my face in his hands, like he was ready to take back everything about not being his type. I stepped out of the way and he nearly stumbled into the wall.

"But not anymore, Jake," I said sadly. My anger was gone, replaced by melancholy. "I used to think you were the best. Funny, cute, I loved being around you. But, we're seventeen now! We have responsibilities, I grew up, and you got - worse."

He clenched his jaw, and bared his teeth at me.

"We're nearly adults," I told him, "act like it. You're not a kid anymore. I'm sorry I got powers and you didn't! I am! I'm so sorry! It's not fair, but you can't hate me for it."

"I'm not your sidekick!" he yelled.

"I didn't say you were! Super Powers don't make heroes, villains are proof of that. Your chance isn't gone just because I got to be one too! You don't need powers to be a hero! " He took a few steps forward and I realized how much bigger and stronger than me he was. The crowd moved back, and for the very first time.

I was scared of him.

He poked me hard in the middle of the chest, and bared his teeth like a dog.

"You weren't supposed to get powers! I was supposed to be the superhero!"

"You still can be!" I must have screamed at the very top of my lungs because everyone took another step back. His eyes seemed to soften, and his hand lowered along with his head. "Jake?" A fist still lay at his side, taut and ready. My gut clenched. "Jake?" His fist grew red, and I fought the urge to step back. I wasn't going to be scared of my best friend. "Jake please. Talk to me." He pushed at my shoulders, rushing through the crowd of people, slamming the door behind him. Ashley tried to reach for my hand, but I just rushed through the crowds after Jake. "Jake!"

He turned each corner as fast as he could. "Stop following me!"

I pulled back at the sting of the cold night air, but chased after him all the same. "Come back," I yelled, "we have to work this out!" I'd lost sight of him, but ran down the street all the same.

"I hate you!" I heard his shout from behind me and turned round, too late.

My head slammed against the street, something in me cracked and splintered. I looked up and he lifted his leg to kick me.

Wait.

Had Jake just punched me?

I blinked.

I was left with the option of block or dodge?If I dodged I'd still have to get back on my feet. If I somehow managed to block, I could counter. Block was the best option, so I took the risk and blinked back in.

My two hands rose up in tandem to cover the tip of his toes. Jake wasn't a guy who knew how to fight, if he did, he would have used his heel. My hands rose up, and before he knew it I'd gripped his high tops, and pulled. His standing leg wobbled and Jake toppled over, groaning in pain as his head hit the floor. Wait a minute. Was there blood in my mouth?

"Bitch!" he yelled pushing himself back up.

"You're calling me a bitch? You punched me!"

"You were asking for it," he growled. His knee came smashing into the side of my leg as he climbed over me, and for a moment I had no idea where I was, or what was happening. Then, I felt his fist come down on my face.

I blinked again.

That was a black eye for sure. My best friend had given me a black eye. How dare he! All I could think about was beating him to a pulp. The image frozen above me was an obvious one to counter. Knee him in the groin. But then what?

I blinked, and he yelled in pain as my heel connected, but he didn't move his hands from my side. I blinked again.

I had to stun him for longer. I thought back to a move my dad had taught me. A punch at the windpipe.

I blinked, and his cries resumed. My hand extended upwards, my middle finger's second knuckle tensing as it collided with his Adam's apple. He made a harsh choking sound and toppled off me, grabbing my ankle like a hand extending from the grave. My black eye started to go blurry, and panic overtook me.

I leaned down and forgot all about well thought out technique, I just bit him as hard as I could. He *screamed* this time and sprinted down the sidewalk. I thought I was free.

A fireball brushed past my head and singed a lock of my hair. Someone knocked me to the ground as fire blared above me. I looked up to see Ashley, out of breath and panicked. Jake screamed, and his body erupted into flames. I shuffled backwards, too taken aback to say a word as Jake stomped forwards. Ashley pulled me up, tugging on my arm.

"Move Fitz!" Ashley told me.

I nodded without looking at him, and ran.

Jake screamed again and the fire on his body flared. A jet came so close to me I stumbled. The vision in one of my eyes was blurry through the tears, the other was swollen. Before I knew it, Ashley was holding me up as I grabbed at my side. He ran into the elevator, setting me down on the benches, hoping the doors would close before a fireball could reach us.

"Who are you calling?" I asked, as he pulled out his phone.

He looked over, still on high alert, and dropped the phone like he'd forgotten about it as he knelt down to me. "Friday, your eye." His fingers reached out, but pulled back for fear of hurting me.

"I'll be okay," I told him. He picked up his phone to call a teacher, but as we sped up in the elevator I saw Jake's fiery trail in the sky. It was too late, he was gone. "We have to tell The Captain," I choked, "we have to tell everyone. Jake is The Figure In The Flames."

———

MAKING THE MOST OF THE NIGHT

I WAS STANDING IN the middle of the school gym, last class of the day, as Coach Flat gave me after school classes on how to fight. No one but Lisa had spoken to me about Jake, no one else really knew him. I shook my head and tried to focus on Coach Flat.

"It's important to know how to take it, because you can't always dodge an attack," he told me. My clothes were covered with sweat, and my hands were wrapped for safety. Coach Flat insisted on boxing as a form of exercise. I wasn't very good, he always told me there was too much emotion behind my blows, and not nearly enough precision. The punching bag was big, but I still managed to miss it from time to time. My stomach was starting to feel really empty. "Take a break, you're making me sad," said Coach Flat.

I nodded and snatched the water bottle from him, drinking as much as I could.

"Knock knock," said Veronica as she strode in, clipboard in hand.

"That's all for today, " said Coach Flat, "eat something, and take a shower, you smell terrible, like really bad, like, I haven't wiped my ass in days bad."

"Thanks, Coach," I said and he gave a thumbs up in response to my sarcasm.

Veronica turned to me, checking her watch. "We need you in a couple hours."

"What for?" I asked, pulling the water bottle from my mouth. I set it down next to my book bag before collapsing onto the floor.

"A charity event at the opera house," said Veronica, "they want some of the new kids there."

"Why me?" I asked her, "there are lots of others."

"One of the teams pulled out, Aya's busy filming, and Ashley just refused."

"Aya's filming? For what?" I asked.

"A drama or something," Veronica replied, "I don't know, I didn't read the script. I haven't got time for that."

"Okay," I said standing up, "so It's David and me?"

"Just this once." Veronica said scribbled something on her clipboard. I unwound the gauze between my fingers as Veronica clicked her pen. "Aya said a designer called-" She said under her breath looking over what she'd written.

"D'fwan?" I suggested, hoping I was right, "yeah, I met him."

"Good," she said with a brief, efficient nod, "you'll need a long, formal dress this time, and hurry it up because it starts at seven."

I picked up my book bag, and grumbled internally as Veronica and I rode the elevator.

"What's the event for?" I asked, hoping there would be food, at least.

"Early cancer screening."

"Cool, cool."

"Very," she drawled and lifted her jacket to protect me from the rain as we passed through the doors to the street and another of the show's huge city busses. This one looked different from the others, it didn't have a giant ad on the side, just a sign saying 'Staff Vehicle'.

"In there," she said, opening the door to a well equipped bathroom complete with shower. Inside, a woman handed me a towel and a selection of pre-approved hair products. "Friday?"

I turned, "Yes, Veronica?" I asked as sweetly as I could, she was beginning to get on my nerves.

"Don't screw this up, you've got two strikes already."

"With all due respect Ma'am," I told her, "you can dress me up however you like, but you can't change my personality."

Veronica ground her teeth, her eyes willing me to catch fire. "Let's make something clear, kid." Her hand wrapped around the front of my shirt, carefully pulling me closer. Anyone looking from a distance would think she was simply holding my shoulder. "Remember who you're doing this for and enjoy the pretty dresses, or your sister gets to skip school altogether."

She loosened her grip and puffed out a breath of air. She really had read my file. She looked like a drill sergeant trying to break one of her new recruits, and of course, that's exactly who she was and what she was doing. I tried not to snap back or grunt, I just closed the bathroom door behind me. At least I wouldn't be there alone. David was always reliable, he was good at talking to people, I could even hide behind him if I wanted.

I cleaned myself as quickly as I could and held onto my clothes in case someone tried to do me a favor and throw them away. I was especially attached to my sneakers. I stepped out to a parade of people all lined up and ready to receive me. Veronica was already on her way out the door.

"They'll take care of you and get you where you need to go, until then I have other people I need to see to because believe it or not, my job doesn't revolve around the *freshman* gold team." She waved goodbye facing the other way, like a lady would to a servant, and the people on the bus flooded me with questions.

"Hold up! Give the girl some air," said D'fwan stepping forwards, with Carol right beside him. "These are the gowns we had for Aya."

I looked at the dresses each person held out and realized the biggest problem was size. Aya was six foot tall, and barley over hundred and ten pounds. I sighed. "I hope you're not too disappointed that Aya couldn't make it."

"Not at all, girl. Don't worry," D'fwan turned round and frantically waved all the dresses away like a fly was buzzing round his head. "Sit down child," he said and motioned me to a seat. I plonked my kicks onto my lap with me. "I think I have *something*. Carol, what about"

"The plum one?" she suggested.

"Exactly." Carol snuck down the aisles of wardrobe, and came running back with a dress in a pink plastic cover. She hung it up high and unzipped it. The color was a rich sangria and the skirt was fluffy like the plumes and petals of a flower, all mixing together in a dark stormy sea. "Get me…"

"The ties?" Carol said, flat toned.

"Nailed it!" said D'fwan, "you and I are just so in sync today!"

"I know!" said Carol as she ran off once again searching through the racks, bringing back the item he asked for.

"Stand up child." I did as I was asked, and he looked me up and down with a careful eye. D'fwan held out his hand, and Carol placed thick velvet ribbon in his hand. "Take off your jacket." I did, and he wrapped the velvet around my waist. "Perfect."

He pulled it away, and handed me the dress. Carol held up a towel for me to stand behind and change as D'fwan waved everyone out of the bus. I pulled on the dress as quickly as I could and Carol did up the fastenings. D'fwan then started winding the velvet ribbon around my waist crisscrossing just under my chest before he ran the last two pieces under my bust in a straight line, and tied it at the back.

I didn't have a chance to see what I looked like in the mirror, I decided I didn't want to in case I wasn't good enough for what he'd put on me. They curled my hair, not that it needed much help, brushed it out, and pinned a strand behind my ear. As the clock in the bus hit six thirty, everyone started scrambling.

The bus started moving at speed down winding roads, and soon came to a sharp stop. I looked out of the window, my stomach turning and jumping. I didn't want to do this, I just wanted to go home. I was going to be sick, really *really* sick! The door opened and David stepped on board in a tux. I had to resist the urge to run over and hide behind him, or cling to his arm like a remora to a shark. He wandered up to me, hands in pockets, and already I felt calmer.

"Hey, Friday." David sang.

"Hey, sorry about Aya not making it." I told him.

"I don't mind," he said as the bus sped off once again, "we spend enough time together already. You look nice."

I tried not to laugh at how much I didn't believe him. I bit my tongue, and reminded myself what most people do when complimented. Say thank you, and then return it. "Thank you, you look great, too," my voice sounded like a robot trying to imitate human customs. I hated compliments, I always felt like saying thank you was stuck up. "Well this is awkward," I finally got out.

"It is," David agreed.

"There's not gonna be a lot for us to do is there?" I sighed.

"Nope." He laughed.

"I hope there's food," I said absent mindedly.

"Me too, I'm starving," he said, laughing. "Hey, if there isn't anything there, you want to get some something from Family Fries on the way back?"

"Definitely." I told him. "I want a nice big greasy burger," just the thought of it made me smile.

Once again, the bus came to a stop and I slipped on my high tops while no one was looking. The skirt of the dress was so long and thick no one would be able to tell.

The bus pulled up a block from the venue and Veronica ushered us into a limo. When we arrived, David opened the door, and I was blinded by the constant flash of cameras as we approached the red carpet. The opera house was breathtakingly enormous from the outside. David took my arm, and stepped out first. He could tell just how nervous I was about the whole thing, so he smiled and we stepped out to a warm reception from photographers who seemed eager to take pictures of us together. A few people shouted, asking where Aya was and all the photographers asked David if he was cheating on her just to annoy him. He held onto me tighter as they took pictures, and I tried my best to smile. He ground his teeth, and they shouted Aya's name again.

"It's okay," I said, "just ignore them."

He nodded, and sucked in a breath through his nose.

"At least this one's got bigger tits!" someone shouted from the crowd. My arm pulled back, and David lunged forward, I held him back with all the force I could, but I stumbled. A hand caught my shoulder as the cameras snapped furiously, and one of Veronica's P.A's caught David, and started pulling him back.

"Ms. Fitz, are you all right?" Captain Fantastic's voice was harsh and sharp as he gazed out into the crowd of photographers, as though he was warning them.

"I'm fine," I replied.

"Why don't you come with me," he suggested, "and leave David to them."

"Sounds like a plan."

The Captain led me away from the cameras walking slowly as though he'd had a lot of practice in situations like this. The inside of the building was huge, even the chandeliers were several stories high. I couldn't see the color of the floor for all the people. Servers walked around with miniature food that no one seemed to eat. The only thing anyone picked off the silver plates was booze.

The room was nearly seven stories high. People in

leotards hung from curtains and for a moment, I thought someone was falling, until I realized it was part of the evening's entertainment, and they were actually dancing all the way up there.

"This is a charity event, right?" I asked. "Do I have to donate something? I didn't bring any money."

A huge smile burst onto The Captain's face as he looked down at me with his faux dad glasses a stylist had clearly told him to wear. "We already made a donation on behalf of the show. You don't need your wallet." For a moment it was almost as though he wanted to reach up and ruffle my hair, but held back once he realized he might ruin it. He gave me another bright smile as David came back, and then he left, moving off into the crowd.

David wrapped his hand in mine, and pulled me over to a sculpture in the middle of the room. "This is an original, " he told me, "made by an artist from the thirties." It was a shiny, almost cartoon-like interpretation of the superhero Stronghold. "You know his real name was Thomas February? Apparently he recruited all the members of the first super group."

"Really?"

He nodded. "They were formed during the war, led by The Captain's mother I think."

"What did they-"

A scream cut through the room. There was a crash, a boom, and more cries. I put my arms in front of David as though I was pushing him behind me, and he did exactly the same. On top of the balcony was a short masked man. The crowd gasped. I looked at Captain Fantastic. He'd pulled out his phone and started dialing.

"Listen up!" The short man yelled and the crowd of guests grew closer, being squashed into one another as men advanced from all sides, rounding us up with guns. "We're here for The Captain!"

Was this a trick? Was this another game the show had decided on? Was this a test? No. It couldn't be. I looked for The Captain, but he was gone. Where was he? The only other person I could see was Veronica, furiously filming the whole thing on her cell phone.

"Give yourself up, Captain, or I kill the first person I see," the short man said, pointing into the crowd. A woman screamed. One of his lackeys stomped down the stairs, gripped her by the hair, and dragged her back up with him.

"Captain! You've got until she gets up here."

The crowd gasped, and David gripped my hand, as though to make sure I was still there. I held the bodice of my dress as my chest heaved, where was The Captain?

"Stop! I'm here." Captain Fantastic stood at the

base of the stairs, dressed in full, and ready to fight. The air returned to my lungs in a rush. "Let these people go, and you can have me."

The short man seemed to consider his proposition. "I think I'll keep one for insurance, " he said and threw the crying woman back to his henchman before leaning over the railing once again. His finger pointed into the crowd not too far from me, and he whispered something to one of his men who nodded. David's chest was heaving just like mine, what were we supposed to do? Were we supposed to *do* anything? We were heroes in training, was it better to stay out of this or not? What if The Captain needed our help? I was so caught up in my thoughts I didn't notice the large greasy man grabbing my arm until it had happened.

"Let her go!" demanded David and a taser shot him through with a bolt of electricity. He fell to the floor, writhing in pain.

"You bastards!" I yelled. "David!" I tried to reach out for him, but the lackey hauled me off.

"Come on girly."

I fought against him, not because I thought I could get away, but on principle. Everyone pulled away from me as they dragged me up the stairs and threw me up the last step and onto the balcony two stories up. The short man in the mask gripped the hair on the back of my head the same way my grandmother had when telling me off. His gaudy golden gun traced my forehead as he forced me onto my knees. It wasn't just any man, it was Short Fuse, and he'd ditched his power for a gun. The real problem though? This time he didn't have an ear bud.

I didn't scream, I was more pissed than scared. The dress I was wearing was expensive, if he ruined it, it wasn't coming out of my pocket.

"Who's this?" Short Fuse asked, "she fought me once before. Your daughter maybe?"

"Let her go," The Captain replied, "she has nothing to do with this."

"What's her name then, eh?"

"None of your business." The Captain's voice was as angry as I'd ever heard it. No. Not angry, panicked.

"Come and get her," said Short Fuse.

"Fine, but let everyone else go!"

Short Fuse gestured into the crowd with his gun, and the men started pushing everyone else out the door. Short Fuse's gun returned to my head and he chuckled. "Not much of a screamer is she? That's a shame."

"What do you want from me?" asked The Captain.

"I'm sick of being beaten up for a job! I want your head on a stake," Short Fuse replied, "see, I know your little secret."

The Captain jolted back, and then straightened again, as though he were correcting an improper fighting stance. "I don't know what you're talking about."

"Oh please!" Short Fuse pushed the barrel of the gun closer to my temple and I tried to stay as calm as possible. "I know you don't have powers anymore! You can try to hide with fancy gadgets, but you're way past your prime, Captain so-called Fantastic!" he spat the name as though it was curse word. What was he talking about? The Captain didn't have powers anymore? "So tell me, how much is this girl worth? How about a fair fight between you and me for once eh?"

"Like you have any chance," I said, without thinking and my eyes bulged in horror as Short Fuse's hand tightened around my hair.

"Did you just say something to me, you little shit?" he asked.

"No! Maybe! Force of habit, I'm sorry!" I gabbled.

"Oh you'll be sorry." He pushed the gun against me even harder, and Captain Fantastic flew up a few steps before Short Fuse was forced to point the gun at him instead. The Captain stopped in his tracks.

"Why won't this girl scream?" Short Fuse asked as he pushed me away, and one of his henchmen grabbed me, acting as the replacement gun to my head.

"You not scared to die, girlie?" the henchman asked. "Answer me!"

"No! At least, not right now. Think about it," I said, "if I die now, I die in a couture gown looking basically as good as I ever will! *Now,* is kind of an ideal moment to die if anything!"

Short Fuse burst out into terrifying laughter, and The Captain rose to the last step.

"Calm down, Friday!" he ordered.

"I *am* calm! Mostly," I replied.

"Look-" A gigantic ball of fire hurtled towards Short Fuse interrupting whatever The Captain had planned to say. The glass of the huge window behind him shattered and Short Fuse was blasted right over the balcony like the ball from a cannon.

Captain Fantastic ran for me, not caring what had just taken Short Fuse away. The man holding a gun to my head, stumbled backward and The Captain socked him right in the face. Another man came up behind him, I stood up, glad I'd worn my sneakers, and head butted the man full on, without thinking.

"No one touches The Captain!" I told him.

"Thanks kid," he shouted back as he kicked one last guy down the stairs and, head-butt complete, I tripped over the hem of my dress and fell right into the arms of Dr. Dangerous.

I pushed away as fast as I could and looked over the balcony to see The Figure standing up, no - Jake! My bones shook. I wanted to shout. I wanted to scream!

The Captain's fist collided with the Doctor's face. What the hell was the Doctor doing? I didn't know where to look. Jake burst upwards in a stream of fire and landed right in front of me. I stepped back, flinching from the flames the Figure had started. Had he come to help? He was *trying* to be a hero, so as I fell onto the floor, and looked up into the flames, I held out my hand, hoping he'd power down before the building collapsed.

"You've done your job," I told him, "Thank you. Please stop, you're gonna burn the place down." For a moment I thought Jake was reaching out to take my hand, but instead his fingers rumbled with blue flame. I scrambled to my feet as a broad jet of fire exploded from his hand and I crawled out of the way as he unleashed more fire towards me. My hand gripped the gun on the floor and I threw it at his head.

Only after I'd done it, did I realize I could have pulled the trigger. I'd been in a life and death situation, and yet, I *threw* the gun at him. It hit him straight on the head. His fire flared in anger. I pulled up my dress and once more got to my feet. The Captain had grabbed a fire extinguisher and ran in front of me covering everything in white mist but his efforts came too late. Flames had sprung up everywhere, engulfing the building's floor.

"Jake, stop this!" I yelled, but he didn't reply. The Captain stood in front of me, sighed, and pointed the fire extinguisher straight at Jake, sending him tumbling over the railing. "Jake!"

"Don't worry, Friday, he'll be fine," The Captain said, "that was just to give us some time to get away."

The building looked like it could fall at any minute. I stood between Dr. Dangerous, and The Captain looking back and forth between them as I watched them decide if they should slug it out. I decided for them. I pushed against The Captain's chest as I pulled at my skirt.

"The buildings burning down. We have to get out," I told him. He looked down at me as though he was still thinking. I gripped him by the collar and pulled him away like an angry mother. I wasn't having any of this, not *now*, not in a burning building. For a moment he looked taken a back, and just as I thought he was running with me, fire crept up from below, and a red hot hand seized his ankle.

"Adam!" I yelled. His hand reached for me as he was dragged downwards into the sea of fire, and engulfed in flame. "No!" I ran forwards like I could jump into the flames as though they were the ocean, but Dr. Dangerous scooped me up, without a care for The Captain. I tore at his clothes, trying to fight him, I don't even know how he held me in the mess of a dress I wore. I saw him frown behind his mask as he threw me over his shoulder and for the first time that night I screamed and cried. I banged my fists against his back, but still, he ignored me. Something sprung from his belt and embedded itself in the building opposite. He gripped me as tight as he could and I screamed at the top of my lungs as we jumped from the shattered seventh story window. I slipped from my place over his shoulder, and threw my arms around his neck. I hated the familiarity, but in the end it saved my life. A red blur crashed into the window just as we swung away.

Dr. Dangerous dropped me in the midst of a deserted street where no one could see. The only light around us came from an orange street lamp, and its reflection in the rain. My dress was quickly soaked through, and my body was cold. I shivered and all he did was look me up and down several times over.

"A thank you?" he suggested.

"Never. You left him."

"He'll be fine. I know The Captain," he said and smiled as though he hadn't carried me away unconscious, or left a bomb in a building. He smiled like it was every day banter.

"Stay, away from me!" I yelled.

"You look very nice in that dress," he told me.

"It's a puffy mess, and I'm soaked from head to toe." I growled and he laughed like we were old friends. "It's not funny."

"It's a *little* bit funny." He smiled.

As I turned to leave, his hand caught my wrist. "Friday…" His gaze changed and a look of something like an iron will flicked across his eyes. He glanced down at the pavement and loosened his grip. "Be careful."

"What's that supposed to mean?" he shook his head at me, and took a few steps back. "Don't leave, please! Tell me what you mean!"

"I can't."

This time, I grabbed him, my grip unshakeable. "Tell me. You work for someone, who is it?"

"I can't tell you. Just be careful," he said.

"It's the gold syringes isn't it? Something's going on, tell me! Who's making you do this?" I asked.

"No one's making me do this," he said, and yanked his arm away. "He's not my boss, but he will be yours."

He loomed over me, reminding me just how small I was. I pulled myself up to my full height and looked him in the eye. "Help me," I pleaded.

"No," his hand twitched at his side, the beginnings of a word of the edge of his lips, but his fist clenched, and the word became "like I said, be careful."

"Why do you care?" I asked him, wanting to hear the answer.

"Because I care about you," he replied.

"Well I care about someone else," I said quickly, like it was some sort of witty comeback rather than an awkward confession. He scoffed and turned his head.

"Yeah I know, the blond, your handler, right? The one on fire?"

"No!" I told him, "why would you think that?"

"Then who?" he asked, leaning down, the edge of his voice turning up. "Who is it?" He didn't believe me.

"His name's Ashley," I said and a playful smile flashed across his face as he pulled himself up to his full, impressive height. "He's one of my team mates," I explained.

"Boyfriend?"

"He hates me," I said, and the silence stung.

"Be careful, Fitz," it sounded like a goodbye. I ran off down the street to the crowd of people being tended by the police and paramedics. Veronica rushed over and pulled me in. It wasn't a hug, it was more like protection. The wail of sirens and whirring city lights was overwhelming.

"Where's The Captain?" Veronica whispered and I shook my head trying to hold back my tears.

"What happened in there?" she asked, "tell me!"

"I can't, not now," I said realizing I sounded lame. She tried to cover up her glare as she backed away but then a red figure emerged from the flames accompanied by someone clad in green. Lisa!

Lisa and Barney walked out of the flames, their faces and skin covered by their super skeletons. Captain Fantastic was with them. The skin on his back was red and covered in blisters, but he was alive. Veronica's arms went weak, and I collapsed to my knees. David found me, and pulled me into a hug.

"Friday! You're okay!" David exclaimed.

"What about you?" I asked, searching him with my eyes, as though I'd find a burn or cut on him.

"I'm fine, I was worried about you, I should have done something." I pulled him into a hug of my own. They loaded The Captain into an ambulance and Lisa climbed in with him. Barney stepped back reluctantly, Lisa waving him away.

"Barney!" I yelled and he jogged over to pull me into a hug.

"From Lisa," he said.

"Is The Captain okay?" I asked.

"Fine," he said, "a gadget he started carrying after

the first reports of The Figure saved him until we got there."

"Thank you Barney!" I said as I burst into tears.

He looked slightly embarrassed. "Thank Lisa," he said, "she's the one who decided to come."

Veronica slapped Barney on the back, and put away the phone she'd been using to call someone about the news. "Do you kids need a ride to the hospital? I'm going to see The Captain."

"Yes!" I answered quickly.

A rare smile crossed her face, "all right let's go. Barney?"

"I have to get home," Barney told us, "Lisa's home that is, I said I'd see to her kids."

Veronica nodded and waved David over as Barney left. Her car looked shiny and very expensive. David stopped me half way there.

"Friday I have something to tell you." David swallowed.

Veronica was already shouting from her car. "Come on kids!"

"Friday, *please,*" said David, " after everything that happened you should know about Aya and me. You know how everyone thinks we're a couple? It's a lie." He licked his lips, and re-positioned himself, thinking about his next words carefully. "All that stuff I say about her in the papers, about her being my girlfriend, it's crap. The producers tell me to say it, they say it makes me seem more manly, more relatable."

"So," I said slowly, trying to work out what he was saying, "why do you do it if you're just friends? I don't understand."

"Friday, I'm gay." He blurted.

"You're what?" I blinked. He slapped his hand over my mouth, and drew me closer the car.

"They brought me into a meeting before my debut, and told me they wanted me to start something with Aya, that people would want a new couple. And they just kept talking, and talking, and telling me how to act. I panicked."

"Why are you telling me this now?" I asked.

"Because after this, I realize you're one of the few friends I have, you should know who I am," David said. "I love Aya, she's great, she's my best friend."

"Just not your *girl* friend?"

"Are you kids coming or not?" yelled Veronica sounding like she was moments from losing it. I saw her piercing gaze from the corner of my eye as she stormed forwards. "Hey, hey you! Yeah, you!" she boomed, nearly shoving David to the pavement as she drove the edge of her phone into my collar bone like a ruler. "What the hell did you think you were doing?"

My back went rigid, and my shoulders pushed back. "I'm sorry, what?"

"Don't give me that crap! You were in there with The Captain, and you can't even be bothered to tell anyone what happened? What do we pay you for? Tell me!"

My fists clenched but Veronica didn't pull the edge of her phone from the hollow of my throat. "You pay me to be a hero," I stammered.

"Bullshit!" yelled Veronica. David didn't have a word to say, not because he didn't care, but because I could tell he'd heard all this before. "You are a piece of merchandise. You were in a burning building with the most famous superhero that's ever lived, and you don't have a story for me? Bullshit! There's something you're not telling me." She waited, still refusing to retract her phone like it was a gun to my head. I wasn't one to be bullied, so much so that my refusal to be told what to do had turned into many a fist fight.

"You're right," I said and she nodded, impatient to hear more. "There is something I'm not telling you, and I'm not *ever* going to tell you."

"You little," she pushed the phone further, I could feel it pushing against my wind pipe. "If you don't tell me, I'll kick you off this team, and you go back to zero, *nothing*."

I was fine with being zero, being nothing. I sure as hell wasn't going to sell out The Captain for some lunch boxes with my face on them. That wasn't a hard choice.

"You don't control me," I told her.

She pushed away, baring her teeth, and just as she reached her army of P.A.'s, she turned. "You're off the team Fitz, go back to blue."

I ran away before anyone could stop me.

———

The Captain sat up in his hospital bed, mostly unscathed save for a few scratches and blisters here and there. His wife Katherine and Black Magic had already been to see him as had Veronica and a couple of his friends. After a few hours it was finally my turn.

He looked up at me and smiled before patting the seat of the chair pulled next to the bed. "More questions that need to be answered?" he asked.

"I got kicked off the team." I told him, blurting it out like a meal that wouldn't stay down.

"I'm sorry, Friday, why?" he asked, moving forwards until he was stopped by the pain.

"Veronica wanted to know what happened in there," I said, studying my shoes.

"And you didn't tell her? Friday, don't lose your place on the team for me-"

"Much as I appreciate the sentiment," I told him, "I did it because she threatened me. I don't work with bullies." The Captain sat back with a small smile, as though he understood my thinking perfectly. I crossed my legs, and sucked in a breath. "So, you lost your powers?"

"I didn't *lose* my powers, Friday, I grew out of them. Some people lose their powers like I did and I suppose I should have retired, but-"

"You mean, you… just, don't have them anymore?" I asked.

"People get older. Things change. It happens. Normally heroes don't work for long enough for people to see their powers decline, but some do. I thought maybe it was coming, but I wanted a successor in place before it happened."

"That's why you started the mentor program, right?" at least that made sense.

"That's right. Can you pass my reading glasses?" I passed over his small silver glasses, being sure not to touch the lenses. "Ah, that's better," he said readjusting them on his nose. "I should have retired a while ago, but I didn't. I can't, not until I find someone to take my place."

"You're gonna get yourself killed, Captain," I told him.

"Then I better find someone soon," he chuckled.

"So am I gonna lose my powers someday?"

"Not necessarily, some find it happens in their forties, some don't," The Captain explained. "Some powers don't decline, they simply change with time."

I shook my head, and slammed my hands down on my lap. "What about Jake? The Figure? I know I don't have any proof, but I swear I found a syringe, and I think people are using them for something!"

"A gold syringe?" The Captain asked and when I nodded he pointed to his jacket where it hung on the coat rack. "There should be a piece of paper in my pocket."

Unfolding the paper, I found a sketch of the same gold syringe I'd found a few months earlier. "This is it. This is what I found," I told him.

"Good. I'm not *entirely* sure what it is, but I think it's something people are using to induce superpowers." His voice was heavy with dread as he spoke.

"What? How?"

"Ten years ago now, I felt the faintest flicker of my powers retiring, so with my friends and fellow heroes, we started to work on a serum, a vaccine if you will, something to stop our powers from declining."

"What happened?"

"It didn't work. We couldn't find a way to save our powers, all it did was-" he broke off as thought unsure of what to say. "Even today, I'm not sure what it did. Friday, you need to understand. Our powers aren't an add on, they're not even a part of us, they *are* us, there's part of our soul in them. The artificial powers from the drug we developed, they're something different; violent, wild, alien and uncontrollable."

"And you think that's what's in the syringe I found?"

"I think some superheroes have been using enhancing drugs," said the captain. "Someone's used the research and created a different drug, one that creates powers where there were none."

"But that's a good thing isn't it?" I asked, unsure.

"If they had figured out how to make someone's powers more long lived, maybe," he explained, "but I think they discovered a way to create *violent* artificial powers. Like those of your friend, Jake."

"There are people running around with fake super powers more powerful than the real kind?"

"It's not that the power's are 'fake', Friday," he told me as he handed the picture back, "it's that powers don't make a hero."

"Why didn't you tell me all of this before?" I asked.

Had it been anyone else, I'd have shouted, but The Captain took my shoulder in an effort to be reassuring.

"I couldn't tell you because you weren't my apprentice."

My heart skipped a beat. "Weren't, as in past tense?"

"Friday, you can learn a lot from Lisa, taking you away from her would be the dumbest thing I could do, but there's no rule that says you can't have two mentors."

I stared at him for a moment, not sure that I understood. "But my power's the worst!"

"It's not your power that matters," he said with slight smile.

"You're just saying that."

"I don't have *any* powers anymore. Doesn't stop me from being a superhero." He pushed himself up, and winced from the effort. "It's not about powers and costumes, it's about inspiring other people to be heroes themselves."

"You're *my* hero Captain." I told him. His smile was so bright, my inner child screamed.

The Captain's eyes squinted at the TV hooked in the corner of the ceiling and he fumbled for the remote like a man looking blindly for his glasses. I reached for it myself, and un-muted the news just in time.

Coach Flat and several other superheroes stood on a stage with cameras flashing as usual. A press conference, only the room was silent.

"Only a few hours ago our Captain was in a terrible accident. I'm told he will make a full recovery, but not for some considerable time. Some of you may be wondering, why a superhero needs a hospital; the truth is our Captain has given us his best years. He is simply too old to continue. Following the latest events in Icon City, he has made the decision to retire."

"They can't do this to me! Frank can't do this!" said The Captain as he lurched from his bed. On screen the crowd of reporters yelled for more information.

"Captain you're going to hurt yourself," I said and pushed The Captain back down.

He groaned, but it wasn't all pain. "I'm not The Captain anymore, didn't you hear?"

"We'll worry about that later," I told him, "right now we need to worry about you."

"No! Friday you don't understand, he-" Coach Flat began to speak again and this time there was someone else on stage with him. Jake stepped forward dragging three men behind him.

"This is my new apprentice," Coach Flat announced, "you may know him, as The Figure In The Flames."

"Call me Hellfire." Jake said and briefly displayed his fire while Coach Flat grabbed one of the men Jake had dragged on stage.

"With The Captain's retirement, I will become the acting head of the Hero Channel, and as you can see, my apprentice is already killing it at as a superhero." Coach Flat gripped the back of the man's head showing his face to everyone. He was a notorious thief but had never been caught; the man was beaten bloody, his eye black, his jaw askew. Tears were running down his face.

The Captain grimaced at the sight and I covered my mouth. It was like seeing a prisoner of war brought on TV to demand a ransom. I had never seen anything like it before, all I could do was try not to vomit. "That's why he can't be in charge," said The Captain in a quiet voice.

"He can't do that, can he? They won't let him!" I looked over to The Captain, hoping to see him agree, hoping he'd tell me what to do, but he said nothing. I tore out of the room into the corridor and grabbing Veronica by the collar, I yelled, "You can't let that man be in charge!" I had meant to sound intimidating, but it came off like a child trying to reach something in an adult's hand. Veronica sighed and rolled her eyes as she scrolled on her phone.

"Listen to me!" I demanded, "he's beaten those men within an inch of their lives! You can't let him do that!"

"Why not?" she asked, turning her phone round. The screen displayed a graph with a line lurching upwards by the second. The line was labelled 'viewers'. "The public sure seems to like it, so I'm gonna keep him, makes good television."

"You can't," I said

"I can, and I will," Veronica insisted. "If I have my way The Captain will never run the hero channel ever again. He's boring."

I stared at her, confused and scared. The Captain had to know what to do. I burst back into his room and he looked at me as though he'd heard the whole conversation. "There has to be something we can do Adam, something!"

On that point we were agreed, "You have to stop him, Friday," The Captain said, but when I asked him what to do, he had no answer. "I don't know, I don't know!" he said, as he grabbed my hand and pulled me down, eyes wide with fear. "Promise me, whatever you do-"

"Captain? Can we come in?" It was a voice I'd never heard before.

"They've come for me," said The Captain, "you have to go."

"What? Who's come for you?" for a moment I had no idea what he was talking about, but then I realized, the hallway was silent.

"Run!" The Captain pushed me as much as he could from the hospital bed, and I grabbed the window sill, ready to jump out.

"Captain? We'd like to come in," the unknown voice repeated.

"Just a minute," The Captain replied, waving me away.

"I don't want to leave you," I told him.

"They won't kill me, they need me, but Friday, promise me you won't hurt him, Frank I mean, or the Doctor."

I pushed away the anger and the fear and focussed on the look in his eyes; a look of life-long regret, and nodded. "Promise."

"Good. Now, run Friday, run!" The Captain cried.

The door collapsed with a bang and I pushed myself from the window, only catching a glimpse as the lawyers and superheroes that worked for Coach Flat rushed The Captain. Every one of the Heroes had a gun in their hands. They weren't taking any chances.

Falling to the grass outside was like jumping off the swing as a kid, I knew the fall wouldn't kill me, but it could definitely hurt. I did my best to land with both feet, and roll. My back ached as I landed on the ground, I hadn't done a roly poly in years. I scrambled into the bushes just as the men above looked out the window. My ankle ached, but it wasn't broken. I crawled through the bushes, the skirt of my dress scraping along the branches until I heard a voice.

"Friday?" a hand reached into the bushes and pulled me out. Ashely patted down my hair, and pulled a branch out as he sighed. "What are you doing out here, Fitz?"

"The Captain! And Coach Flat, he-" Ashley gulped. "-he's the principal now, and he beat some guys up, and The Captain's in danger!"

"Okay, okay," he put his hands on my shoulders, not sure of what to think until he heard the voices coming round he corner.

"Find the girl."

Ashley grabbed my hand and started to run but his legs were so much longer, I couldn't keep up so he picked me up and kept running towards the car park.

"Put me down!" I demanded.

"Don't shout," once hidden, he set me down, and pulled me towards an old rusted car. "Get in."

"Where are we going?" I asked.

"School. Obviously," he told me.

"I can't go back there," I said grabbing the front of

his shirt. He was dressed like he'd been working at Ang's all day, his hair half up, and clad in an old T-shirt. He stopped to look at me for a second, still stuck in my stupid dress, and then looked down at my hand, balling up his shirt just above the waist of his trousers. He sucked in a deep breath, and nodded.

"We'll go to my place, or, rather my Nana's place." I was about to run to the other side of the drivers seat, until he stopped me. "No, stay in the back, keep your head down."

Ashley's car was rusted, but it was no newly bought junker, it had been passed down, still going strong. By the time I thought to ask how long it would take, we were there. Ashley pulled up, opened the door, and the cold air made me curl up against the worn leather seats.

"Xiao-Ley?" called a weathered, shaking voice.

"Nana! Get back inside! It's cold out here," Ashley replied.

"What are you doing here?" his grandmother asked. "It's too late. Go home, you will get in trouble."

"Nana no." the door creaked and the old woman peered down at me, and then back up at her grandson.

"Friday?"

"I'm sorry, Nana." Ashley explained, "She needed somewhere to stay. The school's a bit out of whack right now."

His grandmother tutted, and prodded my cheeks. "Her pretty face is all black and blue." It was an exaggeration, I had a small bruise on the side of my face from Short Fuse, nothing serious. She picked up my fingers, and tutted again. "Why is she wearing such an expensive dress?"

"She had to go to a party," Ashley explained.

"Can she speak for herself?" asked his grandmother with a shake of her head.

"Yes Nana." Ashley sighed.

"Then let her. Why are you wearing a dress?" she asked looking back at me.

"I didn't have time to change…" I said.

"And why are you helping her?" she asked Ashley, slowly straightening her back as though it hurt to lean over.

"Because she's my friend." He pressed out between pressed lips.

His grandmother looked me up and down, lingering a second too long on my chest. She looked like she wanted to laugh as she walked away. "Well, bring her in then."

Ashley let out a heavy sigh, and hoisted me into his arms, as his grandmother nodded in approval. He was warm, and big. The heat from from his body made me feel like a cat, lying in the sun. He moved quickly up the stairs from the restaurant and into the apartment on top. His grandmother's home was decorated the way an old woman *would* decorate her home, with history, pictures, and plenty of furniture from other homes she couldn't bare to part with.

"You take her up and tuck her in," she instructed.

"Yes, Nana."

"Don't worry, she'll be fine in no time." The comment was directed at Ashley rather than me. She tutted again before wandering down one of the narrow hallways. Ashley pushed in the closest door and I caught my first glimpse of his bedroom.

Small and simple, tidy, and old. He hadn't slept there in a while. His grandmother must have been devastated when he moved out. He set me down on his bed and turned on the bedside lamp as I sat up.

"I'll get you some fresh clothes." he said as he rummaged about in his drawers. "Trouble is, I don't have any girls clothes, and I think Nana's would probably look and smell pretty weird." He pulled out what looked like one of the many shirts he used when working downstairs at Ang's, and handed me a pair of boxer shorts he claimed he'd never worn. I nodded and hurried into the bathroom to change. It felt nice not to be soaked from the rain, or wearing a tight dress, but it was only once I put on one of his T-shirts I realized I didn't have a bra.

"You okay in there?" He asked.

"I'm fine!" I hated not wearing a bra, it was so frustrating, sometimes I had to hold the girls in place while I jogged upstairs. I turned to the mirror just to gauge how bad it was, and nearly considered killing myself.

"Are you sure you're alright?" he yelled.

I sighed, pulled on the shorts, and wrapped my arms around my chest in a way I hoped looked natural before coming out.

"Sit down-" he said, "-you can stay here tonight." he looked around the room the same way he had the night he'd made me soup, like he was checking the place for weakness. I nodded sheepishly, and sat on the side of his bed, with my arms still crossed.

"How are you feeling?" he asked and leaned down to take my temperature.

"I'll be fine." in truth, my face stung, but nothing worse. "You've called me Friday twice now." I said biting back a smile.

"So?" he asked, inspecting every inch of my face to make sure there was nothing worse.

"So, you always call me Fitz." I told him.

"Do I?" He scratched his chin. "Huh." his grandmother hobbled up the stairs with a tube of something green, handed it to her grandson, and stood by the door.

"Get well soon." she said as she closed the door behind her, and gave a wink to Ashley.

"What does the wink mean?" I asked.

"Nothing. Ignore her." He said and to my surprise, pushed me down on the bed and pulled the sheets over me.

"I'm not cold," I told him.

"No, but if I put the sheets over you, you can stop covering your chest in a way you think I won't notice." My face flared red as I pulled the sheet a little further up. "Now, don't move," he said. "I'm gonna rub this on your bruise."

"It's not that bad, I don't need tube goop," I protested and tried to sit up, but he pushed me back down.

"Tube goop?" he smiled, trying not to laugh, and continued regardless of my protests. It wasn't exactly soothing, but at least it didn't sting. He rubbed it in carefully and thoroughly before looking at me again. "Does it hurt?"

"Not because of anything you're doing," I replied.

"What about your legs? You jumped out a window."

"They're fine." I mumbled.

"Can I look?" he asked and once again, I told him not to bother. "Friday,"

"Don't Friday me, you never call me that."

"Well maybe I should," he replied, "now let me look."

"No." I said jolting back.

"Friday, please," he said, insisting.

"Why are you helping me!? You don't even like me!" I yelled.

"Are you angry at me?" he asked.

"Yes! Why are you doing this!? Stop taking care of me!" The anger I felt was still there, forming a wall that kept the sadness from becoming overwhelming, only the wall wasn't strong, the anger faded and I cried.

"Friday?" He whispered.

I cried like I should have when my mother died, when I was separated from my father and sister and when I realized my childhood was over. My vision clouded with tears, blurring each color into the next. I crawled over to where Ashley knelt and wrapped my arms around him. I gave no thought to whether or not he would mind, and sobbed my heart out onto his shirt.

"Friday?" It was the most concern I'd ever heard in his voice, and it prompted a word salad of emotions.

"I'm so tired!" I told him.

"What are you talking about?" He asked as his hand came round to rest on my back.

"No one ever lets me be the goofy one!" I said. "No one ever lets me be the screw up. I know you don't like me, but you cooked for me, you went looking for me, you carried me to bed and tucked me in! You're putting weird ointment on my face!" That was all I could say before I collapsed into an ugly, wailing heap. Ashley didn't say a word, he just picked me up, and sat with me on his bed. It was like every inch of awkward had melted away, turned into warmth and comfort. He closed his eyes and rocked me back and forth like my tears were the rhythm of a song.

Once the tears had cleared, he stopped, and we just sat, I'm not sure for how long, long enough for me to feel normal again and for the clock to say two a.m. He leaned into the embrace, his mouth slipping down to rest over my ear as he said. "Idiot."

"That's me." I confessed.

He dropped a kiss onto my cheek that left me more than a little bit shocked. "What was that for?" I asked, looking up.

"For being so sweet." His smile was mind numbing, so beautiful. Like it was something he did every day and I just hadn't noticed.

"I'm not sweet," I protested, "I'm angry and bitter."

It was like his eyes clouded over, the glare of the lamp pressing up against his glasses as he leaned down. It wasn't so much a kiss, he pulled my bottom lip in-between his like he was licking the foam left over from a hot drink. His eyes came into focus behind his glasses as he pulled back, and my pulse quickened.

It was like he could flip a switch to go from the plain gangly boy behind Captain Fantastic to sinfully attractive. Even though his features stayed the same, he'd grown more and more handsome each time I saw him. He chuckled, but not the way I'd heard him do it before, not when talking to fans or producers, this was completely different, it was a deep, satisfied laugh. "You scream, shout, and condescend. Risk you life for a toy, and run into buildings moments away from blowing up..."

Something flicked across his face, something painful. Then there was only hard resolve in his eyes. He pushed me back onto the bed and dropped down onto all fours above me, like a cat carefully walking along a narrow fence. I froze, wondering. Did this mean he liked me the same way I liked him?

He drew closer until I could feel his breath against my lips. I forgot about everything, all I wanted was that kiss.

"And yet," he continued, "the moment I touch you,"

Like he could read my thoughts, his lips stopped hovering above mine and moved lower. He tasted the skin on my neck. As a gasp left my lips, he sighed against my skin, as though he'd been waiting.

"Ashley." I said in a sharp intake of air.

He left hot kisses up my neck as he held onto me, his fingers moving up to my hairline. My hands gripped his shirt, I had to fight to keep my common sense. He pushed closer, like he was on auto pilot, only feeling and wanting, never thinking too long. His lips came down on mine, and I was lost completely. There was no sense of urgency in the way he kissed me, like he wanted to savor every second, like he'd planned it in advance. His hand lifted me up, and stroked the deep curve in the small of my back.

He hissed into his kiss as he dragged me closer down the bed. I grabbed a hold of the back of his shirt as though I needed it to anchor me. I wanted to taste him, his skin was so warm, I couldn't help but touch.

He groaned against me as my hand slid up his back. He pushed his body closer to mine, like everything depended on how close we could get. He pulled at the back of my shirt, my skin still damp from the rain, his hand moving lower while mine searched for every inch of his bare skin. I needed him closer, I needed-

"Are you kids okay in there?"

My hand stopped and Ashley pulled back. My face had turned a bright cherry red. He looked utterly disheveled, his usually organized hair stuck up in tufts, his shirt was pulled up half way and his lips were bright red.

"Yeah, yes!" he replied, "we're fine, Nana."

His grandmother gave a slow sound of approval from outside, as though she'd known exactly what we were doing. He looked down at me like I was something that had to be committed to memory, and I let him.

"I should go. Let you get some rest, but, I was wondering, could I sleep here? On the sofa?"

His eyes searched mine, I didn't want him to leave, I wanted him to stay and hold me a while longer, but the atmosphere in the room came with a sense of dread that was reflected on his face. I couldn't say no, I felt I'd need him next to me in the morning.

"Okay."

He nodded and sat back up at the edge of the bed. Pulling down his shirt he smoothed his hair before turning round again. With a sigh very different from the one from moments ago, he pushed off, placing pillows and cushions on his small sofa.

"Get some sleep," he said and leaning down, he pulled the sheets around me. This was the serious, studious Ashley; he'd locked away the other guy for now. Maybe now I could stop thinking about Dr. Dangerous.

———

The morning sun was heavy, there was a weight on my back. I made to stretch my arms, only to find them held in place by Ashley's. He should have been on the sofa, but had clearly decided otherwise during the night. His eyes opened. He seemed so much more at ease as he woke, compared to the rest of the day.

"Good morning," he said with a yawn.

"So, you decided to switch from the sofa to the bed?" I asked.

"What?" he made to sit up, at which point I realized I was directly on top of him. My arms wrapped around him. He fell back down, but didn't drop his arms.

"What do you mean?" he replied, "you asked me to."

"Asked you to get into bed with me?" I laughed as though the thought was utterly impossible, though I had considered it.

"Yes, you did, at-" he glanced at the clock, "-four in the morning. You started tossing and turning, and sat up to tell me you-" he cleared his throat as though there was something he'd rather not say. "-the point is, you asked me to."

"Okay." I said, though I remembered no such thing.

"You want pancakes for breakfast?" he asked.

"Can I?" I pushed myself up onto all fours, and climbed off him in a way I hoped wasn't awkward. He bolted into his bathroom without so much as a word, leaving me on the bed feeling slightly confused.

For a few hours I'd been able to forget about Coach Flat and what he was doing to Hero High, but now it was time to spring into action, whatever that action was. I certainly wasn't going to decide before breakfast, not because breakfast was more important than the Captain, but because my mother always told me you need to take care of yourself before you can take care of anyone else, and as the days went by, I was beginning to understand what she meant. I turned to pop my head in the kitchen and catch a glimpse of Ashley making breakfast like he considered it a work of art.

"Where's your grandmother?" I asked.

"Girls brunch," he told me.

"By herself? You don't go with her?"

"Trust me, I've tried," Ashley said, "but she's not the kind of woman who wants her grandson following her around ready to catch her."

"She was very nice to me, I just wanted to say thank you."

"You don't have to," said Ashley, who was engrossed in his pancake making. "Just make yourself at home, and I won't be long with the pancakes."

I nodded and looked around the rest of the house. His grandmother kept some fine china and pottery on display. Hanging near the front door was an old, tattered picture of Ang's showing a much younger version of Ashley's grandmother with a woman and a man. The woman was clearly her daughter, she shared the same complexion and had long black hair. The man though, wasn't her son. He was unreasonably tall, wore glasses and had an arm round the young woman. He also had a baby in his arms; could that be Ashley? They were clearly a family.

What had happened to his father and mother? Why did he live with his grandmother before going to Hero High? I peered at the picture taking in every detail. Something about the man looked very familiar. My brow creased in frustration, there was something I wasn't getting, I could feel it in my bones. I walked around a bit more, and turned down a narrow corridor.

Another picture of Ashley's family sat on a book-case. The man and woman were older, the man looked less like Ashley and more like- No.

I looked down. The carpet was worn to the left of the bookcase. Was there something behind it? My hand reached out for the picture frame and tried to pull it closer. It seemed like it was stuck.

"Friday, breakfast's ready!" Ashley sang from the kitchen.

I tugged at the photo and just as I released it something clicked in the wall. The bookcase slowly moved to the side, dragging along the worn carpet. My heart felt heavy with dread.

"Friday!?"

I gulped at the sight of the hidden flight of stairs. For a moment I stood still, checked over my shoulder, and leapt down the stairs before he could come looking and stop me. The lights in the room below sprung into life one bulb at a time; in front of me was Dr. Dangerous' suit, his mask, his gadgets, and lace front blonde wig.

Walls of gadgets were carefully labeled, the place was like a bunker, with food, water, clothes, and a bed to sleep in. The last of the lights flickered on; the room was a lot bigger than I'd thought, it spanned the whole floor plan of the house. My brain cut out, my muscles locked. The man in the picture was the *original* Dr. Dangerous. Ashley was the *new* one.

I had to get out! I jerked forward, hoping Ashley, or

Dr. Dangerous was still happily cooking me breakfast, but it was too late.

His footsteps on the stairs were like the beat of my own heart. First the team, then the school, and now *him*. Ashley's gaze was icy cold, his knuckles white and his fingers wound tight round his spatula. "You just *had* to look." I couldn't breath, I couldn't think. This *couldn't* be Ashley. He shook his head. "I *would* say curiosity killed the cat, but I always saw you as more of an obnoxiously cute border collie."

"You're his son!" I yelled, "you're the one that tried to blow the buildings up! You!"

He pursed his lips, always inching closer. "Friday I can explain, the bomb was *never* going to go off, if Jake had just shown up on time-" he said waving his spatula around.

"You're working with Jake?" I needed time, my mind was whirling, it didn't make sense.

"Where else do you think he got his powers? He stole the gold syringe you left under the floorboard."

"How did you-" the answer was clear from what he'd already said.

"Jake knew you had it, he was with you when you found it. Friday please, let's talk about this!" he said, moving closer.

"Then who are you working for?" I asked, backing away.

"Friday-"

"And on the skyscraper!"

"You've got to understand," said Ashley, "please, Jake just wanted me to talk to you."

"No," I said, shaking my head, "this can't be right. You're working with Jake?"

He cringed, and then nodded. "Friday, please understand."

"No!" I yelled.

"Are you really telling me you had no idea?" he bit his lower lip, and shook his head like he would regret what he was about to say. "You've kissed me twice now, are you really going to tell me you had no idea we were the same?"

A wave of shame hit me. I thought I'd been steering clear of the bad guy, and simply waiting for the good one. Ashley started towards me slowly as I moved back towards his wall of gadgets. I probably *did* know, somewhere in the back of my mind, I mean.

I must have seemed like an idiot, I stood in the rain and told him I wasn't interested because I had a crush on the *other* him.

Oh God, he must have been laughing at me the whole time. He reached out for me.

"Please Friday hear me out, my dad was *killed* by Captain Fantastic."

My back hit the pegs holding the gadgets.

"My mother, and I, we can't let this go." The gap between us had closed, his looming form was over me once again, forcing me to realize just how small I was. But still, it didn't matter, you can't learn how to fight if you don't get knocked down, and I'd been knocked down plenty of times before. I could get out of this. Think Friday, think.

I blinked, stopping everything for a moment. There was a mirror on the opposite wall. If I could figure out where he kept the stunner he'd used on me before, I could get out. I spotted it in the mirror, an inch to my right, and taking a deep breath, I let the world start again.

I lunged for the stunner, ready to plunge it into his shoulder, but he caught my wrist, the nib of the device just a nanometer from his skin. Our eyes locked, and our jaws clenched in a show of sheer strength. His smug smile had gone, replaced by concentration. I did the best I could to stop him from pushing the gadget away, but my muscles were going to wear out any second. There was no getting round it, as much as I liked to fool myself I couldn't match his strength. I had to find another way.

Like the over angry butt-head I was, I stamped on his toes and he flinched just enough for me to push him to the ground and make a run for it.

"I don't want to hurt you!" he shouted, "Friday!"

"Agreed! I don't want you to hurt me either!" I said bolting up the stairs.

"The Captain killed my dad!" Ashley yelled in an unsteady voice, like he was shouting anything he could think of. "Someone has to pay for my family's grief! Friday!" He made a grab for the back of my shirt and I avoided his hand as I bounded up the stairs. "The Captain has to pay!"

I turned round at the top as he stomped on up. "He does, you idiot. Every day of his life. Can't you see it in his eyes?" I stuck to my ground as he slid the bookcase closed.

"Hell no. You're just seeing something that's not there because you've got a schoolgirl crush on him!"

"That's not true!" I insisted, "It's there Ashley, I promise you. What exactly do you think punishing The Captain is going to solve?"

For a moment he paused and I expected some speech about revenge. Instead he simply said, "My mother needs peace." He looked at me like he didn't have room for anything else, like there just wasn't enough in him to keep thinking. He was pleading with me to stop, to just let him be.

"This superpower serum is just going to make things worse!" I told him, "You can't do these things, please-" he reached out his hand as though to catch something behind me, but it was too late. My body rattled and shook with electricity as I collapsed on the floor. Looking up I saw two heroes with hand guns and behind them, Coach Flat and Jake. The Coach patted Jake in congratulation before stepping closer to brush a strand of hair off my face and look down at me properly.

"T.G.I.F."

———

WE SINK

I was inside the Super Structure, the large windows letting in the setting sun.

"Oh look, she's awake," said Coach Flat.

"Do you have to keep her tied up, Frank?" my eyes focused on Coach Flat and Veronica.

"You know she's gonna stop us if we let her go," said the Coach.

"What happened to "convincing" her?" asked Veronica.

"Ask Romeo," the Coach replied and they turned to look down at Ashley, bound, gagged and fully dressed as Dr. Dangerous.

My body jumped; I tried to stand up, only to find I was bound to a metal pillar.

"What did you do to him?" I demanded.

Veronica sighed, and crouched down beside me. "Relax, we're just gonna put on a fight and get Frank here properly accepted as the new principal."

"What do you mean a fight?" I asked.

Jake's boot pounded the side of my head, then he pulled back my hair making the roots sting with pain. "We're gonna kill your boyfriend," he said as he gave my head a painful jerk and wandered back to Coach Flat.

"Now now, Jakey poo," started Coach Flat, "we're not going to kill him, we're going to enact justice."

Only then did I see people shuffling around in the back, their expressions doubtful as they put a set together, piece by piece. Veronica's look was similarly uncertain, she studied the floor.

"Where's The Captain?" I asked.

"In hospital," Coach Flat replied, "where he'll stay until a few weeks from now when he'll tragically pass away from the severity of his burns." He smiled.

"What could you possibly get out of killing Ashley?" I demanded.

"Oh so he's Ashley now? Did he tell you, or did you find out?" the Coach asked.

"I found out." I swallowed.

"Typical. The Captain killed the Dr., and everyone loved him for it. Killing him made Adam the man he is today; the icon we know as Captain Fantastic. Before that, he was just another superhero."

"So what? You're gonna kill the new Dr. Dangerous and hope for the same result?" I scoffed.

Veronica stepped forward, her back was straight and her resolve clear.

"We *will* get the same result, because we'll have the same conditions. The Dr. will take you hostage, and then Frank will swoop in and save the day," she said.

"You fake piece of shit!" I yelled and the technicians stopped in their tracks.

"Keep going!" screamed Coach Flat, and they all jerked back into action. I'd never heard Coach Flat sound so determined.

"What makes you so sure you can beat Ashley in a fight?" I asked and Coach Flat's eyes went wide. It was something he hadn't even considered, he always won.

He picked up a pen from a stage hand, and looked down at me.

"Baby, I'm the king!" he smiled, and the pen in his hand went flat along with the rest of his fingers. Without any warning he thrust forwards, the pen sank into my pillar barely an inch above my head and came straight out the other side taking a five inch long chunk of metal with it.

I caught my breath, and tried to sit up as best I

could. "Baby, I'm the sharpest, flattest, most unkillable man in the world," said Coach Flat, "there ain't nobody can beat me in a fight."

"You sure about that? Isn't that what this syringe is about," I asked, "you being scared of losing?"

Coach Flat squinted and we held each other's gaze for a good few moments. "You know what?" he said, "you're right!" he turned to Jake, "put lover boy in the cozy box we made for him."

Jake nodded and ran off while Veronica reached for the Coach's shoulder. He looked at her hand as though it was burning a hole though the fabric.

"What are you doing? What box?" she asked. He threw her hand off and took a few steps towards Ashley.

"I made a back-up plan. Don't worry, Veronica, I already cleared it with your boss."

"What plan? I need to know!" Veronica demanded.

When he turned, the Coach's smile seemed larger than was natural. "We're going to drown him in the river," he told us, "on live TV."

Veronica stumbled back.

"No." Her hand clasped her mouth. "You can't do that. It's too graphic!" She cried. "The viewers won't stand for it."

"Like I said," the Coach told her, "your lovely little

boss already approved it. Go ahead. Call him." Veronica pulled out her phone. A minute of hushed conversation.

Her face fell.

Her boss… Ord.

"Told you," said the Coach, "boys, take her away."

I struggled against my restraints, but they were so tight I already had burns. The heroes, none I recognized and hand guns advanced on Veronica, pulling her away like a common criminal.

"You can't do this!" she protested, "they'll hate you! He's just a boy!"

The last glimpse I had of Veronica was as she was dragged out the door. A shiver ran down my spine and then I realized something. "They'll never see you the same way," I told the Coach, "you can't *be* him."

Coach Flat frowned and pulled up a chair. "And why's that Fifth Day Of The Week?"

"Because you're a coward. I just realized why he's special and you're not. The Captain's brave. He lost his powers years ago, and he hasn't changed." the Coach's frown deepened, and his gaze grew sharper, as though he was willing me to catch fire. "A cowardly man would have given up," I continued, "he would have run away the moment he didn't have the upper hand. But he didn't. That's the difference between you and The Captain."

"Shut up," said the Coach.

"You're a coward," I yelled, warming to my subject, "you've never had to try! You're the most deadly man alive, it's easy for you, you don't know what it means to be brave! You know you always win, that's why you'll never be another Captain: you don't understand what bravery is!"

Coach Flat reached down and slapped me hard across the face. Before pulling me closer. "The only reason you're still alive is because I can't have *too* many people dying on my first day," he said as he threw me back and then left while I nursed the blood in my mouth.

Jake wheeled out a large see-through box with several small, interior cameras. They weren't just planning to drown Dr. Dangerous, they were planning to capture his death in high definition close up. Ashley's eyes were fixed on me and nothing else, like I was keeping him calm.

Jake turned to me, slapped the box, and smiled. "This beauty right here, we molded it out of one of the world's strongest substances," he said and turned to Ashley, still bound on the floor, "you'll try, but you can't kick it, break it, or shatter it."

With the help of the black clad thugs, Jake pulled Ashley up and threw him into the box. Ashley struggled the whole way, he refused to make it easy, but it made no difference. They'd just put the top on as Coach Flat swaggered back into the room wearing his old costume, the one he'd worn years back when he was Captain Fantastic's sidekick. His suit had shorts and a big white star, along with puffy gloves and shoes. The costume was a joke, but that in some ways was the point; he wanted to wear it while he killed someone.

The Coach took his place under the lights, on the set the stagehands had built, as Ashley, in the transparent box, was rolled up to the window. They were going to drop him from the fourth floor into the river.

One of the thugs moved behind me and covered my mouth as Kevin the cameraman, the one I'd told to run in the park, counted down for Coach Flat. I could see the hurt in his eyes, as though he blamed all of this on himself. The lights above him spun, and a jingle played.

"Welcome to our lunch special here at Hero High," said the Coach, "and do I have a treat for you! As the new acting principal until our beloved Captain returns, I've already been hard at work; the evil Dr. Dangerous had been captured at last!"

The crew behind him clapped shakily as the sign

above them flashed 'applause'. The camera panned over to Ashley as he banged against the box.

My eyes watered, and I screamed behind the hand that silenced me.

With a push Ashley sailed out the window and splashed into the river below.

Every screen in the city focused on the inside of the box where Ashley, still stunned by his impact with the river, struggled against the slow rising water. Coach Flat threw off his cape and pulled me up the pillar I was bound to.

"Watch," he said, but I couldn't, so instead, I blinked, and everything stopped.

I caught my breath, and tried to steady my heart. I felt like I might die from the stress of it all, but I couldn't give in, I was not going to watch Ashley drown, hell no. I might not be Adam Armstrong, but I knew I'd find a way to make Coach Flat regret what he did to Dr. Dangerous, and I sure as hell wasn't going to let history repeat itself.

Think Friday think! How could I get through that box? It was one of the world's strongest substances, but what was holding it together? Glue? No. They said it was molded. The hinges

*where white, I couldn't tell how they were
attached.*

*I wound my memory back further, watching
everything I'd seen play out once again. They'd
sealed him in with a lock. It wouldn't be a
tumbler, I saw wires, numbers, and what?
Plastic explosive. So, the box would explode if I
tried to open it from the top. What could I do!?
How could I break him out?*

*I sat there in silence, for what seemed like
forever.*

*Not bothering with memory, or possible
scenarios.*

*I settled in the darkness as I thought everything
through.*

*What was I missing? Frustrated and angry I ran
my memory back further and further until I
reached the point where the flat pen flew
through the pillar. How had that been possible?
Why was the pen flat? The Coach could make
other things flat? Of course! His clothes flattened with him, which meant his power applied
to more than his body, it applied to things he
touched. My memory sped forwards again and
found the pen, flat against the ground, it was at
least ten minutes since he'd thrown it, and it*

was still flat. That pen would be flat on this
floor until the floor no longer existed.
It was an honest to God eureka moment. Coach
Flat could cut through anything, that's what
made him so deadly, and if he could affect
things within a certain radius of his body, then I
could steal his power!

I blinked the world back into action, and looked straight up at him. If he was going to use his power, I'd have to make him angry. I looked directly at the box, and did as he said, I watched, and I showed no emotion. It wasn't long before he yanked at my restraints.

"Cry!"

I did nothing, hoping against hope my last ditch effort would work. "You little-" he raised his hand, thin, deadly. I turned. Stuck a finger in the air, touching his hand with mine.

The air popped.

It was strange, I could feel it. I spun my arms round, dodged his chop, and kicked him back with my heel. Using my new flat finger I cut my restraints and confused one of the heroes by chopping the tip off his gun. The few seconds I gained were just long enough; I kicked Coach Flat to the ground and still dazed, he thrust his flattened hand at me.

I ran forwards making for the window. Jake moved to intercept, I was *sure* it as all over.

Kevin the cameraman, *my* cameraman swooped in, and tackled Jake to the ground.

"Run, Friday, run!" He yelled, and held Jake off just long enough for me to get the lead. The camera crew cheered.

I leapt out the window. I hated heights. I dived into the hole Ashley had left.

It was painfully cold. But shock kept me alert. The light of the sun barely penetrated the water. The yellow on his wig shone as he sunk lower. The plastic off the box twinkling in the light. He was so far down. How would I ever reach him? I wasn't strong enough to pull it back up.

I wasn't going to give up now. I'd die if I had to.

I pushed through the murky water. It seemed like he was sinking fast than I could swim. Ashley's eyes found me, and I pushed harder.

I grabbed the sides of the box like a ledge. I wanted to take a breath. My lungs were almost empty. I shook my head, and showed him my flattened finger. His eyes widened, he moved back, there was only an inch or so of air left in his box.

I pushed my finger into the box. And pushed. It cut like butter. Something told me with Flat's powers I could cut through anything like butter. Soft butter I mean. Just to be clear.

Ashley's fists banged against the box before I'd even finished cutting. I almost wanted to tell him to calm down. Then I looked up.

The light of the sun as becoming a pin point. Was there an opposite to a fear of heights?

Ashley slammed his way out. The box filed with water. I carefully cut his ties. The light was so slim, my air...

You know when you're a kid, and you try to stay underwater for as long as you can? There's a moment when you feel empty. When you can't think about anything else but the surface. That moment had been a while ago.

My eyes were fluttering closed.

There was nothing left in me.

I was gone.

Like the light.

My eyes opened to a furious Ashley pulling at my chin. Everything focused again. I don't know how. We pulled at each other. Swimming, charging, pressing against the code water.

My chest was on fire. Collapsing in on itself. My body demanded I open my mouth but I knew if I did...

So close!

We pushed up, up, up. I had never been so focused in my life.

AIR!

The crowd roared. Ashley and I climbed onto the concrete. He went limp in my arms, and the crowd went quiet again. He wasn't moving. Whispered moved around me. They were actually rooting for Dr. Dangerous. I nudged him.

"You don't need CPR," I told him, "I can see your chest moving up and down." I groaned, collapsing next to him.

He sighed and opened an eye. "Worth a try."

"Idiot."

He laughed before turning over and coughing for good measure. The crowd, held back by barriers, let out a sigh of relief. I shook my head at him, how could he be so relaxed?

"What, we're friends again?" I asked him.

In answer he locked his arms around me and the heat of his superpower chased away the chill of the ice cold water. "We were never *just* friends. Besides, I knew you'd save me." He smiled. I took a moment. A moment until the crowds picked up again. I looked over.

Coach Flat was running towards us, pushing fans out of the way. His hand raised. Like butter.

I pushed Ashley away.

And pushed up. He swung his arm. I ducked. Could have died there. The crowd gasped.

He moved to slice my legs, I stumbled back. Could have had a surprise amputation.

My power slowed things down for a fraction of a second. A new way to use it I realized.

He slammed his hand towards my chest. I blocked it.

Then he fattened his arm I heard the pop, and drew my body back.

My arm, he was going to slice my arm in half!

I was falling. Lisa, from nowhere kicked him. Flat popped his whole body this time. Save for his feet. I look dup from the ground at a paper thin man.

A boom echoed through the crowds. Air pushed me back. I gulped. Barney stood next to Lisa. We were dead. We couldn't stop him. He was deadly to touch.

His hand popped back. Then his arm. His legs.

"Shit!" He screamed. He closed his eyes and it all flattened again.

He was close to his limit. All we had to to do was distract him a little longer. Until he needed his serum.

I lunged forward. Flat darted out of the way. He knew I could hurt him. He'd never faced a real enemy and he was *scared*.

He doubled back, holding his hand out to Jake, "Gimme the syringe!" Jake fumbled in his pockets. Pulled out a gold syringe. He slung it across the courtyard.

Lisa ran.

And caught it.

"Not today, Satan!" She yelled.

"Yes, Lisa!"

She threw the syringe to Barney. Flat's whole body popped back. His instinct was to fight.

But he couldn't. Without his powers, he wasn't super.

And if he wasn't super, he had no courage.

Instead, he tiptoed backwards. Lisa raised her finger and tutted. Flat turned and sped off down the street where he collided with Barney. Barney grabbed him. Lisa ran to help.

"Get off me!" Flat yelled. Barney was only *just* strong enough to hold him down. Lisa pulled him to his feet. People started to clap.

I breathed a sigh of relief, and ran back to Ashley.

"Don't worry, we'll get you back to the Super Structure, warm you up." I smiled rubbing his shoulders.

"Promise?" he said, eyebrow raised.

"Shut up." I looked away to see Coach Flat being

bundled into a van as the police pushed people back. Flat was screaming. I couldn't make out what. But I could see confused looks on the faces in the crowd, and then I heard it.

"Play the tape!" Flat cried. The people who'd tazed me nodded. I got to my feet, what the hell was this? It was too late; every screen in the city flashed into life.

And every single one showed the same looping video. Stories above me, looking down on the city square, the screen showed security camera video of Dr. Dangerous pulling me in for a nice *long* kiss.

Why? Why though? What difference would it make now?

Then I saw the fireball hurtling towards me.

"How could you?" Jake screamed, "he's a super villain!"

The crowds began to back away, but Jake just turned around to the school. Lisa ran for Ashley while his back was turned. Lisa dragged Ashley away.

"Leave them alone Jake!" I said, "they didn't do anything." he turned back and looked me in the eye. He sent a blast of red hot fire towards the students. A warning shout. It flew over their heads. They all screamed.

"You should have thought about that before you kissed him!" he yelled.

"You've got no right to be upset!" I said inching forwards.

"Bitch!" he trained his fire on all the students like a hail of bullets, backing them up against the building. A fountain of fire mixed above them.

"Jake stop this," I cried, "stop being, *this*!"

"You think you're better than me just because you got super powers!" He spat.

"No!"

"So what if I had to get mine from a syringe!" he yelled. The fire above the students stopped. He turned to me.

"Jake, stop!" I yelled again, but he was way past the point of control.

"Everyone should know just how un-heroic you are!" he said and the fire that encompassed his body flared with his anger.

"You see her?" Jake said to the crowds, "you want to know how she got her powers?"

"Jake no!" I yelled, hoping against hope that he wouldn't cross the line.

"She killed her mother! She's a murderer! And *I'm* the bad guy! I'm not the bitch sucking face with a supervillain!"

My fists clenched. My nails drew blood from my palms. He stepped towards me, and gripped me by the chin. The crowd waited. His grip was distraction enough, the students ran

"You threw a stupid tantrum in the car and she died in the crash. You killed her!"

"I don't remember," I told him.

"Convenient, isn't it?" he said and his face twisted into a smile.

"I was eight!"

"It doesn't change the facts," he said softly, "you're still a murderer!"

My fist reacted by itself, ready to bloody his nose and make him pay, but all I could see were memories.

Jake was my first friend, my first crush, my first refuge. Funny, sweet, kind. He made the days I couldn't stand to be alive, worth living. He'd made me smile for seventeen years.

Why was he making me cry now? Why had this happened? I loved him with all my heart, I still do. I wasn't *in* love with him, but I did *love* him. But just because you love someone, and you know no matter *what* they do you'll always love them.

But it doesn't mean you keep coming back when they call, and it doesn't mean you're obligated to give them a third or fourth chance.

I realized, love isn't an obligation.

My fist stopped. An inch from his face. He smiled. He'd won, in a way.

I chose to be a superhero.

I chose to *change*.

But being a superhero hurts.

I felt a tooth loosen. The side of my face felt numb. When you're hit like that, it takes a moment to understand. I stumbled backwards. The wave of pain was like another punch, but I stood back up and straightened my shoulders.

"I'm not going to fight you," I said.

"No, you're not," he said as he nodded to the his band of heroes with hand guns and they rushed towards the crowd. The grabbed at random people, pulling them from behind the barriers.

Dozens of them, each had a gun to their heads. Hostages.

"You're gonna let me kill you. And if you don't, they die."

I laughed. It had all come to this?

I looked at him, and nodded. "It won't make you a hero. Isn't that what you want, to be a hero?" I asked.

There was a moment when the realization crossed his face; and then satisfaction.

I'd lost him completely.

"Heroes aren't real," he said. He hit me again. In the

gut. It felt like my organs had been thrown up into my throat.

He grabbed my shoulders, slammed his knee into my stomach.

Blood trickled off my lips. People in the crowd gripped each other tighter. Another voice, pleaded with him to stop.

He slammed my head into the ground. My vision wobbled as he stepped away with pride. My eye was swollen, my mouth numb, every inch of me had to be cracked or bruised or worse. I pushed up with my good hand, and stood.

He'd said he was going to kill me, I didn't plan to die lying crying on the ground.

Jake gripped me by the back of the head and slammed his knuckles into my nose. It splintered. Blood spilled over my face. All the screens in the city were focussed on me. Bruised and bloody. Beaten to a by my best friend. I was trying not to cry.

"So this is you trying to be a hero?" he asked, with a smirk.

I spat the blood from my mouth, my vision was blurred with blood and tears.

People in the crowd were crying. For me.

He pushed at my shoulders, and I fell. There was nothing left in me.

I couldn't fight him. Adam had killed Dr. Dangerous and regretted it the rest of his life. I wouldn't make the same mistake.

Never. I could never kill Jake.

If I resisted, innocent people would die. He stepped on one of my legs with all his weight. I heard the bone snap. I screamed. All around me, people in the crowd were crying out for him to stop.

I tried to speak but my voice was gone. Instead I wrapped my fingers around the leg of his trousers. I wanted to say, 'I love you, stop this, this isn't you' but he shook me off with a kick.

Jake screeched, his fire sputtering, jolting, burning my skin. The flames all around him grew larger and larger, like a star.

"You're not a hero!" he screamed into the crowd. I'd never seen him so angry. And I could barely see as it was.

But a small voice from behind Jake disagreed.

"She's *my* hero!"

A little girl, in a blue cape made out of a weathered towel stepped forward. A garden hose in hand.

June with her stuffed bunny, in hand. The girl I'd saved.

She gave Jake a fierce glare, and water erupted from the spout on the hose. It was nothing like enough, a water pistol trying to put out a house fire, but she stood there. Despite the blood and pain, I couldn't help smiling.

Jake screamed as he used whatever power he had left, flinging it all at her. My hand reached out. There was nothing I could do.

She was going to die.

I couldn't save her this time.

June.

But, I wasn't alone.

The bright neon yellow of a fireman's jacket dropped over June protecting her, while someone pulled her away in the nick of time. A heavy jet of water pounded Jake into the ground. For a moment I was lost in confusion.

Firemen and women lined up with their hoses, dousing Jake in water his fire couldn't escape. Men and women ran, talking the people holding hostages. They prying the guns from their hands. A medic hoisted me up.

A crowd of everyday people surrounded Jake, scared, but brave.

They held him down. Jake couldn't fight them all.

June's blue cape swayed back and forth in the wind.

People crowded round me, each one wanting to make sure I was still breathing.

June held out her hand as I was pushed into the ambulance, I wanted to take it, but the pain was too much.

My hand shook as I tried to lift it. My vision narrowed to a pin point. My hand fell short.

Everything went dark.

———

EPILOGUE: CLEAREST BLUE

I blacked out in December, and woke up in June. My father and sister were both by my side when I opened my eyes. My father crying with relief and my sister collapsing onto the ground. My father had practically lived in the hospital for all those months, and The Captain, who'd been my roommate for several days, had got into the habit of reading me the headlines every day without fail.

My flattened finger was three dimensional again thanks to a helpful hero.

I spent a day having the doctors look me over, clearing me to leave, telling me I needed a wheelchair, in case the leg Jake had broken acted up. My father agreed, and offered to pay, but in the end Hero High covered all of my treatment. Only a day later Veronica stormed into my room, unscathed and unfazed by what had happened, telling me I had a party to go to.

It was only five in the afternoon, the sun was still high in the sky as Captain Fantastic helped me into a wheelchair I didn't *really* need, and my father and sister stood nervously at the side. Veronica insisted I keep the wheelchair near by in case and I had to admit, although my legs weren't ruined, I probably didn't have the strength to stand for *too* long. As far as injuries went, I was in pain, my nose sat wonky now, and one of my teeth was fake.

Regardless, I considered a protest, but The Captain just shook his head. D'fwan and Carol stormed into my hospital room, immediately claiming it as their own and Veronica leaned down to explain.

"We need you to look nice, and Aya said you liked these people, whoever they are."

"Sugar, I'm so glad you're okay!" D'fwan yelled, placing the back of his hand on his forehead like an overdramatic stage actor. Carol cleared her throat behind him, and he stood up quickly.

"And Carol was also worried."

She nodded in agreement from behind him.

"Leave us!" D'fwan said clapping his hands together.

Veronica frowned, but dragged everyone out all the

same. D'fwan wheeled in a small suit case, and slammed it down on the bed.

"Now, I know we've given you designer dresses, but I was hoping you'd do me the honor of wearing one of *our* designs," he said pursing his lips and raising his chin proudly.

"Of course."

"Good, 'cuz I only brought one." he said laughing.

Carol pulled out the dress, and held it up to me. It was short just like the other one they'd given me, but much fuller in the skirt because the fabric was abundant and thick, it looked cloudy, like frosted glass. Every inch was threaded with beads reminiscent of glittering ice. The richness of the blue changed depending on the angle, giving the dress a high, demure neck and ending it an elegant split cape, not too long for me to trip over.

"It's beautiful," I said. And it really was.

"We figured blue was your color, and well, the cape was Carol's idea."

"I love it."

"Put it on!" He clapped.

I stepped out of the chair, and left to change. As soon as it was on D'Fwan and Carol started pressing down the edges, checking it from all angles.

"Perfect."

I stepped out of my hospital room, happy to never

come back, and Veronica motioned everyone down-stairs onto the bus. The Captain helped me on board, and my dad and sister sat opposite.

"Where are we going?" I asked Veronica.

"Park celebration." She said.

"What for?"

"You'll see." She groaned.

"Captain?" I said after a half hour of driving.

He hummed in reply, turning to me cheerfully.

"What happened to Jake, and Coach Flat?"

He paused, and took a deep breath. "Frank is in The International Heroes Group holding facility," he told me, "Jake is awaiting trial since he has no access to the serum."

"Has he asked about me?"

He shook his head. "I'm sorry, he hasn't said a word."

The back of my head hit the seat as I looked up into the blue sky though the sun roof. "What about Ashley?"

The Captain cleared his throat, the sound made my head shoot back up. He leaned over to whisper. "Actually, I decided to keep him on."

"What? Why?"

"Because I believe there's still a chance we can help him. He's the son of the man- The point is, I knew that when I accepted him into the school, so I don't know why it makes a difference now. And besides, we don't actually have any proof he's been doing anything illegal."

I sighed, trying to decide exactly how I felt.

"I'm proud of you," said The Captain, "but you know that wasn't the end. From here on out, you'll always have to take the high road."

"I know."

"I'll help you, and so will everyone else."

"Thanks, Captain."

"Adam," he said, correcting me with a smile.

"Thanks, Adam," I said, and smiled back.

Veronica hurried off the bus, pulling The Captain with her, insisting I stay put, until someone brought my wheel chair. The Captain pulled it up, wheeled me out, and thousands of cameras caught my pursed lips and look of distaste. He steered me through crowds of people shouting questions, with my family behind me. Somehow it felt a lot easier to deal with than if I'd been walking by myself. Was that why Veronica had insisted?

I noticed the pillars of balloons, and families enjoying sandwiches on the summer green grass. The Captain steered me towards a stage with several other students, and the mayor in the middle. Two men gripped the wheels of my chair and hoisted me up on stage. Aya took over the handles, and David stood guard. They were both dressed to perfection. The Mayor tapped the microphone, and began to speak to the people. David leaned down to me, his stupid visor in place per Veronica's request.

"Need us to catch you up?"

"Please."

"We switched teams," he told me, "we're all blue now."

"Ashley?"

Aya titled her head, and chimed in. "For some reason The Captain transferred him to the Pink team. We still talk, but, you know, we don't have much time nowadays."

"You guys liking the blue dorm then?" I asked.

"Loving it, the gold dorm was way too stuffy for me."

"We already moved your stuff back in," said David, nodding in agreement. "No pressure though, you don't have to get back to work straight away."

"It's okay," I said, "I don't mind."

"Good, because we have some applicants for the blue team!" Aya said over the mayor. Lisa and Barney stepped on stage, but only Lisa stepped towards the mayor who dropped two medals round her neck. This was the first time I'd seen Lisa in a dress, and she looked breathtaking.

"For the apprehension of Coach Flat and for long term heroic service. Ms. Kisaragi, you are the longest serving superhero. We're proud to have you in our city."

Lisa nodded and waved to the crowd as they clapped. Her kids ran to her, pulling her into a hug before she pulled them over to me. Lisa leaned down as others were called onto stage, and threw her arms around me.

"I'm proud of you, kid," she said.

"You're proud of me? You're the longest serving superhero."

She smiled and took a place behind me like Aya and David, her kids doing the same before waving hello to me. In front of the mayor this time stood the entire fire department, the policeman who'd cuffed Jake, the medic who whisked me away, and finally June and Kevin, *my* cameraman. Each one received a medal for their heroics, and a thank you from the mayor.

My father and sister rushed on stage, my dad taking the handles of the chair from Aya to wheel me forwards, but I stopped him half way, and stood up. I wanted to do this on my own two feet.

Everyone nodded, and I stepped forward. The

Major cleared his throat and read, once again, from the teleprompter.

"Ms. Friday Fitzsimmons, it is my honor to reward you for your heroic actions, though you are *already* a superhero."

The crowd chirped with laughter.

"For your actions I would like to award you-" He reached round for the wooden box a stage hand held out to him, and pulled out a medal, a golden comet etched onto the round surface. "-The medal of heroic free-doms." He pinned it onto my dress, something I hoped D'Fwan and Carol wouldn't mind, and turned back round to another box. "And the blue heart."

The crowd erupted, the mayor clapped and the music in the park started to play once again. The Mayor held out his hand to me, not because he had to, but because he wanted to, and I shook it firmly.

"Thank you very much Ms. Fitzsimmons, I hope we'll be seeing more of you in the future."

"Thank you Mr Mayor."

D'Fwan and Carol spent the afternoon dancing, and handing out their cards, Lisa pulled out a picnic basket for everyone that the kids nearly single handedly devoured. The captain introduced us all to his wife Katherine. It was a lovely party, I expected people to clear out after an hour or two, but they didn't. When I asked why, Aya told me there were going to be fire-works and as we waited, June found me, and jumped onto my lap. A lot of people gasped in horror, but I didn't mind, and it didn't hurt at all.

"I didn't hurt you did I?" June asked.

"No June, it's fine."

"I'm glad you're okay Friday, and…" She looked over her shoulder at her dad who gave her a knowing nod. "I'm sorry I made fun of your name," she said with an infectious giggle.

"Don't worry about it, it is a silly name, but my mother was a bit of a hippy."

My teeth clenched, holding back tears at my own willingness to bring her up as June hopped off my lap and her dad picked her up. The people around me quieted as I sucked in quick breaths, trying not to cry. My dad hurried over, kneeling down beside me, taking my hand. He grabbed my face, and forced me to look at him.

"Stop this," he told me firmly.

I shook my head, unsure of what he meant.

"Stop hurting yourself trying to prove something," he said.

"Dad?" Tears were trickling down my cheeks.

"I don't blame you, I never blamed you," he said. His teeth clenched the same way mine did when I wanted hold things back, "so just stop, stop, hurting yourself. You don't need to prove anything to me, you're my daughter, I love you." He pulled me down with a firm kiss to my forehead as my sister pulled me into a hug. We all cried, tears of sadness, and relief.

The sky began to darken, and the mayor made another appearance, this time his jacket was gone and his sleeves were rolled up, he'd come to say the fireworks were ready. People starting making their rounds through the crowds handing out flashing toys and snacks. Once our tears had dried, I patted the arms of my wheelchair, and spoke up.

"Hey guys, I'm just gonna go get a better view."

They all nodded to me as I stepped out of the chair, and went off on my own up the little hill in the park hidden by the cherry trees where I sat on the park bench and watched the sky explode with color.

"Friday?"

My head turned a little too late as Ashley settled on the bench next to me.

"The Captain told me he decided to keep you on."

He turned to me smiling, clear and genuine, like the truth hadn't changed a thing.

"What do you mean? Why wouldn't he?"

I frowned at him as his gaze shifted to the sky.

"Because you're a supervillain," I said with a certainty I didn't know I had.

The truth was he had absolutely no proof he was Dr. Dangerous.

He laughed like I'd just done something cute and pulled the bag beside him up onto his lap.

"Nana wanted me to be prepared," he said, pulling out a thick blanket before laying it over my legs. "I don't know what you're talking about, Friday. Try to stay warm, I know it'll be summer soon, but the nights are still chilly."

He patted the blanket like he was tucking me in. My glare was fierce and confident. What was he trying to do? He leaned over his bag again, and took out a canteen.

"The Captain told me you've haven't eaten anything, so I brought some soup from the restaurant."

I nearly took it but my hand retreated at the sound of someone coming up the hill.

"Hey Ashley, you coming down for the party?"

A blond boy, only a few inches taller than me jogged up the hill as Ashley set down his canteen on my lap.

"I'll be down soon," Ashley told him, "I just want to make sure Friday's okay."

"Friday? You mean Fitz?" The blond boy looked at

me his eyes wide open, and smiled much the same way The Captain did. He hurried forwards and shook my hand. "My names Luke, I'll be Ashley's team mate next year, it's great to meet you!"

His cheerful disposition and white smile were a cliche; he was perfect for television.

"I'll see you next year, Ashley, we'll be next to the apple tree, join us when you're ready." Luke hurried down the hill, and off into the distance to sit down with his friends.

"The Captain made me the leader of a freshman team," Ashley explained.

"I see. Maybe he thinks it'll do you some good," I said.

"Well, I should be going," said Ashley as he put an arm round the bench, and blocked out the light the same way he always did. "You'll be the leader of the blue team come next year. You ready for some competition?" he asked.

"The captain will keep giving you chances. I won't," I told him.

His eyes went cold, no playful sparkle left. I wanted to let this continue like nothing had happened, but I couldn't let him brush it off, no matter how much I wanted him to convince me.

"Oh?" he said taking a strand of my hair in his fingers.

"I'll put you in jail," I warned him, "and your kisses won't stop that."

He sat still for a moment, the gears in his head turning, resulting in a sly smile that just made me hot.

"Really?"

He took me by the chin, so close I could feel his breath. His lips hovered over my skin, reaching just below my ear. He gave me a single chaste kiss, it was small but still, it made me shiver. As he was about to pull away I gripped the knot of his tie, and leaned into his ear.

"I'll put you in jail because when the time comes, you'll *want* to go."

I released him, and he pulled back slowly, his sly expression gone. His eyes took in every inch of my face, and then my dress. Over the pops and shrill whizzes of the fireworks, and the conversations of the crowd, his expression softened.

"This is my favorite, of all your dresses," he said, "it's made of the clearest blue, just like your eyes."

I nearly forgot where I was, too caught up in looking at him. The pop of a firework brought me back, still dizzy from his presence.

"Aren't you tired, Ashley?" I asked.

He dropped his hands, and nodded as though he'd caught even himself off guard. "Eat your soup," he told me, "and don't think for a second just because you know the truth, that I won't be scolding you and making sure you eat everyday."

"I'm okay with that," I replied, "but I won't forget."

"You don't have to."

"How can you be both of them?" I asked as he stepped away.

He smiled, and nodded again, more sure this time. "Eat your soup, Fitz." Without another word he stood up, leaned down to give me a kiss on the cheek, and left to find his new team mates. I opened the canteen, and took a careful sip. It was delicious.

————

Friday's husband sits down next to her, never taking his eyes off her. Without realizing, we've spent the day in her family restaurant, watching the sun go down. The sky now is dark and calm as I gather my things, and thank the captain for her time.

"Do you have enough, Claire?" she asks.

"More than, but-" I hesitate, unsure of what she'll say since I've taken up her whole day listening to stories and asking questions.

"What?"

Her husband finally looks at me, but only to give me a quick smile that's mostly a formality.

"isn't there any more?" I ask.

Fitz gives a quick inaudible laugh, and bites her lip.

"There is, but it's a nice book end, don't you think?"

———

ACKNOWLEDGMENTS

First off, I'd like to thank my family for being supportive in my effort to write a book. I know it may not be your thing, and this book may be too girly, or whatever it is, it doesn't matter, thank you for believing I'd finish it. If you hadn't, I'm not sure this book would exist.

Second, I'd like to thank everyone on Tumblr who followed me throughout the writing process.

I'd also like to take some time to thank all my inspirations for this book, and the pieces of media that have made me the storyteller I am. The Caves of Steel by Isaac Asimov for being a better book than I'll ever be able to write, Tiger and Bunny for coming up with something new in the superhero genre, Kamen Rider Fourze for teaching me you can be a superhero without hurting people, and Shugo Chara for showing me protagonists are allowed to have personalities. Oh, and I'd like to thank 'The Selection' for opening my eyes to how wonderful writing and reading romance can be.

And lastly, I'd like to thank you, if you're not a family member, thank you for taking an interest, and reading all the way to the end, unless of course you just skipped to the acknowledgments. I'm assuming you didn't though because I don't know of anyone who buys a book to read the acknowledgments. I can't imagine that's a particularly thrilling part of the book.

I'd also like to thank my test readers, who were kind enough to read my book even though I'm a nobody. You guys are great, thank you so much.

I should also thank my friends on "THE COUNCIL" for being so supportive when I told them about this book. I love you guys, you mean so much to me. And if you're reading this, HI! And second of all, I hope you liked it, if not, it's okay, you don't have to lie to me. I'm a big girl.

A quick special thanks to everyone I consulted while writing this book.

Lesley Rice, my mum, who read this over and over again, helping me fix my weird sentence structure, and making me *not* look super dyslexic. Thank you.

Tiffany, from "THE COUNCIL", who helped me

with Chinese terms of endearment. I know it was only a short conversation, but you should still be thanked Nut. Thank you.

Alexander Charalambides, BROTHER!!! (That's a Metal Gear reference.) Who read this over and was brutally honest, because unlike me, he's actually good at writing. Thank you.

My dad, Stelios for proof reading, and for telling me what he knows about fixing watches.

And special thanks to, insilentscreams-swift, Davinaikr, geekygirl34, and mashybeans.

Anyway, back to you reader, thank you very much, for your money (jk), your time, and your consideration. Just the fact that someone I don't know might take an interest in a story that only six months ago existed exclusively in my head is unbelievable. So, I guess all that's left to say is, I hope you liked it.

ABOUT THE AUTHOR

Mina Chara is an artist, writer and student of design. Born in London in the UK she now lives in New Hampshire in the USA with her family and two dogs.

Hero High: *Figure In The Flames* is her first novel compilation. The book is also available in paperback.

You can learn more about Mina and the characters she creates by visiting her website, Goodboybooks.com where you can join her reader community.

You might also like to follow her on social media.

Mina Chara's Friday Fitzsimmons Series

A teen joins the cast of her favorite reality show and tries to be a hero.

Hero High: Figure In The Flames

Hero High: Heartbreak Rebellion

Alexander Charalambides Formula Q Series

High speed racing in space, with flying cars, a kick-ass heroine, a talking dog and a cowboy.

Formula Q

Pace Laps

Alexander Charalambides K.I.A. Series

A teenage girl sets out in search of the truth about her parents and learns more than she expected.

K.I.A.

The Beagle Briefing

Alexander Charalambides Black Blade Series

A young man gains possession of a legendary sword and is swept off on a quest by three unusual modern day wizards.

Black Blade

Secrets of the Black Blade

Golden Void - Coming soon in May 2020

Alexander Charalambides Vampire State Series

A young woman must choose between wealth and power and remaining human. The answer's obvious, until she meets Vincenzo.

Vampire State

Vampire State II - Coming Autumn 2020

Made in the USA
Monee, IL
05 July 2021

72971185R00256